Brush with LOVE

Brush with Love

Lisa McKendrick

BONNEVILLE BOOKS

An imprint of Cedar Fort, Inc.
Springville, Utah

ISBN 13: 978-1-4621-2125-0

Published by Bonneville Books, an imprint of Cedar Fort, Inc.,
2373 W. 700 S., Springville, UT 84663
Distributed by Cedar Fort, Inc., www.cedarfort.com

LIBRARY OF CONGRESS CATALOGING-IN-PUBLICATION DATA

Names: McKendrick, Lisa, 1965- author.
Title: Brush with love / Lisa McKendrick.
Description: Springville, Utah : Bonneville Books, an imprint of Cedar Fort, Inc., [2017]
Identifiers: LCCN 2017018710 (print) | LCCN 2017023489 (ebook) | ISBN 9781462128518 (epub and moby) | ISBN 9781462121250 (perfect bound : alk. paper)
Subjects: LCSH: Man-woman relationships--Fiction. | GSAFD: Love stories.
Classification: LCC PS3613.C554 (ebook) | LCC PS3613.C554 B78 2017 (print) | DDC 813/.6--dc23
LC record available at https://lccn.loc.gov/2017018710

Cover design by Katie Payne
Cover design © 2017 by Cedar Fort, Inc.
Edited and typeset by Hali Bird, Jessica Romrell, and Nicole Terry

Printed in the United States of America

10 9 8 7 6 5 4 3 2 1

Printed on acid-free paper

To my husband, Richard McKendrick.
Thank you for being awesome.

"These people became so real to me, I had to stop myself from adding them to my prayers!"

—Diane Tolley, author of *Daughter of Ishmael* and *A House Divided*

"Just the right book for relaxing by the pool or on the beach. A satisfying romance with a handsome stranger, triumph over past trials and a touch of nostalgia."

—J.A. Matern, author of *British War Children*

"A heartwarming tale that proves that sometimes, the unexpected things in life are the best things in life. McKendrick paints a beautiful story, reminding each of us that people, and our relationships with them, are the greatest masterpieces of all."

—Heather Chapman, author of *The Second Season* and *The Forgotten Girl*

Prologue

I wanted to forget, so I said I couldn't remember. It was easier that way, or at least that's what I told myself, easier to say that my life began the day Edward and Lois Huish adopted me. But the truth was I remembered everything. I remembered my fingers gripping my mother's long blonde hair, and the way she gently pried them off as she handed me to the stern woman. I guess I actually don't remember everything, because I can't remember the stern woman's name. But I remember well the slap across the face she gave me when I wouldn't stop crying for my mother to come back. After that, I stopped crying, and, terrified beyond words, stopped speaking.

When you're three and won't say anything it's difficult to defend yourself. But I wasn't interested in defending myself, I was interested in survival, and though I was little, I understood that surviving Bushkaya orphanage #3 hinged on my ability to blend in, to disappear among the metal cribs, dirty walls, gnawing hunger and loneliness. If someone dipped their spoon in my soup, I didn't object, and when a child (or several children) skipped me in line, I didn't protest. Instead I studied them, the harsh eyes, the defiant set of the jaw, the turn or bump in a nose, the smudge of dirt across a cheek, knowing before I'd ever tried that I could recreate it.

Paper in a Siberian orphanage isn't wasted on three-year-olds, so my palm became my paper, and my finger a pencil, a way for me to sketch, to find beauty in that miserable place and lose myself in it. The frosty breath of children huddled in conversation, a shaft of light falling into a room, a pile of broken toys. If I focused long enough I could slip away, my finger almost casting a spell, as it moved across my palm, sometimes in shorts spurts, other times creating long lines extending beyond my hand, rubbing as if blurring what'd been drawn.

I could also escape through the window, not literally, of course. (Where would I have gone?) But I liked watching the street. It was a dreary street—wide and snow-packed with squat buildings on either side—but as the sun made its arc in the sky, the colors changed, white turning to gray, and the sky burning orange.

"Clearly, she's not all there," the stern woman said to one of the workers when she noticed me at the window or sketching on my palm. And she was right, I wasn't all there. As much as I could, I escaped into art, and memories of little things, like my mother kissing my forehead before saying good night. As much as I could, I left that place.

Still, a year later, I don't think I was ready for Lois Huish to rescue me, to yank me from what was familiar—Russia, the orphanage, my window—and plop me down in suburban America. American speech sounded to my ear like the clanging of an empty can, and my new mother's unreserved love felt like a blasting fire hose I was being asked to drink from. I had stepped from darkness into a light both glorious and garish. It would take getting used to, and, to be honest, seventeen years later, I was still getting used to it—still squinting and rubbing my eyes, trying to adjust, trying to feel like I belong.

Chapter One

A sea breeze rippled through the wedding canopy making it billow softly. Constructed from tulle and twigs (and carefully concealed zip ties), the canopy was a temporary, flimsy shelter whose one purpose was to look pretty, and with the Florida gulf shimmering behind it, and seagulls fluttering white against a coral sky, it did look pretty—very pretty, if you were willing to overlook the guy to the left in a Speedo practicing yoga.

"Isn't this romantic!" gushed Ingrid as a harpist strummed and wedding guests drifted in, filling up the rows of folding chairs.

I looked at Mr. Downward Facing Dog and scrunched up my nose. "I suppose," I said.

Ingrid swatted at a sand fly, slapping her hand hard against her neck. "I don't think there's anything more beautiful than a beach wedding," she said with a sigh.

An airplane pulling a sign advertising all-you-can-eat ribs Sunday at the Rib Doctor was circling overhead. "They're all right," I said.

Ingrid nudged me, her shoulder bumping into mine. "Quit being blah," she said. That's the one downside to having a perky best friend—they tend to insist that you're perky too.

I nudged her back. "I'm not being blah," I said, sounding ever so slightly, I hate to admit it, blah.

A seagull perched itself on the chair in front of us and Ingrid discreetly shooed it away. "You're like Eeyore on downers."

"Only next to your Tigger on uppers."

Ingrid shook her head. "You're impossible," she said.

"I suppose I am," I said, doing my best to sound like a certain gloomy stuffed donkey.

Ingrid gazed at the sky, the surf, and the sand, appearing to ignore the flotsam and discarded cigarette butts. "Lana, what could possibly be better than getting married at the beach?" she asked, more like demanded. Her hands were on her hips.

I patted her leg. "Ingrid, I'm not trying to knock beach weddings," I said, watching a jogger trudge through loose sand. "Even with Latin pop music pulsating at a distance, I can honestly say, this is a beautiful wedding. Not what I would pick, but beautiful."

Ingrid looked up just as a wisp of her amber hair caught the breeze, making my fingers twitch, as if they sought, of their own accord, a pencil and sketch pad to capture her in that moment. "What would you pick?" she asked, shaking a TicTac from its container and popping it in her mouth.

"Oh, just a place," I said, waving away her offer of tiny minty freshness.

Ingrid clicked shut the little container. "And where would that place be?" she asked, her brown eyes wide with curiosity.

I took a deep breath. There was no reason to feel nervous. This was Ingrid, for heaven's sake. Inga, Binga, Bottle of Ink—my best friend since high school. The girl who knew me better than anyone. So why was it so hard for me to say something like, *Look, you know I'm Mormon, and for Mormons the most romantic place to get married isn't the beach; it's the temple. That's where I plan to get married one day, and if you'd like to learn more I could totally hook you up with some missionaries, assuming your very Catholic mother doesn't kill me first.* Just bam, lay it out there. No hesitating, no awkwardness. We talked about everything! Well, to be honest, not everything. Not Siberia and not my religion. It should have been easy to bring it up in conversation. I loved my religion, but when it came to sharing it, I caved. Not far from where we sat sand crabs were burrowing into the shoreline, hiding, trying not to be noticed. Why, when it came to my testimony, was I sometimes like that? Like a sand crab doing its best to avoid detection.

I started to get up. "It's nowhere, not important, but hey," I said, jutting my thumb over my shoulder, "maybe I should go grab another confetti cone before things get started."

Ingrid tugged my arm, pulling me back into my seat. "Wait, I want to guess," she said.

"Guess what?"

She clapped, quick and quiet. "Where you want to get married!"

"Uh, you're not going to guess it."

Ingrid waved a hand in the air as if to erase my doubts and, as she did, thwacked a guy scooting past us, spilling his beer onto his shirt. "I'm so sor—" said Ingrid, cutting her apology short to gaze into his eyes, which wasn't surprising. When it comes to boys, Ingrid falls hard and fast. Plus, he did have beautiful eyes. They were periwinkle blue and seemed almost aglow against his tan skin.

"It's fine," he said blotting his shirt with the napkin that had been wrapped around his beer. Sitting just a few seats down from us, he turned once more to Ingrid and smiled. And in return she bit the knuckle of her index finger, which, whether he understood or not, was her way of saying she'd be happy to cover his dry-cleaning bill.

"Oh my gosh, what do you think?" she said as she chewed her fingernail.

"What do I think? I think it's weird they started serving alcohol before the ceremony, but I guess nothing says beach casual like tipsy guests."

Ingrid poked me in the side. "Do you think he's cute?"

"I think fluffy bunnies are cute."

Exasperated, Ingrid sighed. "Then handsome, do you think he's handsome?"

I didn't need to glance at the guy in question to assess his features, because the artist inside me had already done that—strong jawline, good shoulders, eyes a little close together, but other than that good facial symmetry. "Yes," I said, "he's handsome."

"You have to get me his number!" she declared.

"I'm not your fairy godmother," I said.

"Come on, Lana, it's not like I'm asking you to turn a pumpkin into a carriage. Wait!" she cried. "That's it!"

"That's what?"

"The kind of wedding you want."

Ugh. What was the use of your best friend spilling beer on a fairly handsome stranger if it didn't make her forget your previous conversation? I scowled. "Fine," I said, throwing my hands up. "What kind of wedding do I want?"

"You want to be a Disney bride! Bejeweled ball gown, Cinderella's carriage, and his and hers mouse ears for the cake topper!"

"Not even close," I said.

"That's too bad," she said, sounding a tad wistful. "It would be the perfect way to shrug off your life-is-serious-business look for a day."

"I do not look like that" I said, my voice an indignant whisper.

"Not once someone gets to know you, but you're a tough nut to crack—complicated. Sort of like a coconut."

"You realize that didn't make any sense," I said.

"What I mean is tough on the outside, sweet on the inside." She bit her lip. "But not flaky. Okay, it's not a perfect comparison."

The corners of my mouth curled into a faint smile. "So I don't go great with shrimp?"

Ingrid tutted. "Make fun all you want, but you don't go through all four years of high school with someone without getting to know them, and—"

"Billy Martinez," I said, interrupting.

Ingrid raised an eyebrow. "Who's that?" she asked.

"Someone we went through high school with that you don't know."

"Who cares about Billy Martinez?" she cried.

"Well, clearly not you."

Ingrid poked me again. "My point is, I know *you*, Svetlana Feodora Huish," she said, then struck with an idea, snapped her fingers. "You want a garden wedding! Bohemian dress, lights twinkling in the trees, burlap banners, candles flickering in mason jars, vintage lace, a little poodle as the ring bearer and—"

She was on a roll, I probably should have let her keep going, but I didn't. "Wrong," I interrupted, loud enough that a lady sitting in front of us turned to look.

Ingrid pressed her fingers to her temples and thought for a moment. "A barn then," she whispered as a string quartet joined in with the harpist, and the wedding planner, white flip flops thwacking her heels, hustled down the aisle to make a few last-minute adjustments.

I leaned toward her. "No," I whispered.

"A cliff's edge," she whispered back.

"Still no."

"Bungee jumping."

"Be reasonable."

"Glad you feel that way," she said as the groom in an untucked tuxedo shirt, black pants, and bare feet took his place under the canopy. "On your wedding day you should be putting your trust in each other, not a gigantic rubber band." Escorted by the groomsmen, the bridesmaids began their slow walk down the aisle. "Now that I think of it," said Ingrid in hushed tones, "aren't Mormon weddings supposed to be boring? Well, not boring, but drab?"

"Where did you get that from?" I asked.

"Not sure."

"I never told you Mormon weddings are drab."

"No, you hardly tell me *anything* about your religion. I know you can't wear bikinis."

"There is no Mormon bikini police, apart from Sister Wilkins in my parents' ward."

"I'm just saying that your religion seems to have a lot of rules."

A group of onlookers had gathered at the fringe of the wedding, some taking pictures with their phones, others chatting, waiting to see the bride, none of them connected in any way to the happy couple. I fidgeted with my sleeve. "Any religion has rules," I whispered.

"If you want to wear black, will they let you?"

"Why would I wear black to my wedding?" I asked."

"Because that's all you ever wear," she said.

A flower girl trotted down the aisle, scattering fistfuls of rose petals. "She's adorable," cooed Ingrid. I smoothed my (black) pencil skirt.

"I do not always wear black," I said, a slight edge to my voice.

"Lan, for as long as I've known you you've even kept your butter blonde hair black."

It's not black, it's Burnt Espresso," I said.

"Burnt Espresso is why the Goths kept inviting you to sit at their lunch table."

"That happened once."

"Well, it never happened to me."

I was speechless, and not because we'd gotten shushed from behind. Black was chic, sophisticated, and a huge chunk of my wardrobe. Best friend or not, Ingrid had struck a nerve, and my usual reluctance to talk about my religion went temporarily on hold. I took a deep breath, and said, "The only place I'm getting married is in a Mormon temple."

The quartet and harp, cranking up the volume, began playing the wedding march, and the minister asked us to rise.

Ingrid looked at me. "You mean that castle thingy you have a picture of in your room?"

"Yes."

Ingrid thought for a moment. So, how's the catering there?" she asked.

"There's no catering; you have the reception somewhere else."

"That's asking a lot of your guests," she whispered as the bride and her father, arm and arm, approached the petal-strewn aisle.

"It's honestly not that big of a deal," I whispered back.

"So why the temple?"

"Because marriage there is forever."

Ingrid's mouth fell open. "That's so sweet," she said, her eyes misting. "Count me in. I want to be there when you get married forever."

"You'll have to convert first."

"Wow, you really do ask a lot of your guests."

Slowly, taking in the moment, the bride made her way toward her groom.

"Sweetheart neckline," whispered Ingrid, dabbing her eyes with a tissue, "empire waist, chiffon skirt, tattoo discreetly hidden—she looks beautiful."

"If weddings needed commentators, you'd be perfect," I whispered as the bride kissed her father on the cheek, took the hand of her groom, and we took our seats.

"I would be perfect at it," she whispered back. "I love weddings."

I looked at the scene in front of me—the bride and groom under a wedding canopy at dusk. She did look beautiful—*they* looked beautiful, though I could have lived without the groom's bare feet.

"Well," whispered Ingrid as the minister spoke of true love, "let me know when you find your forever guy."

Tears pricked my eyes and I brushed them away with the back of my hand.

Ingrid handed me a tissue. "A softie on the inside, just like I said," she said, and I smiled like my tears had something to do with the bride's personalized vows to her groom. But my tears weren't for what was happening, but rather for what I feared never would. Would I ever find someone I loved so much I'd want to be with them forever? And assuming I did, would he feel the same about me?

I sighed and watched the sun sink lower on the horizon. Where in the world was he, my forever guy? One thing was certain, he wasn't at Yale. Four years there and all I'd gotten was a degree in fine arts. My social life had been fairly nonexistent, which wasn't surprising. Ivy League schools aren't exactly LDS dating hot spots. Still, I could have decoupaged a small suitcase with all the temple wedding announcements I'd received while there, each one adorable, sweet, and super annoying. *Tada!* they all seemed to say to me. *Look what we've done that you haven't! We've gotten engaged! Look how cute we are together! Now go put on your sweats and eat some ice cream.*

Sure, I had gone out on a few dates, but flirting didn't come naturally to me, and to make matters worse, neither did smiling. Lois, my mother, blamed this entirely on Siberia. She said the cold there can freeze your heart, and that though it had been seventeen years since the day she bundled me up and carried me away from Bushkaya Orphanage #3, she was convinced mine was still thawing. Parents as loving as mine should have melted any Siberian ice still clinging to me years ago, but according to my mom, such things took time—time and miracles.

Speaking of miracles, for me to get married, it was going to take a few. Not only was I bad at flirting, but after spending a few more days with my family in Florida, I was heading to Nantucket Island where the only fish in the sea would be . . . fish. I was going there for a six-week post-graduation mentoring program made possible by the famed Ethel and Chester Wilmington Trust. It was an honor to be chosen. Every year hundreds of art students applied for this coveted opportunity. Getting picked could, if things fell into place, be a life-changing experience. More than one art career had been launched through the program. Of course, you had to be willing to give it your all, and I was. Totally. I told myself I should be glad that I hadn't met the right guy yet and could focus on building a name for myself as an artist. There would be plenty of time later for falling in love.

What I needed to do now was work! And get used to feeling lonely. Actually, loneliness was good. Artists needed to suffer. It got the creative juices flowing, even if it did occasionally lead to an early demise. I told myself to forget about guys; that sooner or later the right one would surface. But apparently I was a terrible listener, because despite my best efforts, my heart longed for him—my guy. Like a compass's needle forever finding north, my thoughts returned to him.

The maid of honor handed the bride a hanky as she, repeating the words of the minister, promised to love, honor, and cherish her groom until her last breath. The couple turned to face their guests, and the minister, suddenly sounding like an announcer at a monster truck rally, pronounced them *HU-U-USBAND AND W-I-I-FE!* The couple kissed, then, hand-in-hand, walked down the aisle, stopping just once for the bride to remove a piece of confetti that had landed in her smiling mouth.

After the wedding party had made their exit, Ingrid stood and stretched. "Time to go find me a martini and you a tall glass of milk."

I touched her arm. "Go ahead. I want to get some fresh air."

"But we're already outside."

"Fresh*er* air then."

Before Ingrid could open her mouth to protest, Mr. Slightly Beer-Spattered Shirt tapped her on the shoulder. "You ladies heading over to the party?" he asked with just a touch of a Florida drawl. Sophisticated Surfer wasn't a look she'd ever gone for, not with her weakness for three-piece suits, but there he was, dressing up chinos and Havaianas with a linen shirt, and Ingrid was getting a dreamy look in her eye. He put his hand to his sticky shirt. "By the way, I'm Riley," he said.

Ingrid giggled. "I'm Ingrid," she said.

"And I'm staying here," I said as I waved hello. "Just for a little while, to watch the sunset."

Ingrid, alternately, smiled at Riley and shot daggers at me. "This is Lana," she said with a sweeping gesture, "my *best* friend," her emphasis sending me the message, *Lana, you have to come with us! You know I don't like flying solo!* This was true, in any social situation, but especially when first meeting a guy. It was the reason I was attending this wedding. I didn't even know the bride and groom. They were friends of Ingrid's from Florida State.

Yes, I was Ingrid's best friend—the one who had known when to let go of her hand when she was learning how to surf on the simulator at Swell Concoction, the one who had gently nudged her (she called it shoved) off a waterfall in Georgia. Sometimes, as best friend, it was my job to push her out of her comfort zone, especially when I wanted a moment to myself.

Riley shook my hand, earning points as he did for having a firm grip. Weak handshakes annoy me. "Nice to meet you," he said.

"Nice to meet you too," I said. "Why don't you two head over to cocktail hour."

Ingrid cocked her head. "You should head over with us," she said.

"I would," I said sweetly, "except I don't want to. Not just yet, anyway."

"Birds of a feather stick together," said Ingrid.

"Birdy can spread her wings."

"Are we still talking about cocktail hour?" asked Riley, his eyebrows scrunching together.

"More or less," said Ingrid. She took a step and her stiletto sunk into the sand, knocking her off balance, but Riley was there to catch her. Ingrid gave him an embarrassed smile then let go of his arm.

"I'll see you over there soon, I promise," I said.

They headed toward the glowing tent, and then, at last, it was just me and a glorious Anna Maria Island sunset. Well, the guy in the Speedo was there too, but at the moment he was sitting cross legged on his towel meditating, hardly a distraction.

I took off my heels and walked closer to the water's edge, enjoying the soft sand between my toes. The sky was now broad strokes of burnt orange, broken here and there by clouds turned in the fading light the color of dishwater, a color as murky as my future. I smiled. Here I was, a Yale grad and Wilmington Trust recipient, and I thought my future was murky. Maybe there was something to Ingrid's Eeyore comparison. My future was bright, a dazzling kaleidoscope of colors, but instead of my pulse quickening with excitement, it did so with panic.

School was now done, that routine that had made me feel rooted, that place where I'd belonged. It was time for me to step into the world, to make my mark. Yes, the next six weeks I'd be spending in Nantucket, but after that, where would I go? Where did I fit?

"Heavenly Father," I whispered into the breeze. Some people collect shells at the beach, I like to collect moments, quiet ones where I can pray unnoticed. There is something about looking out at the water and the sky that makes me feel heard, and right then, I needed to be heard.

"Father," I said again, "please help me to figure out my life. To understand where I should go, what I should throw myself into. There are so many potential projects, so many places I could live. I know it should be exhilarating, but it's overwhelming. And I'm scared to be alone, but more scared that I'm scared to be alone. Does that make sense? I don't want to end up with someone simply because a vacancy needs filling. I want to find him; help me to find him. And until I do, please watch over him, keep him safe, and preferably unattached. I know you're there, and that you love me. I'm still working on loving me, but I'm grateful for the progress I've made, and I'm grateful—along with so many other things—for this sky tonight. As an artist, it teaches me. One day I hope to paint like you. In the name—"

A loud *Ohmmmmm* filled the air.

I turned around to see Captain Speedo standing on one leg with his hands flared zombie-like in front of him. He waved at me, which made him wobble.

"Hi," he said.

Ugh. "Hi," I said, which was generous of me. Usually a guy has to be wearing more fabric than it takes to make a shower cap if I'm going to talk to him, but hey, I was trying to be nice.

"Can I have your number?" he asked, wobbling some more.

Why did I try to be nice? "You can have my sweatpants," I said.

"Should I take that as a no?" He asked, his toe touching down for just a second to help him regain his balance.

Dude, assuming you were a wayward teen, you could be my father. "'Fraid so," I said, then smacked my lips in a way that said, *we're done here.*

He shrugged. "Stay centered," he said, wobbling back and forth.

"I will," I said. "I definitely will.

14

Chapter Two

Ingrid was pouting. She was sitting on my bed absently thumbing through *Trendy Bride* magazine, and jutting her lower lip. "I just don't understand," she said.

I shoved a pair of jeans into my bulging suitcase. "Why you're looking through a wedding magazine when you're not engaged? Yeah, I don't understand that either."

She looked at the ceiling and huffed. "You know what I mean," she said closing the textbook sized magazine, "why do you have to go?" she asked.

"Maybe I forgot to tell you, but I won a dumb prize. It's no big deal. Only two former first ladies were there to hand it to me."

Ingrid sighed. "It *is* a dumb prize. If it weren't for that thing you could move to Tallahassee with me. We could hang out together on the weekends when I don't have homework. I could totally get you a job at Applebee's."

"You know you're talking crazy now."

Ingrid fell over on the bed and reached for my hand. "I know, but I don't want you to go."

I rolled my eyes like her dramatics were wearing me thin, but the truth was, I loved that Ingrid hated for me to go. I had made friends at Yale, but no one had protested when it was time for me to pack my things. I squeezed Ingrid's hand. "Ing, it's only six weeks. After that I have no idea where I'll end up, but we'll, for sure, see each other at Christmas."

"Maybe by then Riley will have texted me back," she said, sitting up, checking her phone, and flopping back down. "I hate guys," she moaned.

"You didn't hate him at the wedding," I said, raising my eyebrow.

Ingrid burrowed into my pillow and groaned. "Why did I let him kiss me!"

"Because he's cute," I said. "You always kiss the cute ones."

She sat up. "I don't always kiss the cute ones."

I gave her a withering look.

"Okay, fine, I do always kiss the cute ones." She sat up and pointed a finger at me, her hair thrown wildly about. "I need to make them earn it! Require that they take me on a minimum of three dates before I even consider giving them . . . Well, that's asking a lot. Maybe two dates, two awesome dates . . . unless they're super busy with work or school, then maybe just one, one incredibly amazing date involving dinner before they get a kiss from me."

"Or you could just meet them at a wedding and kiss them before dessert is served."

Her hands flew upward. "Why won't Riley text me?"

"You texted him five minutes ago."

"And what could be more important than texting me back?"

"I don't know, you said he's a firefighter. Maybe a building is burning somewhere. What did you ask him anyway?"

"What's his favorite sandwich," she mumbled.

"How dare he leave you in suspense."

"So insensitive," she said, diving for her phone as it vibrated. "It's a Cuban. I think I love him."

"How sweet. Your mutual love of deli meats has brought you together."

My mom rapped her knuckles softly on my open bedroom door. "Hello, my lovelies," she said, her knitting tucked under her ample arm, "Daddy says it's time to start heading to the airport."

"Don't let her go, Mama Huish!"

Mom smiled, making her chin double and her kind, grey eyes sparkle. "Wouldn't I love to keep her here, but our girl has places to go to and pictures to paint. We're so excited for her—excited and proud."

A drip fell from the frozenness inside me. My mother had a way of doing that, slowly, steadily thawing my iciness, and—though she didn't know it—making me feel ashamed of myself. She had wanted me, despite the stern woman telling her I was an idiot.

Don't pick that one, the stern woman had said. *That girl never speaks.* But Mom had been undeterred. *Her teeth are chattering*, had been her reply through an interpreter. *Who can talk when their teeth are chattering!*

I was as fragile as a newly hatched bird fallen from its nest, and she had nurtured me tenderly, patiently, completely, and yet sometimes I just wanted her to take a little time to make herself look pretty.

If Ingrid had planned to fling herself onto my suitcase to keep me from leaving, it was too late. My dad was already wheeling it out of my room. He ducked a little as he crossed the floor, trying to make himself less noticeable. Dad was many things—smart, kind, funny—but he was not one who enjoyed the spotlight, even if it fell on him just because he'd entered a room to grab a suitcase. My dad was a behind-the-scenes sort of man, which, as a security consultant, suited him well. Thin, short, and with a full head of gray hair he kept meticulously parted on the side, Dad was a listener, which worked out well since he had married a talker.

I'm a listener too, and so from the beginning we understood each other, silence at times our shared language. Dad hadn't planned on me. When my mom, while accompanying him on a business trip to Siberia, had said she would be spending the day looking for nesting dolls he had taken her at her word. It was a story my mother loved to tell.

My escort, Irina, was taking me to yet another tourist shop, she'd say, *when I saw a building with a child looking out a dirty window. What's that? I asked, and when she said it was an orphanage, I shouted, "Stop the car!" The driver didn't speak English, but he slammed on the brakes all the same. Irina tried to tell me we wouldn't be able to go in, we didn't have an appointment, the orphanage wasn't on our schedule, but I told her, I had to try. Of course, as soon as I got out of the car, I nearly froze on the spot, it must have been forty below, but with Irina trailing behind, scolding me, I dodged traffic, walked up to the front door of the orphanage, and rang the bell.*

A woman's voice crackled over the intercom. She didn't sound like the friendly sort, but after hearing through Irina that I was an American interested in perhaps donating supplies (you have to think on your feet!) to the orphanage, the door buzzed open. The woman was willing to walk me around to see the orphanage, or more to the point, its urgent need of everything. I had just started to think about blankets, how I could surely knit several each year to send, when I saw her, our girl.

Her blonde hair was tucked inside a knit cap and she was sucking the corner of a thin blanket. She said nothing; she didn't even cry when I picked her up, just touched my cheek with her cold hand and looked at me, her green eyes too sad and wise for such a little one.

"She's coming home with me," I told them, and she did. It took some doing, but that's exactly what eventually happened—she came home.

Of course, Ed thought I was out searching for souvenirs, but when I called him and said, "Eddie, what would you think if we brought home a little girl?"

Mind you, we'd just driven Louis, the youngest of our boys, to college. Some men wouldn't have it. But Eddie said, "That's fine." Just like that! As if all I'd asked was to buy a fur cap. And those two are a match. From the beginning, they've been like two peas in a pod.

Mom checked her watch. "Just another minute to say good bye, you two, and then we need to skedaddle. Our girl's got to catch a plane to Nantucket!" As mom hurried off, Ingrid grabbed my hand.

"Promise me no matter how successful you become, Lana Huish, you'll always take my calls," she said, sadness tinging her words.

I raised an eyebrow. "I'll be sure and tell my personal assistant to never put you on hold."

She grabbed my other hand, "Lana, I'm serious."

"Seriously off your rocker. I'm an artist, not a pop star."

"But you're going to be a star. You'd be famous already if it weren't for Lois. I love your mother." My mom. She liked to conceal tissue boxes in crocheted covers and mask her iron will in folksy kindness, but there was no mistaking it was there, especially when it came to my art. She wanted me to have a balanced childhood, and for her that meant me playing soccer and softball terribly (I'm no athlete) in addition to developing my talent as an artist. And it also meant that my work wasn't for sale.

She persuaded some of the finest artists in the southeast to take me on as a pupil, but when art dealers tried to convince her that my *astonishing talent* needed representation, the answer was always no. A sweet smile, but no. One art dealer accused her of squandering my rare gift. Work such as mine needed to be in galleries!

She'll have the rest of her life to work, she replied, *but right now we're focusing on not squandering her childhood.*

And so I divided my time between painting and bench warming, the one solitary, and the other actually a good way for a quiet girl to make a friend, a best friend as it turned out. Our freshman year of high school, Ingrid and I played soccer together, and it was tough to say who was worse. Ingrid apologized when she stole the ball and I didn't like getting kicked in the shins, two things that not only tested the limits of Coach's blood pressure medication, but had him convinced we lacked the killer instinct. And if there was one thing Coach loved it was killer instinct. As a result, we both spent a lot of time on the bench. It was there where I first gave Ingrid a timid smile, and where she, while twisting a strand of her amber hair around her finger, first got us talking.

"What are you thinking about?" she'd asked, bumping my knee with hers.

"Play of light," I'd said. "What about you?"

"My latest Snapchat" she'd said with a giggle.

"What you should be thinking about is the game!" Coach had snapped, but then again, Coach always snapped. As soon as he turned around, Ingrid pretended to shout, opening her mouth wide enough for a dental exam, which made us laugh, and instant friends.

The afternoon sun, which had been shining through my bedroom window, slid behind dark clouds, making it feel like someone had switched off the light. "Everything's going to change, and it's going to be terrible," Ingrid moaned.

I pulled her to her feet. "You sound like a really depressing fortune cookie," I said.

"Friends grow apart, Lana. It happens all the time."

"You falling for a cute boy happens all the time. Friends grow apart on occasion, but that's not going to happen to us."

"I know it's stupid, but it feels like you're going to dump me."

"Strangle, yes. Dump, no." The garage door hummed, signaling that Dad was pulling the car onto the drive way. I held out my pinkie. "Come on, it's time for a promise blitz."

Ingrid locked her pinkie around mine. "Can I go first?" she asked, her natural cheerfulness returning. I rolled my free wrist, telling her to hurry. "Okay, promise me we'll always be friends, not just acquaintances, or Christmas card buddies, but friends."

"I promise," I said, glad that it was my turn, because it was a chance for me to say what had been on my mind since I'd watched her lean toward Riley, a guy she barely knew, and kiss him. I'd teased her about it plenty, but the truth was it concerned me. Was Florida State changing her? "Promise me you'll stick to The Plan."

"The Plan!" she said, before exhaling sharply. "I'm the one who wrote The Plan. It's my baby!"

I tightened my grip on her pinkie. "And even cuddly hamsters sometimes eat their young."

It was true that Ingrid had been the one to write (scribble) The Plan on the back of a stolen wedding card, all thanks to her sister deciding to move back home a few days before her wedding.

"Why should I have to give up my room to her!" she had cried as we, one day after school, sat in her family's living room surrounded by wedding presents. "They've been living together for two years. What difference does it make to stop a few days before the wedding?"

"I guess it's tradition," I told her with a shrug. "The groom not seeing the bride—"

"Trust me, the groom has *seen* the bride. No, you know what this is, she said, pointing a finger at me, "this is Krissa kicking me out of my room so that she can *pretend* to be a virgin. And the weird thing is she's beginning to believe it. The other day at her bridal shower I heard her say she was nervous for the wedding night. I couldn't help it. I threw a carrot stick at her."

"Look, I know you're mad," I said, taking a wedding present in hand and fiddling with its curly ribbon, "but all you can do is hang tight, the wedding will be over soon enough."

Reaching toward me, Ingrid ripped the card off the present in my lap, making me jump a little with surprise. "No," she said, "there's something more I can do—*we* can do."

I cocked an eyebrow. "Steal her gift cards?" I asked.

Ingrid tore open the iridescent gold envelope, and took out the card. On the front were two champagne flutes, and inside, nothing more than congratulations. "Give me some credit, Lana. I'm mad, not looking to commit a misdemeanor," she said. "I just needed something to write on . . . and to get out a teensy bit of aggression. Ripping felt good. Hey, do you have a pen?"

"Dumb question," I said, setting the present aside and reaching into my messenger bag. I always carried with me a sketch pad and a crocheted pouch filled with pens and pencils.

The back of the card was blank, and at the top of it, Ingrid wrote, THE PLAN, underlining it more than once. My pen flipping between her fingers, she thought for a moment. "So what's our plan?" she asked.

I raised my hand. "First, I'd like to make it clear that I have no idea what we're doing."

"We're making a pact."

"If it involves blood or spit, I'm out."

"What it involves is not ending up like Krissa."

"Engaged?"

"No, pretending the wedding night isn't going to be just more of the same. When we wear white, Lana, we're going to own it." Ingrid click, click, clicked the pen. "So how about this, she said, "We, Ingrid and Lana," writing as she spoke, "promise, no, vow to stay virgins until we're married." Ingrid bit her lip. "Is that too much? Too crazy?"

I shrugged. "Sounds good," I said, not mentioning that since I intended to get married in a Mormon temple that was my plan anyway.

Ingrid pointed to what she'd just written. "Do you think we can do it?" she asked, squinting.

"You realize you're talking to a girl who's never even been—"

"Kissed!" finished Ingrid, clapping a little as she said it. Her first kiss had been to Theo Walincowski on the bus home from middle school while everyone had snickered. Theo, or Dolphin Free, as she liked to call him, had smelled of tuna, and after their kiss had smiled so wide she could see lettuce stuck in his braces.

That I hadn't kissed anyone yet meant to Ingrid that I had dodged the Theo bullet, or something equally as awkward. She was convinced I should be patient, and that when it happened, whenever that was, it would be, as she put it, super romantic! I loved her for not mocking me, but wondered if she was up for the challenge.

I put my hand to my heart. "I know *I* can do it," I said. "The question is can you."

Ingrid bit her lower lip. "I think so," she said. "Maybe, possibly."

"You sound like The Little Engine That Couldn't," I said.

"It's just so unheard of. They'd never admit it, but even my parents . . ." Instead of finishing that sentence, Ingrid pretended to throw up.

"Living on Mars is unheard of," I said, snatching the wedding card and pen from her fingers, "staying a virgin until you're married is not."

"You really think so?" she asked, a note of hope in her voice.

"I know so," I said, thinking instantly of couples I knew who'd succeeded at doing so, but there wasn't any way of talking about them without mentioning church, so I left it alone.

And we did stick with The Plan. Of course, I had intended to all along, but for boy-crazy Ingrid it was no small thing, especially once she started attending Florida State. Standing in the center of my childhood bedroom, her pinkie interlocked with mine, Ingrid sighed, worry clouding her brown eyes. "You realize they think I'm odd."

"No one thinks you're odd."

"My sorority sisters do," she said, then chewed her lower lip. "At our softball awards ceremony, they gave me a trophy for being MVP, most virginal player. It was funny, but still."

"You said it before, they're snobs. Who cares what they think?"

Ingrid tugged my pinkie. "But Lana, what if I really like a guy, and he really likes me?"

I tugged back. "So."

She tugged. "And we're practically engaged?"

I tugged. "So!"

She tugged. "We are engaged?"

I tugged and gave her a withering look.

She tugged. "He's heading off to war?"

I tugged. "No."

She tugged and let out a deep breath. "Okay, fine, but you have to promise—"

"You know I'm sticking to the plan," I said, interrupting her.

"Right, but when you get your first kiss," I rolled my eyes. "Promise you'll call me."

"The rate I'm going, I'll be calling you from the retirement center. "Ingrid," I said, trying to make myself sound a hundred years old, "guess what just happened . . ."

"That kiss is coming like a freight train."

"So it's going to kill me."

"No, just knock you off balance."

"It's never going to happen."

"It's totally going to happen, and would have already if you weren't such an Oliver Twist."

"Huh?"

"An artful dodger," she explained, poking me in my shoulder.

I didn't try to deny this. She knew me too well. "Fine," I said, "when it happens I'll call you."

"Your dad hasn't honked the horn yet," she said tightening her grip on my pinkie, so let's keep the promises coming."

"Sure," I said, "promise me you'll stop using emojis at the end of your texts."

"Promise me you'll ask a flight attendant where the loo is with a British accent during the flight."

"Promise me you'll friend request Theo Walincowski." With her free hand, Ingrid pinched me. "Ouch!"

"Promise me the next thing you buy won't be black, and that we'll see each other at Christmas."

From the driveway, we heard Dad give the horn a quick tap. "I Promise," we both said, and after one last hug, we headed outside.

Chapter Three

Whenever I fly, my four-year-old self likes to tag along. That little girl who boarded a plane and left Siberia—it's as if she's buckled next to me, tugging at my sleeve, and insisting that I remember. And so I do. I remember the stern woman giving me two cold kisses—one for each cheek—and handing me to Lois, explaining as she did that this was my mother now and to forget about the old one. "She's certainly forgotten about you," she had said, words that stung worse than any slap. I told myself I would never forget her, but the world beyond Bushkaya Orphanage #3 was so breathtaking that, sitting next to Lois and staring out the oval plane window, I wondered if my memory of my mother would, like a wispy cloud, fade to nothingness. Her long hair, the point of her chin, the curve of her lips—would I forget it all? Almost without thinking, I began to do what I always did—sketch on my palm with my finger.

Other than to mock, no one usually noticed my sketching. But there was nothing usual about Lois Huish, this woman who had gone looking for nesting dolls and found a daughter. For our long flight out of Russia, she had brought a backpack filled with things to keep me busy, but in it no paper. So she handed me the napkin from under her drink and a pen from her purse. It was amazing, seeing the lines I was drawing instead of just imagining them, or rendering them temporarily in dust. Though the paper was flimsy and the pen odd to grip in my little fist, I drew my mother. Not perfectly, but well enough that Lois's mouth fell open. She said that had she not seen it, she wouldn't have believed that a child so young could produce such a drawing, and on a napkin! She knew it couldn't have been a fluke. Still, just to make sure, she grabbed a stack of napkins off a passing beverage trolley, handed them to me, and for the rest of the flight I drew pictures. With my new mother by my side, I drew until my hand cramped and I fell asleep.

When you step off a plane with a pillow hugging your neck, the last thing you're thinking about is smiling for the camera. The flight from Tampa to Nantucket had been long, and had included a three-hour layover in Boston, and a short, bumpy flight on a regional jet, But finally, late in the afternoon, I touched down in Nantucket, safe and sound. The wind whipped my raven locks as I stepped down the plane's short flight of stairs and onto the tarmac. I was travel worn, beat, exhausted, and by the time I got to baggage claim, surrounded by paparazzi.

Okay, that was an overstatement, but there was one guy there with a video camera, and for some reason, he had it trained on me. I eyed him with suspicion then smiled at Chester and Ethel Wilmington who were standing beside him. I had met the Wilmingtons once before in New York at the gala where I'd received my award, and was happy to see them again. Stooped yet energetic, the Wilmingtons were a couple whose fifty-plus years of marriage had melded them into an unstoppable white-haired team. They reminded me of Santa and Mrs. Claus, only thinner and philanthropically focused on art, not toys. With them was a thirty-something African-American man dressed in a white t-shirt and jeans. It was an outfit that said, I'm just an ordinary guy, but his gold wristwatch begged to differ. Moguls and hip hop artists wore that watch. Who was this guy?

"Welcome to Nantucket!" warbled Ethel Wilmington, clasping her chilly, small hand in mine. "We're so delighted you're here!"

"Such a pleasure," said Chester Wilmington, whose hand seemed just as small and chilly as his wife's. "We've been looking forward to your stay, even if it is going to be short. But Mr. Zaugg will explain that."

"Lefty Zaugg," said the man in jeans and t-shirt, his smile filled with charisma. "Of course, my mother named me Demetrius, but my brothers and sisters called me Lefty because I wanted whatever they left on their plates. Can't blame me for having a big appetite. Still do," he smoothed his shirt against his flat stomach, "only now it's for success."

I peeled off my neck pillow. "And why is there a camera guy?" I asked softly.

"Well, if I had my druthers there wouldn't be. No offense, Julio," said Ethel. The cameraman, who was apparently named Julio, said nothing but raised his hand to let us know that none was taken.

"An unnecessary expense, if you ask me," said Chester.

"Our vision for the mentoring experience has been one that other than hobnobbing with the locals, is mostly a quiet—"

"And cheap," interjected Chester, one chilly finger raised.

"Affair," finished Ethel.

Lefty let out a breath, whistling as he did. "With all due respect, art isn't quiet. It's commotion, chaos, convergence," he said, his hand gestures more like interpretive dance. "It's color, and the absence of color. It's mashing what offends with the sublime."

"I have no idea what he just said," whispered Chester to Ethel.

"That makes two of us," whispered Ethel to Chester.

Make that three of us, I would have mumbled if Julio hadn't zoomed in for a close up.

"And that's okay," said Ethel. "We don't pretend to understand the creative process. We're not artists, we're enthusiasts!"

"Fiscally responsible enthusiasts," clarified Chester.

Ethel softly swatted her husband. "Enough about money," she admonished, then, suddenly aware of Julio, turned toward the camera and gave a tentative smile. "We don't pretend to understand the creative process," she said, alternating between looking at the camera and me, "which is why we, along with our board of trustees, are willing to grant Mr. Zaugg's request."

"And what is Mr. Zaugg's request?" I asked as Lefty glanced at his watch.

"The freedom to change," said Chester.

"Change what?" I asked.

"Everything," said Ethel. "Until now our artists and mentors have stayed with us at our seaside home for the six-week program, which, of course, has been no trouble at all," explained Ethel.

"The arrangement has saved us a lot of money," said Chester, his hand to the side of his mouth as if sharing a secret.

Ethel rolled her eyes. "All he thinks about is money," she said apologetically.

Chester patted his wife's arm. "Which is why we're billionaires, my dear," he said.

"And so what happens now?" I asked, glancing at Lefty who was glancing at his watch again.

"Mr. Zaugg takes the money and runs," muttered Chester, earning an elbow nudge from his wife.

Lefty flashed his winning smile. "I'm an advocate for the unseen, a disciple of discovery, a celebrator of the real estate that lies outside the box—"

"Here he goes again," mumbled Chester.

"—What art have we yet to create because we haven't reached beyond the ordinary? As mentor and student, we are going to eliminate the expected and embrace the unexpected."

"And how are we going to do that?" I asked, trying to not sound annoyed. What was wrong with the way things had been done?

"You're going to tap my watch."

"I'm going to what?" I asked as Lefty turned his wrist to show me his watch's face. It wasn't what it had been, just your average diamond encrusted luxury timepiece. Now the Swiss movement was gone, replaced by a black screen, on which flashed the names of cities and towns. Quebec. New York City. Paris. Brussels. Berlin. Detroit. Globe. Lefty slid his finger around the rim of the watch and the cities flashed so fast I could barely read them.

"Lana Huish, in my watch is a list of cities, roughly fifty. Julio, get up close. I want to make sure we get a shot of this." Julio zoomed in, his camera focused on Lefty's wrist. "Some of the places you've heard of, some perhaps not, but all of them have one thing in common—they're each home to artists who have been honored by the Wilmington Trust in one way or another, and all have agreed—"

"This part was my idea," interjected Chester.

"To have you stay

as their guest for the next six weeks," said Lefty. "Of course, you'll come back to Nantucket for the Wilmington Museum Gala in the fall where your art will be on exhibit, but where you experience your mentorship depends on which city you pick."

My heart lifted. Maybe changing everything about the program wasn't such a bad idea. "Well, in that case, I pick Paris. It's a great city. I won't be able to set up an easel in the Louvre since I'm not already on the waiting list, and it's like a year wait, but I could roam its halls when I'm not painting elsewhere. And there are so many places to paint in Paris, Musee D'Orsay, Sacre Coure—"

"No, no," said Lefty, smiling as he cut me off. Did he ever not smile? "Yes, you get to pick where you go, but by tapping my watch. When you tap the list will stop, and that's where you'll go. Simple as that. He tapped his watch, and the speeding list of cities stopped on Rome. He tapped again and the list sped up. Then again, and New Orleans appeared. "You see, there's nothing to it."

I bit my lip and stared at the whir of cities passing across his watch's face. "And are you coming with me?"

Lefty's already bright smile brightened. "That's funny," he said, pointing at me. "No, you're going to do *you*, and I'm"— he put his hand to his heart—"going to do openings, first in Helsinki, then Berlin, then Tokyo. Come to think of it, Tokyo is on your list of possibilities. Tell you what, if you end up in Godzilla's stomping ground, we'll meet for Sake."

"I don't drink," I said, which Lefty either didn't hear or ignored.

"But not sushi," he continued. "In my opinion, raw fish is a reward for sea lions after doing tricks. But don't worry, you won't be alone. Julio's going."

Julio, still peering through the camera's lens, twisted his hand over and under.

"Looks like he's on the fence. We'll work that out later, but right now, it's time to tap. Are you ready, Lana?"

"Not really," I said.

"Well, how can anyone really be ready for such a moment? cried Ethel. "In my day, you would have at least spun a wheel or thrown a dart at a map. Even while wearing a blindfold that would have been preferable to just tapping a watch. Technology makes everything more frightening!"

Chester took Ethel's hand. "Now, now, Mother."

Lefty clapped like a coach trying to motivate his team. "Okay, Lana Huish!" he said, extending his watch toward me. "Let's do this! I've got a plane to catch!"

Anxiety rose up inside me. Lefty was leaving? My mentor was ducking out? "Wait a minute," I said, grabbing him by the arm. "You're taking off right now? Right this minute?"

Lefty's eyes went wide. "Lana Huish, he said in almost a whisper, "you tapped my watch."

"But I didn't mean to tap your watch!" I said, my voice suddenly high and squeaky. "I didn't mean it. I was just grabbing your arm. It was a gesture, not a tap."

"Does it count?" asked Ethel.

"Of course it counts!" cried Lefty. "Lana Huish, you have tapped."

"So where am I going?" I asked, too stunned to beg inwardly for Barcelona.

Lefty looked at his watch, then brought it to his face for closer inspection as if what was written required deciphering.

"What does it say?" asked Chester.

"For heaven's sake, don't keep us in suspense!" cried Ethel.

"Just say it," I said.

"Bluegill, Idaho. You're going to Bluegill, Idaho," he said, his smile so wide I could have counted all his teeth.

I gulped. "No, Ida—No," I stammered.

"No," said Lefty, "Idaho. Bluegill, Idaho."

Chapter Four

Bluegill. I pressed my palms to my temples and watched as my suitcase made a lonely turn around the carousel. The other passengers had already claimed their luggage, and there mine was, as solitary as I was bound to be in a town called Bluegill. I let out a heavy sigh.

"It will be great," said Lefty, rubbing his hands together. "Idaho's great, or so I hear. I've never been, not enough Korean take-out. But Julio's going." He pointed at Julio. Julio gave him a thumbs down. "Can I take that as a maybe?" he asked.

Julio turned off the camera and looked at Lefty directly, instead of through the lens. "If she had picked someplace worth visiting, sure. But Bluegill, Idaho? No way, man."

Lefty smiled, "Come on, be a friend."

"You told me I'd be going to Honolulu."

"It was a possibility," said Lefty, his smile now as wide as the Cheshire cat's. "How about a week? Julio shook his head. Three days. It might give us just enough for a documentary."

"A documentary!" cried Ethel. "How is she supposed to concentrate if you're filming a documentary?"

Lefty's smile tightened. "Julio's great at blending in."

"At a Puerto Rican wedding," said Julio.

"We'll pay you time and a half."

"What!" cried Chester.

"Not doing it."

"Here, here!" said Chester.

I folded my arms. "Come to think of it, maybe I won't either," I said. With Lefty changing everything, did I really want to do this?

"Oh dear," said Ethel, pressing her hands to her wrinkled face.

Lefty looked at his watch, which now displayed the time. "Can we talk about this?" he asked, gesturing toward the luggage carousel—a distance just far enough away that our conversation wouldn't be heard.

I shook my head as if saying *no*, but followed him.

"What is the matter?" he asked me, turning his back to Julio who had started filming again. I suppose even a documentary maker likes a little privacy.

"What's the matter?" I cried "You're my mentor, and before I can even claim my luggage you're taking off for Helsinki or Berlin or wherever you're going! I thought you were supposed to teach me!"

"Teach you? Have you taken a look at your work?" cried Lefty, his hands flying upward. "I started out a tagger, a tagger with considerable talent, no doubt, but still a tagger. Sure, I studied at the Sorbonne, but you Lana, you paint like a Rubens, a John Singer Sargent. What exactly do you think I can teach you?"

"I don't know! I'm sure there's something!" I said, but with less fire. His compliment had softened me.

Lefty rocked back on his heels. "Look, I'm an artist, but I also graduated from La Guardia Community College with a degree in finance, and if there's anything I can teach you it's this, art is business. You're a talent, Lana Huish, a rare one, but right now no one knows you. You've hoarded your paintings.

"I haven't hoarded them!" I said, because there was a difference between my mother storing them in an air-conditioned warehouse and hoarding. Wasn't there?

"Well, you haven't sold them, especially to the right people. You have zero provenance, zero buzz about who owns one of your works. Collectors like to keep up with The Joneses. So, you go to Bluegill, Idaho, and let me go find Mr. and Mrs. Jones."

"You don't have any of my paintings."

"I've got the three you submitted for this mentorship."

"They're supposed to be hanging in the Wilmington Museum!" My bag crawled past, within arm's reach, but I was too mad to care.

Lefty threw his hands in the air. "And who's going to see them there—a museum five hundred miles from anywhere that is only opened Wednesday through Saturday from 11 to 4?" Unable to think of a response, I bit my lip. "I'm taking them where the buyers are, starting with Helsinki," said Lefty as he looked at his watch again. "And not to be rude, but I gotta split. My plane is boarding in five."

"You can't sell them, you know."

"I know, I know," he said, shaking his head, "you *donated* them to the museum. Paintings aren't sticks of gum, Lana Huish. You shouldn't give them away."

"I was being kind!" I said. And I was. It wasn't required that submitted works be given to the Wilmington Museum. But the Wilmingtons had been so excited about my paintings, I think, because they understood them. Last year's recipient, Phillip Fellows, created art out of Kleenex. *We're delighted with your work,* they'd whispered to me at the ceremony after I'd received my award, *Philip's art makes us want to sneeze.*

"Kindness has its place," said Lefty, "but it never bought a villa in the South of France."

"I don't want a villa in the South of France," I said, only because the thought of owning one had never occurred to me, but even as I said it I felt something within me, something small, like a seed splitting open. Come to think of it, maybe I did want a villa in the South of France, or if not that, the freedom to live the life I wanted. Who wouldn't?

"Lana Huish, do you want to be successful?" he asked, sneaking another glance at his watch.

"Of course!" I cried.

"Then let me take your work and go find Mr. and Mrs. Jones. That's who you want. That's how a canvas covered with paint turns into something worth millions. Rockefeller's Rothko sold for over 70 million, not just because it was a Rothko, but because it was David Rockefeller's Rothko. You get what I'm saying?"

Provenance wasn't new to me. Of course I knew that certain people buying your work created buzz that drove prices up. But I had thought it was something you waited for, not forced into being. I rubbed my temples. "Fine, go and find Mr. and Mrs. Jones. But let me tap your watch again. Just once. Okay twice. Gary, Indiana's in there."

Lefty folded his arms, tucking his watch out of sight. "You got your tap."

I threw my hands in the air. "What exactly am I supposed to do in Bluegill, Idaho for six weeks!"

"You're supposed to paint."

"Is everything all right?" asked Ethel, her hands cupped to her mouth.

"Yes!" cried Lefty, drowning out my mumbled *no*. Everything was not all right! My mentor was ditching me, and I was heading to Bluegill, Idaho to paint what, potatoes?

"So when will I see you again?" I asked as I grabbed my suitcase.

"That's going to depend," said Lefty.

"On what?"

"On Mr. and Mrs. Jones."

And with that my mentor shook hands with the Wilmingtons, gave Julio a pat on the shoulder, and left. And for a brief but absurd moment it all came back to me—my mother prying my little hands from her sleeve, the stern woman's grip on my shoulder, my ineffectual tears. Why did it feel like yesterday? And why did those memories still have the power to make me cry? I brushed away tears and watched Lefty walk away.

"It will be all right," said Ethel, placing her arm around me and giving me a squeeze. "I'm sure Bluegill is lovely in June."

Bluegill. I was going to Bluegill. I could have gone to Paris or Rome, but that's not what I'd tapped. I'd had one chance, one shot, and completely messed it up. It didn't matter that Julio was slowly walking around me, filming me from every angle. I buried my head in Ethel's shoulder and cried.

Chapter Five

I stayed for two days at the Wilmingtons' just long enough to know that if Lefty hadn't decided to shake things up I would have loved doing my mentorship in Nantucket. Luxury is easy to get used to. It was a short stay, but with full use of the most awesome art studio on the planet (sweeping views, surround sound, and their maid Cecile at the ready) I was able to finish one painting—a portrait of the Wilmingtons, which they loved, so I gave it to them, even though I could hear Lefty in my head. *Paintings aren't sticks of gum, Lana Huish.* Yes, the Wilmingtons were billionaires, but they were the nicest, not to mention most frugal, billionaires you could hope to meet. And so, I gave them the painting, and in return they gave me six weeks in Bluegill, Idaho.

Why did six weeks in Bluegill feel like a jail sentence? Almost like six weeks hard labor in some dreaded place like Siberia. I smiled. "It's like I'm headed home," I muttered as I sketched the businessman seated across the aisle from me. "Home, sweet home."

In the history of aviation, I was likely the only traveler who had ever left Nantucket with Bluegill, Idaho as their final destination, and with good reason. There was no straight shot from one to the other. It would take me all day to get to Seventy-Two Dogwood Lane, the home of LeVan and Rosemary Hitchpost.

As the short bio I'd been given told me, LeVan Hitchpost had graduated from Columbia University in 1965 with a degree in fine arts, and had, before retiring, divided his time between painting (western art was his specialty) and civic duties. His connection to the Wilmington Trust had occurred later in his career. He was awarded a grant by the trust that had made it possible for him to spend a summer painting at the Grand Canyon, and had, as the bio explained, taken with him his youngest grandson.

"Rosemary will be delighted to meet you. She's stepped out for a moment," he'd said when I'd contacted him. The committee was of the opinion that Lefty was supposed to contact my host family, but Lefty said he was swamped, and so that fell to me.

A cool breeze greeted me as I walked out of the airport to wait for my Uber. Mr. Hitchpost had offered to pick me up, but when I called him, he said his wife, Rosemary, had just stepped out (she seemed to do that a lot), and that if it weren't too much trouble, could I find a ride, just someone to drop me off. "While you're here, you can use Ruth," he'd said. She's a good truck."

A truck named Ruth. This intrigued me. I had only ever driven a 2004 Civic with cigarette burns on the upholstery from the previous owner. My car had never been my friend. It had gotten me where I'd needed to go, that was all. But I liked the idea of driving a christened truck, especially since the trust wasn't springing for a six-week car rental. It would be part of the whole small-town experience, and so I told Mr. Hitchpost I'd be happy to use Ruth during my stay, and booked an Uber to Bluegill.

"You the one needing a ride to Bluegill?" asked the driver of a gray four-door sedan so boring, it seemed guaranteed no one had bothered to give it a name.

"That's me," I said.

The trunk popped open. "Do you need help?" he asked.

I tossed my suitcase and backpack inside. "I got it," I said, glad to sit in the back and relax. After a long day of travel, I was tired—tired of pretzels and Ginger Ale, of gate changes and overhead bins, of flight attendants smiling while telling me what to do in the event of a disaster, but mostly I was just tired. All I wanted to do was get to Seventy-Two Dogwood Lane and fall asleep, so I was glad someone besides me was driving. And besides, Ingrid was texting me.

Guess what!!!!!!!

Riley asked you out.

Yes, for Saturday! How'd you know?

The seven exclamation points gave it away.

Oh, please.

Just take this slow.

I am! But it's hard. He said I have nice eyes. How am I supposed to not fall for that?

Find a way.

Where are you anyway?

In the back of an Uber driving past potato fields.

Is that safe?

I'm fine. He's listening to NPR

Still, don't fall asleep

Okay

So is it beautiful?

What?

Idaho!

Everything has beauty

Quit talking like an artist.
Would you want to live
there?

I'd rather kiss
Theo Walincowski

I'm going to take that as a
no.

Please do

The afternoon sun was peeking out from behind a dark cloud, warming my face and making me drowsy. I stared at the potato fields. Their vastness, like the waters of the gulf coast, reached to the horizon. *A spud ocean*, I thought, which made me think of Anna Maria Island, Ingrid's friend's wedding, and whispering a prayer as I looked out at the water dappled with the last light of day. I had prayed for guidance, and here I was, in an Uber heading to Bluegill, Idaho. Life was funny.

I closed my eyes and sighed. Oh well. All I needed to do was get through the next six weeks, and then get on with my life. I could handle six weeks. I'd dealt with worse. *Thankless child*, said the stern woman while shaking her finger at me. *Would you have preferred fending for yourself on the street? We provided for you! And, perhaps, if you hadn't spent all your time staring out the window, you might have noticed you weren't the only child left to our care. Dealt with worse!* I felt a tap on my shoulder, but ignored it. Ingrid was right, it wasn't smart to nap while being driven by a stranger, but despite that good advice, I had fallen into a drooly slumber, and when the tapping turned into shaking, I bolted awake. "What, what, what!" I cried.

"Sorry to startle you," said the driver, "but are you sure this is your stop?"

I squinted. "No, this is it," I said, pointing at a mailbox with Hitchpost, Seventy-Two Dogwood Lane painted in block letters on its side. And that's when I noticed the house's windows were boarded shut.

I leaned forward. The house was abandoned. Deserted. I gulped, my heart pounding like I'd just sprinted rather than driven up the empty street. What was happening? Had I written down the address wrong? Where was I supposed to be? And why did my phone always lose reception when I really needed it? I looked at the house. Seventy-Two Dogwood Lane. It had been beautiful once, that was easy to see. Care had been taken in building it. A white, two-story Dutch colonial, it was placed just far enough off the road to provide privacy, but not too far back to ruin the picturesque quality of it by the road's curve. A modest row of daisies grew in the garden beds, and the lawn had been recently cut. This house had been abandoned, but it was still cared for. Someone was looking out for this house.

"I don't know, it looks empty to me," said the driver, fingering the hoop in his ear.

"It's supposed to look empty," I lied.

The driver turned around and gave me a skeptical look. "Why?"

"The owner doesn't like solicitors."

"Or neighbors," said the driver, his neck popping as he turned his head to look up and down the street. "Doesn't seem to be anyone else out here."

"Some people just aren't persons people. People people. People persons," I said with a shrug, like there was nothing odd about me jumbling my words or someone living in a house that looked prepared for a hurricane. "Thanks for the ride," I said brightly.

I slammed the door and started toward the abandoned house.

"Would you like your bags?" asked the driver, popping the trunk. I only had a small suitcase and my backpack with me. The rest (my painting supplies) was being shipped to Seventy-Two Dogwood Lane. I could have easily pulled my things from the trunk, but the driver did it for me. "I'm Carl, by the way," he said, shaking my hand. "Nice meeting you, and be sure to give me a call the next time you're in need."

"I will," I said, and looked at his business card. "Carl Holdman," I said, glancing at him and then back at the card, "Your Friend On The Road."

"Do you think it's too much?" asked Carl.

I tucked the card in my pocket. "No, I like it," I said.

"Glad to hear it," he said, climbing back in his car. And that was when it hit me—this guy wasn't dangerous, and the smart move would be to come clean, tell him I needed a ride into town so that I could make some calls and figure out what had gone wrong. But I had told him I was in the right place. I had told him that someone inside that shuttered house was waiting for me. And so I reassured myself that just around the corner there was probably a house or a corner market, and I waved Carl good bye.

Chapter Six

It took just a minute of walking to realize suitcase wheels weren't meant for rough country roads, so I decided to stash my suitcase behind the house, just in case someone drove by and felt inclined to swipe it. As if. No one was out here, except me, some birds, and a few hyperactive squirrels. Around the back I discovered LeVan Hitchpost's art studio. A stone path connected it to the house, and though the house's windows were boarded, the studios were not. Two rolling glass doors, the kind used in auto repair shops, were at the front of the studio. The other sides were windowless and white planked like the house. Ivy grew along one side of the studio, reached to the roof line and crept across the glass doors.

"That needs to be cut back," I said, as if someone were there to hear, and I had something to do with Seventy-Two Dogwood Lane. I pulled some ivy away from the glass front and looked inside. This was no Wilmington studio, but it had the essentials—a small kitchen, a long table, some chairs, a cot for when you needed to rest, and it faced North to allow for the best lighting all day.

On the back wall, hanging from industrial clamps, and hidden behind scaffolding, were three huge canvases, roughly 12 x 5 feet. All three had been under painted a soft red, a good technique for adding richness to color, and across the first two, rendered in thin paint, were drawings. "What an ambitious project," I said as, squinting, I tried to decipher the drawings, and puzzled over why the artist (LeVan Hitchpost, presumably) had abandoned it.

I propped my suitcase against the glass front and headed down the road. It was a good studio, I thought as I walked in the direction Carl had gone. A tad masculine, yes, and out of the way, but I liked the glass doors, the way they could be rolled up on pleasant days. Having a preference for small to medium-sized canvasses, the studio was larger than I needed. This was a muralist's work space. I wasn't a muralist, but the studio felt right, and I looked forward to working in it.

Beyond the bend, I had expected to see a house. A little store would have been fantastic, but at least a house, some sign of life. There was none, and in the distance, nothing but a fork in the road. I squinted, trying to see if I could spot Bluegill, Idaho, but it was impossible to tell what lay ahead. Both roads were covered in loose gravel and appeared equally untraveled. I stared at them, a hand pressed to my forehead, as I felt panic rise inside me. Thoughts, directionless as I was, raced through my mind. *Why did I let Carl drive away? I shouldn't have fallen asleep! I could be miles outside Bluegill! Maybe I should say a prayer. I hate my phone! I'm thirsty! The sun is setting! Which way should I go? I should definitely say a prayer.*

My mind was as disjointed as an orchestra warming up, and in the midst of that din, I said a hasty prayer, half expecting the clouds above to reconfigure themselves into an arrow pointing left or right. But nothing happened. No impression, no voice from heaven, just the distant sound of a stream gurgling and the rustle of the wind through the trees. "Left or right?" I closed my eyes and repeated that question until it turned from a prayer into a rhythm. Still nothing. I opened my eyes. I had to make a decision. I couldn't stand here forever, and so I took off down the road to the right, in the direction of the stream because I was thirsty, not considering, until it was almost dark and I'd still spotted no one, that maybe I should have stayed put.

I had dressed for the plane, not walking endlessly on a winding country road, and my flip flops were beginning to rub the skin between my toes raw. To make matters worse, the temperature was dropping and my yoga pants and thin sweater were doing little to keep me warm. I was tired, lost, and, because I'd been unable to find that stupid stream, incredibly thirsty. Tears stung my eyes, and though no one was there to see, I fought to keep them from sliding down my cheeks. This was not the time to fall apart. This was the time to turn around, and in the dark, find my way back to Seventy-Two Dogwood Lane. In the morning, I'd search again for help.

Thin clouds slipped across a crescent moon as I headed back in the direction I'd come. At first the setting sun had turned the sky a crisp azure that heightened the sparkle of the stars. But as it sunk below the horizon, the colors deepened, silhouetting the surrounding peaks and revealing more stars in an already crowded sky. I had never seen so many stars! Turning around and around, I let their beauty envelop me, and as I did the distance between me and them seemed to shorten, as if these heavenly bodies had rushed to greet me. Taking in the stars, I forgot I was lost and hungry, that I was cold and miles from shelter. I forgot about Lefty Zaugg, the Wilmingtons, and waving Carl good bye. But most all, I forgot to check for oncoming traffic.

By the time the truck in front of me screeched to a stop, I could have reached out and touched its bug-covered grill.

The driver flung the door open and rushed toward me. "Are you Lana Huish?" he asked, sounding desperate.

"Yes," I said.

Lacing his fingers behind his neck, he bowed his head, and then went all upset parent on me. "Why are you standing in the middle of the road? You could have gotten hit!" He said, stopping just shy of shouting.

"I was looking at the stars!" I said, defending myself when, deep down, I knew I should have been apologizing. "You're wearing black! I could barely see you!"

"Well, you should be more observant," I said, but without conviction, because Ingrid was in my head with her hands on her hips.

He'd killed the engine, but left the headlights on. Their light outlined his tall frame, but did little to reveal his face. "Me, more observant!" he cried. "You should have seen me coming!"

"You were going too fast!" I said, squinting, trying to discern his features. I was pretty sure I spotted a big nose and broken teeth.

He raked a hand through what looked like a mass of greasy hair. "I was going fast because I was worried about you! I found your suitcase, but not you! You shouldn't have left the house!"

"I was trying to find help!"

"First rule of survival: stay put until help arrives!"

"First rule of hospitality: don't board up the house!"

The driver hung his head, and though I couldn't see his face, I could sense sorrow crowding him, making it hard for him to answer back. I shrugged off the impulse to tell him I was sorry. So, we stood there in the dark, neither speaking, until a voice from inside the truck broke our stalemate. "Is everything all right?" asked a girl, poking her head out the open truck window.

"Everything's fine!" said the driver, his voice an unpleasant mix of frustration and sarcasm. Then he let out a long breath, as if to take a moment to calm down. "Look, it's late. We should go," he said, sounding tired. He was trying to give me an olive branch, and, to be honest, all I wanted to do was hit him over the head with it.

I folded my arms. "I happen to not be in the habit of getting into cars with strangers," I said, imagining, as I did, Carl saying, *Well, I wouldn't exactly say that.*

"I'm Walt Hitchpost," he said, and reached out to shake hands. "My grandfather is your host."

Host. Why had he said it like it was a joke? I considered telling Walt to get lost. But, that would have been rude, and stupid, because, at the moment, *I* was lost. Like it or not, I needed his help. I extended my hand, and he gently enclosed it in his. I'm usually a firm handshake sort of girl, but there was something about his gentleness, the way he held his strength in check, that made me feel protected, and I liked it. I liked it a lot. A cluster of shooting stars blazed across the dark sky, and my heart flung itself into my ribs, which, I told myself, had nothing to do with Walt. Shooting stars, not handshakes, had that effect on me.

"Welcome to Bluegill, the pearl of Idaho," he said, sounding like a tour guide who hated his job. There was no denying it. His touch had conjured inside me the beginnings of happiness, a wispy, fragile happiness, but now it was gone. Walt Hitchpost obviously didn't want me here, which shouldn't have hurt, because I didn't want me here, but it stung all the same.

He slid my backpack from my shoulders. "You can just drop me off at a motel," I said, as I followed him to his truck.

"Don't be ridiculous," he said, stowing my backpack in the back of the truck beside my suitcase. "You're our guest."

He opened the door. "I don't want to be a bother," I said.

"Too late," mumbled the girl in the truck, her eyes on her phone. I don't know what made me dislike her more, her sassy remark, or that her phone had service out here. "Let's go home," he grumbled, taking me by the arm to help me into his truck because it had been lifted. I smirked. Lifted trucks were so high school, the sort of thing the 4H-Club boys did to show off. I was in the middle of mocking him inwardly for having one when the dome light blinked on and I saw Walt Hitchpost for the first time. It wasn't just that he was good looking, though he was certainly that, there was something familiar in his intense brown eyes, something strangely reminiscent about the slope of his slender nose and the curve of his lips, the rightness of the top of my head reaching just to his shoulders. The impression left me feeling stunned and disoriented. Did he remind me of someone? Had we met before? Or was it—the thought made me blush—that I just wanted it to be so?

If Walt Hitchpost was president of the Bluegill, Idaho welcome wagon, this girl was vice-president. Her cold shoulder made it clear she didn't want me there either. Still, she seemed happy to have an excuse to slide closer to Walt.

Walt shut his door and started the engine. He then took a moment to rub his face and exhale sharply before putting the truck in drive. Walt looked exhausted, and knowing I was the reason why made guilt, like an itchy blanket, settle over me. "Lana," said Walt, tilting his head to the right, "this is Shailene Stock."

Shailene's eyes didn't leave her phone screen, but she wiggled her fingers to say, *Hello.*

"Hi," I said, my finger moving discreetly across my palm in my lap as I sketched Walt in my mind, and considered how to capture his eyes. Their intensity intrigued me; *he* intrigued me. How old was he? He couldn't have been much older than I was. Why was he here, in Bluegill? Why hadn't he moved on to someplace more exciting? And why did I care? I thought of what Ingrid would say about his work boots, his truck. Probably something like, *You can do so much better, Lana.* This made me smile, since, first of all, he was angry I was here, and secondly, he wasn't up for grabs, at least not if Shailene had her way.

I turned my attention to Shaliene, glad the glow from her phone provided just enough light for me to study her on the sly. She was beautiful, I had to give her that, even if I didn't want to. Everything about her was long—her arms, her legs, her dark hair, her face when acknowledging me. What's more, she was long on girly glamor. Rhinestones were everywhere. Well, not everywhere, but they were stuck to her shirt and her fingernails, sparkling in the dim light like she'd just gotten off work at the tiara factory. She had pretty eyes, which later I would find out were an annoyingly piercing blue, and though blessed with creamy, flawless skin, wore her makeup heavy, like the girls who work behind cosmetic counters. I was certain I had her figured out, until she mentioned killing a bear.

"I killed a bear last week," she said, which I assumed meant she'd recently gone crazy in the stuffed animal aisle at Toy R Us, until she added, "right in these woods."

"Quit trying to scare her," said Walt, his voice low.

"But it's true!" she said with a laugh, his little chastisement, in her mind, an opportunity to flirt. She moved closer to Walt, the side of her leg now brushing his. Shailene flipped her hair off her shoulder and continued. "I was hunting with Britney when I saw him by the stream." Suddenly I was glad I hadn't found the stream. "He came charging when I sounded my predator call, and I got him with my bow, maybe fifteen yards off."

Hmm. Shailene had killed a bear, a charging bear, and with just a bow. She wasn't who I thought she was, not entirely, which was irritating. The girl had depth.

"He weighed over six hundred pounds."

I wish you weighed over six hundred pounds, I thought.

"And, of course, didn't have the sense to just drop, but had to run down into a ravine. That's where I found her. It made harvesting the meat—"

"A total bear?" I muttered softly, not intending her to hear me, but she had, they both had. Shailene ignored me and got back to telling her story. Walt didn't say anything either, but I saw his eyes crinkle with a trace of laughter.

" . . . It was definitely a two-person job, getting in and out of there with our kill. The rocks, and the mud, our equipment, a few rattlers we had to pick off. But we did it,"

We emerged onto Dogwood Lane, turned left, and winded our way down the mountain.

Walt pointed out a small, distant cluster of lights he said was Bluegill. I knew nothing about this town called Bluegill, which was fine. My time here would be short, and soon I would be on to places meant for an artist—Paris, London, Madrid. Few people earned a living painting oil on canvas; I wanted to be one of them, and I was willing to work hard to achieve it, to do what I needed to earn it, even if it meant—I stole a glance at Walt—staying in Bluegill for a while.

Chapter Seven

My mom likes to compare artistic talent to an untamed mustang. Its wild side is majestic, but in order for the horse to have a relationship with people, it needs discipline. Lois Huish didn't believe in artists answering the muse's call any hour day or night. According to Mom, an artist needed sleep, time with friends, and plenty of exercise. The muse could swing by later, when it was more convenient. It took some doing, but I got used to this approach to my craft—me ruling it, not it ruling me. My artist friends at Yale envied my ability to "clock in, clock out," as they put it, never staying late in the studio, sacrificing sleep for art. So, they would have been stunned by my first night in Bluegill, Idaho.

After dropping off Shailene at Flintlock, her parent's mansion on the outskirts of Bluegill, we drove in silence to a modest home a block east of Main Street.

"This is it," said Walt, slowly opening the front door to keep it from squeaking. The house was dark, except for a night light glowing in the hallway. Still, I could see enough of the front room, its plush carpet and velvet couches, to know it looked like a snapshot from the seventies. "Gramps is asleep," Walt whispered, sounding relieved.

Walt led me to a bedroom, halfway down a narrow hallway. He opened the door, but didn't turn on the light. "Can I get you anything?" he whispered, placing my things inside the room.

My stomach growled. "No," I whispered.

He bent closer a little closer. "Sorry," he said, his voice softer still, "for, you know, before."

I wanted to say sorry too. I had, after all, raised my voice at him. It seemed the right thing to do, but having him so close to me, my thoughts scattered. I cleared my throat. "Good night," I whispered. He hesitated for a moment, and then left, quietly shutting the door behind him. I knew I'd sounded rude and should apologize, but I needed to collect myself, clear my head. And I needed to sketch.

I worked through the night, sketching Walt Hitchpost against a star-filled sky. The more I revealed his face the less the stars shone. I tried it dozens of ways, some with his eyes in full view, and some with him barely visible, and the stars taking dominance. As I sketched, I replayed in my mind the events of the day, and found myself dwelling on the things Walt had said that had angered me. Yes, he had apologized, but like the dimly sparkling stars in some of my sketches, I put that in the background, choosing instead to place, front and center, the fury in his eyes, and the clench of his jaw as he shouted, *The first rule of survival is stay put until help arrives!*

Heart pounding with indignation, I tore a page from my book and started sketching Walt again, this time with his face contorted in anger, his mouth wide, his teeth bared, and his eyes filled with rage. As the night went on, I added more detail, spit flying from his mouth, smoke coming from his ears, sketching and sketching, until the birds began to sing outside, the first light of day appeared, and the pencil fell from my fingers.

Hours later when I awoke, I looked at the ceiling, and was struck with a sense of unfamiliarity. My eyes flitted around the small room now flooded with daylight, taking in the empty bookcase, the bare walls, the patchwork quilt draped over me, and, with effort, the events of the previous night began to crawl through my mind—getting lost, Walt finding me, the frustration and worry in his eyes, shaking Walt's hand, Shailene sliding closer to Walt in the truck, dropping her off at Flintlock, sketching all night, page after page, not bothering to change clothes, brush my teeth, put in my retainer, just allowing myself to sketch and sketch.

There was a gentle knock at the door.

"Hey," said Walt, "Can I come in?"

There was no time to make myself presentable, but that didn't stop me from hastily rearranging my hair. "Sure," I said.

Walt opened the door, and though I had spent the whole night sketching him, it surprised me to see, once again, how tall he was.

Good morning," I said, as it occurred to me that my face was probably smudged with mascara.

"More like good afternoon," said Walt," pushing the door open wide. "It's almost two o'clock."

I looked at my phone. It was black; I'd forgotten to charge it. "Wow," I said, blushing. "No worm for me."

"Huh?" said Walt, gripping the top of the threshold.

"The early bird gets . . . never mind," I said, trying not to notice his biceps, flexed and tan, were stretching the limits of his t-shirt sleeves.

He gave a lopsided grin. "Speaking of birds, I promise if I were one, I wouldn't be an angry one."

"I'm sorry?" I said, not understanding.

Walt grinned and picked up my picture of him hopping mad, the one I'd ripped from book. It had fallen to the floor. You know, the video game," he said, scrunching up his eyebrows. I opened my mouth, but he didn't give me a chance to respond, which was fine, because what was there to say? "Gramps!" he shouted, turning toward the kitchen, she's awake! Gramps!"

"Jehoshaphat!" warbled LeVan Hitchpost, shuffling across the thick carpet. My face burning with embarrassment, I brought the quilt to my chin, wishing I had the nerve to pull it over my head, and keep it there until Walt and his grandfather gave up and left. Walt placed a gentle hand on his grandfather's shoulder, and stepping aside, made more room in the doorway. LeVan Hitchpost stood before me. He was thin enough his suspenders were a necessity, not a style choice, but he appeared strong, and his grey eyes shone with happiness. "A new student!" he said, tossing his hands in the air, "and a pretty one at that. So pleased to meet you. My grandson's pleased too; He combed his hair."

I looked at Walt just as his eyes shot to the ceiling. Walt's embarrassment renewed my strength to face this situation, and I threw off the blanket and stood before LeVan Hitchpost. He was taller than I expected. "Nice to meet you too," I said.

We shook hands. "Rosemary will be so delighted to know you're here. Are you ready to begin your lesson?" he asked, his hand still clasped in mine.

"Lesson?" I said. "I thought we were just painting together. You don't need to worry about teaching me."

"Not today, Gramps," interjected Walt. "Lana wanted to see Bluegill today." I was about to say, *I did?* until I saw the look of pleading in Walt's eyes, asking me to play along, and so instead, I said, "That's right, I did."

Walt gave me a look of thanks, and, in return, I nodded. It was a simple thing, but it felt special, a shared secret between us.

LeVan scratched the back of his head. "The children need shoes," he said, his voice grave.

I looked at Walt, hoping for an explanation, he gave none.

"You just bought the children shoes," said Walt, patting his grandfather's shoulder.

"And Rosemary," said LeVan. "She brightens her old dresses with scarves, never complaining, but I know she'd love something new to wear." LeVan wrung his hands. "I need to finish a painting."

"You're selling a painting tomorrow," said Walt, reassuringly.

"I am?" he asked. "Which one?"

"True Horseman."

He frowned. "That will fetch a pretty penny," he said, taking on the tone of a shrewd businessman.

"So, you'll have plenty for buying shoes and dresses."

LeVan stared at the floor and nodded. "That's good to know," he said, then he turned to me. "And you say you're my student?" he asked, as if I'd just sprung this on him, instead of the other way around.

Why did his grandfather think I was his student? My mentor was schmoozing in Europe, LeVan was supposed to just give me a place to work and sleep. Not that I wasn't willing to learn from LeVan Hitchpost. I knew next to nothing about western art, and every artist had something to teach. It wouldn't bother me to have him instructing me while I painted. I was good at filtering out distractions. If it made him happy to think I was his student (and it appeared to) then so be it. "It's an honor to have a chance to learn from you," I said, which seemed to make Walt breathe easier." LeVan smiled, and I noticed one of his incisors was lined with gold. "Well, I'm just an old cowboy," he said.

"An old cowboy who can paint," said Walt.

LeVan chuckled, his frail body shaking as he did. "An old cowboy who can paint," he said, both pleased and humbled by this description. He folded his arms and smiled with satisfaction.

From what I could tell, Walt was the kind of person who found it easy to shrug off awkward moments. He seemed to have already forgotten our shouting match, and my less than flattering picture of him. For me, however, they replayed in my head like an awful short film I couldn't escape. He was over it and I was kicking myself in the shower, wishing the water wasn't already cold, and LeVan wasn't at the door, knocking.

"Are you done?" he asked as Walt told him not to rush me.

"Almost," I said.

I dressed quickly and gathered my wet hair in a ponytail. Walt and LeVan were seated in the kitchen, waiting for me. The kitchen was small, but in a corner next to the table, room had been made for an easel. A small canvas had been placed on it. Next to this was a collection of paints and brushes. All was pristine, untouched, as if just purchased from a store.

Walt helped LeVan to his feet, then looked at me. "You're wearing black again," said Walt. It was just an observation, but still.

Together we walked the short distance to main street. LeVan, despite his age, kept a brisk pace. The outing appeared to invigorate him. He seemed eager to get to town, and, *take care of matters*, as he put it. Walt walked beside his grandfather, attentive, trusting him enough not to take him by the arm, but not enough to abandon his careful watch over him. With his focus on LeVan, Walt didn't try to strike up a conversation with me, which was perfect, since talking with him made me feel, or lack of a better word, wobbly. Assuming the worst, I hadn't bothered to google Bluegill, figuring if I had to see it I'd wait until it was absolutely necessary. It was going to be dreary, no question about that. Who, after all, would want to live in a small Idaho town? Apparently quite a few people. Downtown Bluegill's prosperity surprised me. Stepping onto Main Street I realized this was not a town down on its luck. Pleasant shops were in abundance, their windows lined with pansies and begonias, and outside their doors, water bowls sat filled for passing pets. There were, of course, a few eyesores, shops sitting empty, but every town had their share. Truth was, Bluegill was a charming town, bustling with activity.

At LeVan's insistence, we stopped first to see Norm in Ace Hardware. A bell jingled as we entered the store, and a wiry man in his early sixties, with a tablet in hand, stepped forward to greet us. "Well, hello, Sir," said Norm, shaking LeVan's hand, "I was wondering if you were coming today."

LeVan rubbed his hands together. "Of course, of course," he said.

Walt and Norm shook hands. "Hello, Norm," said Walt.

"Good to see you," said Norm. He gave me a quick smile then turned to LeVan. "Mr. Hitchpost, Sir, it appears that you've brought someone with you."

"She's my student," said LeVan, a tinge of pride in his voice.

Norm shook my hand. "Norman Lawson," he said.

"Lana Huish," I said.

"Lana will be here for six weeks," said Walt.

"So, you've come to learn from the best," said Norm, folding his arms and rocking back on his heels. "If there's anyone who knows painting, it's Mayor Hitchpost."

"Mayor?" I asked.

"Gramps was Mayor of Bluegill a while back," said Walt.

"That's what they tell me," said LeVan, his eyes fixed on the shelf in front of us. "The pool toys are out of order," he said, his thin white eyebrows knitted with concern.

"As are the bolts on aisle six," said Norm.

"Could you use some help?" asked LeVan, his jaw a little more square.

"If you can spare some time," said Norm.

"I don't mind rolling up my sleeves," said LeVan, standing up a little taller.

"Here, Gramps, let's get your apron," said Walt, his hand hovering just below LeVan's elbow as the two walked to the back of the store.

Norm rocked on his heels. "So, you're an artist," he said.

I smiled. "Yes, I am."

"You'll be in Bluegill for the barn dance," he said, trying, I supposed, to just make conversation

"That's nice," I said. "Never been to one."

"I'm sure you'll want to prepare a few words, all considered."

"I will?" I asked, wondering if at barn dances speeches by newbies were customary, but just then, Walt appeared, making my heart flip

"He's already hard at it," said Walt, shaking Norm's hand. "Thanks so much."

"Always a pleasure to spend time with Mayor Hitchpost."

"We'll be back in an hour. We're going to go grab something to eat," said Walt, making me feel even more wobbly. How was it possible to simultaneously want and *not* want to be alone with someone?

"We should probably take Mister, I mean, Mayor Hitchpost with us, don't you think?" I croaked.

"He's fine," said Norm, dismissing us with a flick of his wrist.

"This is what he does," said Walt. "He'll be fine. Thanks again, Norm."

"Take your time," said Norm, his eyes fixed on his tablet.

Walt opened the door. "After you," he said.

I walked through the open door and fell into step beside Walt. Part of me wanted to flee, but, as a calmer part of me pointed out, when it came to boys, I always felt that way. I was prone to panic, prone to escape, and yet despite that deep-seeded inclination, part of me wanted to stay.

Chapter Eight

Walt and I walked a few doors down to Faye's Luncheonette and took two stools at the bar. Faye's Luncheonette was a beautiful relic from the 50s. It had a checkerboard floor, chrome-trimmed seats, and a large metal sign hanging behind the bar that said in fancy script, Hinckley Dairy—Savor The Deliciousness!

An Asian man with Hien Bao on his nametag handed us our menus. Lean with dark hair peppered gray, Hien Bao wore, beneath his spotless white apron, khakis and a lime green golf shirt with Faye's Luncheonette embroidered on one sleeve.

"Afternoon," he said. "Where's Boss?"

"He's helping Norm," said Walt, "This is Lana. She's staying with us."

Hien Bao shook my hand and looked at Walt. "You guys together?" he asked, his accent on the thick side.

"Hien! No! She's here to paint with Gramps!" said Walt, color rising to his cheeks.

Hien shrugged. "Why you no together; she pretty," he said.

Walt put his elbows on the bar, and cradled his head in his hands for a moment. "We just came here to eat," he said, sitting up and looking Hien Bao in the eye.

I smiled at Hien Bao. "But thanks for the compliment," I said. Most days I try not to stand out, but it felt nice to have Hien Bao say I was pretty.

Hien Bao cupped his chin and gave me a closer look. "Wear different color, even prettier," he said.

My smile stiffened. "And for the fashion tip," I muttered as an image of Ingrid gloating passed through my mind.

Walt handed back the menus. "We'll take two house specials," he said, before Hien Bao had time to say anything else.

Hien Bao shouted in a language I didn't recognize to someone in the kitchen as Walt excused himself to use the bathroom. I was expecting Hien Bao to rush to help another customer, but, instead, he looked me over and said, "You work with Boss. We love Boss."

"I've just met him, but he seems like a nice man."

"You coming to dance?"

"The barn dance? Yes, it sounds like I'll be here, so, sure."

"You should speak."

"Is that a *thing* here, giving speeches at barn dances?" I asked, but Hien Bao didn't reply. Another customer had walked in and he rushed to greet them, just in time to give me a perfect view of Walt walking toward me. He was tall, strong, and slightly tan. Nothing not to like about any of that, but he also dressed like a cowboy, Lee jeans and a plaid shirt, which was new for me, and he'd been pretty annoying out there on that dark, lonely road. *Be reasonable*, I told myself. *Don't fall fast for this guy.* Walt slid on to the stool next to me and flashed me a smile. "So, how's it going?" he asked.

"Just chatting with Hien Bao," I said.

"About what?" he asked, which would have been a perfect opportunity for me to mention the barn dance, but just then Walt looked into my eyes and, as if a trap door had opened, my thoughts fell away.

"Are you sure you're okay?" asked Walt.

I shook my head to clear it. *Do not fall fast for this guy! Show some restraint!* "Totally. Uh, so what are we having? What's the house special?" I asked, my tone casual though my heart was pounding harder than necessary.

"A cheeseburger and fries," he said. "When'd you last eat?"

"I shrugged. "I think I had some peanuts in Chicago," I said

Walt slapped the counter. "You need calories. Hien Bao!" he said, flagging him down, "this girl needs a chocolate shake." He turned to me. "I'm assuming you like chocolate." When I nodded that I did, he added, "And make it a large."

"Thanks," I said.

"You should have said last night you were hungry," he said, his words almost a chastisement.

I unfolded the paper napkin cocooning my utensils. "It was late, you were worried about your grandfather. It didn't seem like the right time to whip together a sandwich," I said.

Walt stared at something in the distance, his mouth turning down in a frown. "Sometimes Gramps . . . can be difficult," he said.

Sadness sat between us, creating what I was certain was a wall. "I don't want to pry," I said, smoothing the napkin in my lap.

Walt shook his head. "Look, there's something I need to tell you, but just know it doesn't change anything. We still want you here."

"What is it?" I asked, possibilities of what he might say swirling through my mind.

Walt cleared his throat. "Gramps has Alzheimer's," he said, trying to sound matter-of-fact, but not succeeding. He was clearly heartbroken. "Or at least that's what they're calling it for now," he said, continuing. "Medical science isn't paint by numbers, nothing's exact."

I wanted to touch his arm, tell him I was sorry, do *something* to comfort him, but we barely knew each other, so my hands stayed in my lap. "I see," I said.

He rubbed his index finger across the scruff above his lip, "It's not easy," he said, "but sticking to a routine helps."

"So what's the routine?"

Walt drummed his fingers "We keep it basic," he said. "Gramps wakes up, eats breakfast, I give him his meds, then he walks to town, stopping in the shops to say hello and lend a helping hand. Around noon, we meet at home for lunch, more meds, and about the time he lies down for a nap, I head back to the farm. I wish when he woke up he painted, but for the rest of the day he checks the mailbox." Walt covered his mouth and coughed, a short quick outburst that seemed meant to toughen him against what he'd just said. "All considered, we're fine. Gramps is still Gramps, he's just forgotten certain things. If life were a book, the way I see it, he's still got the book, it's just some pages are missing and others have multiplied."

"Does Mrs. Hitchpost help?" I asked.

"You mean Britney?" he asked, bitterness edging his words.

"Who's Britney?"

"My brother Hank's wife, and no, if I weren't here, she'd put him in a care facility."

"I'm talking about Rosemary. Your grandfather's mentioned his wife. Is she well enough to help?"

Walt's face fell. "That's one of the things he's forgotten."

"I'm sorry?"

"My grandmother died fourteen years ago, along with my parents."

"Oh," I said, my voice barely a whisper.

He swiped his finger, once again, above his upper lip. "Dad was piloting a Cessna 172. They were on their way to Boise, and there was fog," he said. Walt would have been a young boy when the accident happened, and though time heals, there are certain losses (I knew this only too well) that leave behind such a deep cavern of pain, that ever feeling whole again seems too much to hope for. And now, his grandfather was sick. And with Alzheimer's, if it actually was that. There was but one expected end for such a disease. Unlike his grandmother and parents, this would be a long good bye. I looked at Walt, the pain apparent in his eyes, and wondered which was worse.

I gripped the sides of my stool, and tried to think of something helpful to say. "So, have you found him a home?" I asked.

"He has a home," said Walt, his jaw tense. "He's not sick."

I gave him a puzzled look. "How can you say that?" I said.

"He's not bedridden or hooked up to a breathing machine."

"No," I said, "but he thinks his wife is alive."

"Are we arguing again?"

"No," I said, and pressed my lips into a thin line, "this is just a lively discussion."

With the two of us glaring at the counter, Hien Bao appeared with my chocolate shake. He placed the frosted glass in front of me, along with two straws. "Two straw," he said, "just in case things get lovey dovey."

I handed Hien Bao the extra straw. "One will do, thank you," I said, stiffly.

He slid the straw into his apron pocket. "Play hard to get, even better," he said.

I opened my mouth to deny this, but before I could speak, Hien Bao was off to help another customer. I sunk my spoon into the frosty chocolate, stirred, then took a delicious, brain-freezing spoonful. "So," I asked, my hand pressed to my temples, "what else can he not remember?"

"Put your tongue to the roof of your mouth," said Walt.

"Why?" I asked, pressing against my temples harder.

"Just trust me," he said, his voice slightly gruff and slightly sweet.

I did as he said, and felt relief, which I shouldn't have found annoying, but did. "Thanks," I muttered.

"You're welcome," he muttered back, mimicking me.

There was a playful glimmer in his eyes, but I ignored it, and continued pressing him for information. "You said that pages are missing, and others are multiplied. What does that mean?"

Walt spun his butter knife on the counter, and stopped it. "Look, if we stick to the schedule, he's fine," he said.

"Don't avoid the question."

He spun the knife again. "I'm not avoiding the question."

He spun the knife, but this time I stopped it, my hand smacking down on the twirling utensil. "You're certainly not answering it."

"Here we go, here we go," said Hien Bao as he placed before us two monster-sized burgers with fries.

Despite the mouthwatering smells rising up to greet me, I stared at my food, my hands in my lap.

"What are you doing? asked Walt, leaning toward me.

I didn't answer.

"If," he propped his elbow on the counter and rolled his wrist, "you're waiting to pray, I should tell you I prefer doing that in my head when I'm in a restaurant," he said.

"I'm not waiting to pray."

"Then what are you doing?"

"I'm waiting for you to answer my question."

Walt looked at me. "Lana, it's nothing I can't handle," he said.

"If that's true," I said, "then you should be able to talk about it."

Walt let out a long breath. "Fine," he said, "we *sell*," He made quotation marks, "True Horseman around once a month. He doesn't remember donating it years ago to the Wyoming state capitol. Most days, in his mind, he's a young father struggling to become a successful artist and also take care of the needs of family. He has no memory of serving as Mayor, even though he is credited with saving this town. "And who does he think you are?"

"His brother, Walt, the one I was named after. "Now let's eat!" Walt stole a french fry. "You weren't needing that one, were you?" he asked, grinning.

"Guess not," I said, his playfulness surprising me, the way it allowed him to hurdle past an argument and get on with being happy. I liked to stew, withdraw, and sketch unflattering pictures. And I never took a French fry without asking. Watching him from the corner of my eye, I slowly bit into my burger.

Walt picked up his spoon, his eyes darting between me and my shake. "Do you mind?" he asked, his voice full of little boy hopefulness.

"Help yourself," I said, and pushed my shake toward him. Walt helped himself to a heaping spoonful.

"So good," said Walt, sliding the shake back to me. "Glad that's over with."

"Sampling my shake?"

"Telling you about Gramps."

"But there's more I'd like to know."

Walt took a bite of his burger. "He's not all there," he said once he'd had a chance to swallow. "End of story."

"You can't be serious," I said, then, after some doing, wrapped my mouth around my burger and took a bite. My annoyance with Walt momentarily went on hold as juices dripped down my chin, and I chewed, savoring—as the sign above us said—the deliciousness. After a few more bites, I blotted my mouth, ready to go back at it. "There's more I need to know about your grandfather."

"Like what?"

"Like, why, with your grandfather sick—"

"Gramps isn't sick," corrected Walt, pointing a French fry at me.

I pressed my napkin to my lips. "Okay, if some of his *pages* are missing and others have multiplied, why did you let him sign up to be a host?"

Chewing, Walt raised his index finger, letting me know he needed a minute. "I did and didn't agree to it," he said, "Try the fry sauce."

I dipped a few French fries in the sauce and bit into them. "That is awful," I said.

Walt stopped mid bite. "Not liking Faye's Luncheonette's fry sauce is like not liking America," he said.

"That's not it. I like it too much," I said, dipping a few more fries and stuffing them in my mouth. "I came here to paint, not gain fifty pounds."

"Who says you can't do both?"

I dunked another fry in the sauce. "Very funny," I said, rolling my eyes.

Halfway through my burger, I pushed my plate from me. "I can't eat anymore," I said, wishing I could unbutton the top button on my pants.

"Do you mind?" asked Walt, waiting for my consent before sliding the rest of my burger toward him.

"Help yourself," I said, surprised that I wasn't weirded out this guy I'd just met was helping himself to my food. I could count on no hands the number of times I'd given Ingrid a spoonful of my shake.

"But back to my question," I said, watching Walt finish off my burger, "why did you let your grandfather sign up for this?"

Walt curled his napkin into a ball. "I have our mail sent to a P.O. box to make sure Gramps doesn't misplace something important," he said, keeping his eyes on the crumpled napkin. So, I saw the Wilmington Trust's letter, asking if, as a former grant recipient, he would be willing to sign up to possibly be a host."

"Does he remember receiving the grant?"

"No, but he understood that he'd been asked to help a fellow artist, and he felt honored. The letter explained that there were Wilmington Trust alumni all over the world willing to host you, and that where you ended up would be left to chance."

"Lefty's way of shaking things up," I muttered.

"That part Gramps didn't understand. According to him, you were coming here to learn from him. I didn't try to correct him on that. I figured once we'd heard you were heading somewhere else, I'd come up with an explanation that would satisfy him. It didn't occur to me that you'd pick Bluegill."

"I didn't *pick* Bluegill," I said.

"Still, you coming here, what were the odds?"

"Yeah," I said. My stomach tightened as I thought of Paris, but then another thought occurred to me. If I'd ended up in Paris, I wouldn't be talking with Walt, and I liked talking with Walt, even though we sometimes disagreed.

Walt continued. "I kept checking for an email or letter from the foundation, but there was nothing." My face reddened and I chastised myself for not doing more than calling. "Gramps spoke with you while I was still in the fields, and gave you his old address."

"Seventy-Two Dogwood Lane," I said.

Walt nodded. "We moved into this rental when his memory started slipping, but he still considers Dogwood his home. When I came home from work yesterday I found him packing his suitcase. He said he was going to meet his new student."

"Did you believe him?"

"I didn't, until a few hours later when a guy named Lefty called to see if you'd arrived. He said he was checking on you, and that you should have arrived at Seventy-Two Dogwood Lane hours ago. That's when I grabbed my keys and ran."

I wanted to ask him when in the midst of his panic he'd swung by Flintlock to pick up Shailene, but decided against it. "So you were banking on me ending up somewhere else," I said. He nodded, which, surprisingly enough, stung a little. It shouldn't have. *I* had banked on me ending up somewhere else!

Walt raked a hand through his hair. "But we're happy to have you; it's no trouble," he said. "We can push aside the kitchen table and make room for another easel."

"My supplies are being shipped to Dogwood," I said, stunned that he would suggest his grandfather and I set up shop in a tiny kitchen, especially when there was such a good studio within driving distance.

"I'll bring them to you."

I pushed my shake away too full for another spoonful. "I'm not painting in your kitchen," I said.

"Where are you expecting to paint?" he asked, sliding my shake toward himself while looking to see if I'd disapprove. I didn't.

"At your grandfather's studio," I said.

Walt drained the glass of its creamy contents. "That's not possible," he said, sounding resolute.

"Of course, it's possible. Your grandfather said I could use Ruth. We could drive up there—"

"Ruth!" cried Walt. "Have you ever driven stick?"

I sat up a little straighter. "Not yet," I said.

"Well, she's not the truck to start on, let me tell you. And then there's his schedule, his medications—"

"I'll help with that," I said.

"—And me being close enough to him to check on him. Dogwood's a half an hour from the fields. There's no way around it. You're going to have to paint in the kitchen."

"I absolutely have to use the studio," I said.

"Why?" he asked, tossing the straw back in the glass.

"Because," I said, laughing at the absurdity of his question. "I'm not spending the next six weeks painting in a small, poorly ventilated kitchen."

Walt took a bite. "That sounds egotistical," he said as he chewed. "Just saying."

On the counter, a pot of coffee was percolating, simmering like my blood. "So I'm egotistical because I want to paint in an actual studio," I said.

"You work on small canvasses! That's what we were told," he said.

"I shouldn't *have* to work on small canvasses!" I said.

"What are you planning on?"

"I don't have to explain that to you."

Walt shook his head. "I can't have you all the way up at Dogwood. It's summer. If I'm not in the fields, I'm filling in as a river guide for Stock Outfitters."

"As in Shailene Stock?" I asked, my voice a little too pleasant. "That's right," said Walt, sounding puzzled. "You do what you want," I said, the happy rafting moments they, no doubt, shared making me stubborn. "Your grandfather and I need that studio."

"It's not gonna happen."

"Yes, it is, and we're going to use Ruth."

Walt laughed. "Over my cold, dead body."

"I'd prefer to drive around you, but suit yourself."

Walt and I looked at each other, our jaws set, but before either of us could say anything else, Hien Bao was there, handing Walt the check. "Anything else, lovebirds?" he asked.

"That's all," said Walt, glaring.

"It was delicious," I snapped.

"Come back soon," said Hien Bao. Eating out is good for romance."

Walt handed Hien Bao some cash, and before he could offer up any more relationship advice, we left.

Chapter Nine

Bushkaya #3 was harder on me than I liked to admit. I preferred to gloss over my time there, not bring it up at all, or, when necessary, sum it up in a sentence. *Yeah, I spent a year in a Siberian orphanage, but then the Huishs adopted me, so that was cool.* I reduced it when I could to a foot note, though doing so didn't change anything. I was still haunted by those memories, still frozen inside, wanting to love, but forever pulling back. As soon as I joined the Huish family, Lois set to work chipping away at my walls. Morning and night, we'd work through my check list: wash face, brush teeth, say prayers, give hugs. My hugs were always stiff, barely what was required, and, to be honest, not much had changed. I was better at pretending it, but I wasn't better. I still felt trapped, as if I were inside a block of ice—unable to wrap my arms around someone, or have them wrap their arms around me. Unable to leave Bushkaya #3.

As we walked home, I didn't feel much like chatting, or, if I'm being honest, behaving pleasantly in the smallest way. I was stewing over my conversation with Walt, and I wanted to keep stewing indefinitely. I briefly imagined myself giving Walt the cold shoulder for the next six weeks. But that would have been childish, and I was never childish. Not even as a child had I been childish, so I couldn't start now. No, I would talk to him eventually, but for now I wanted to just listen to him talk with his grandfather.

"True Horseman is my finest work to date," said LeVan, furrowing his brow.

"Lionel Smithson says it's a masterpiece," said Walt.

LeVan smiled and color rose to his weathered cheeks. "Well, I don't know about that," he said, "but I won't go soft on the price."

"Stand your ground," said Walt.

"If they want it they'll have to come up and meet me. I'm not going down."

"Don't go down."

"But the children, and Rosemary . . ."

"Then again, you have to consider your family."

"It's one thing to say you're going to provide for your family through your art, but quite another to actually do it. This isn't a life for sissies."

"No, and you're doing it."

"Where's the buyer from?"

"Texas. Oil money." "Then I definitely won't go soft on the price," he said, and the two of them laughed. LeVan's laugh was genuine, which didn't surprise me, but what did was that Walt's was too. He must have had this conversation a dozen times, and yet he wasn't speeding through it like a tedious exercise. Walt was just enjoying talking with his grandfather, and it made me melt a little. And then there was the way he watched out for LeVan, never letting his guard down, always ready to catch him if he were to fall. It chipped away at something inside me, and as we neared home, I found myself joining in the conversation.

"Thanks for doing that," said Walt, as, once home, we stood near the mailbox, letting LeVan check and recheck for mail.

"What, let you eat my leftovers?" I asked.

"Coming downtown with us. It meant a lot to my grandfather," he said, causing a pang of disappointment to ripple though me that he hadn't said it also meant a lot to *him*.

"Happy to do it," I said, and was about to say more, but then bit my lip. Why did I always have more things I wanted to say than the courage to say them?

"And don't worry, no one else here is as odd as Hien Bao. I take that back, Oby and Yarrow, the owners of Spatula are sort of out there too."

"They named their store Spatula?"

"It's an organic restaurant, famous for its buckwheat pancakes. They also own Ottoman."

"A store dedicated to an ancient Turkish empire?" I asked, scratching my head.

"Close," he said, "they make handcrafted furniture and gifts."

"Yeah, that makes a little more sense," I said, wishing I could politely excuse myself, and groan with embarrassment. Of course it was a furniture store! But then Walt smiled, crinkling his eyes in that adorable way, which made me smile, and everything better.

"You never know," he said, "there are stores that sell just candles. Why not one filled with stuff about a random time in history? You could have the faces of conquerors on coasters. It might work."

We smiled and I shielded my eyes to see him. "So, how's business going for Spatula and Ottoman?" I asked, a note of skepticism in my voice.

"You'd be surprised. Spatula was just featured on the Food Network's Backroads Bon Vivant, and Ottoman can't keep in stock its cutting boards, especially the one shaped like the Bluegill fish. And it's not just Spatula and Ottoman. The Dapper Dog Grooming, Annabelle's antiques, The Crusty Loaf Bakery—business is good all over Bluegill. It's what Gramps envisioned. Because of him, this town really is the pearl of Idaho," he said, sadness dulling his eyes as he watched his grandfather opening and closing the mailbox.

I was about to reach out to Walt, and tell him I was sorry his grandfather was slipping away, this man who had accomplished so much, but Shailene's truck screeching to a stop beside us got there first. Getting out, she walked up to Walt, leaned in, and pressed her manicured nails against his plaid shirt. "Hey," she said, her eyes fixed on Walt.

"Hey," I said, like I hadn't realized she was talking to Walt.

Shailene looked at me like I was a thing of curiosity.

Walt gestured toward me. "Shailene, you remember Lana."

Shailene gave me quick smile. "Sure," she said, then returned her attention to Walt. "Dad said to come see if you're free. Pallets of new rafts just arrived, and he's paying overtime to get them ready for tomorrow," she said, emphasizing the word overtime.

"We can't," he said. "We're having a dinner tonight for Lana at Hank and Britney's."

Shailene coiled a loose curl around her finger. "Brit and I talked about that," she said, "and we've decided it's okay to cancel since we're getting together at Flintlock tomorrow for lunch, if that's not a problem." Shailene glanced at me.

Walt folded his arms against his body. "Last time I talked to Brit she said the lasagna was in the oven," he said.

Shailene nudged Walt in the side. "I told Brit to bring it tomorrow," she said. "We can add it to whatever Mom's whipping up. But seriously, we need you tonight. Gramps can keep your friend company."

I wanted Walt to dig in his heels, to tell Shailene she wasn't going to have her way, but he didn't. He looked at me, and then at the ground. "If I'm gone for a few hours will you be okay with Gramps?"

So she says jump, you say how high? Is that how it works? Is what I wanted say, but I didn't. Of course, I didn't. Compared to Shailene Stock, who was I to Walt Hitchpost? No one. He hadn't mentioned her at Faye's Luncheonette, and I didn't get the vibe they were currently a couple, but that didn't mean they hadn't been one at some point. Maybe they'd crushed on each other in kindergarten, swapped sappy notes in middle school, or been each other's first kiss in high school. Other than lunch, we'd shared nothing. Well, that and a handshake. Still, I didn't have a claim to Walt Hitchpost, and it was stupid for me to feel like I should.

"We'll be fine," I muttered.

"I'll try to be quick," he said, before climbing into Shailene's truck.

Shailene's truck roared to life with a throaty rumble. "I wouldn't expect him back before midnight," she said through the open window. Then she smiled, punched the gas, and sped away.

They were no longer in sight, but I stared down the road, in the direction they'd gone and let frustration and fear build inside me. Walt Hitchcock had left me. Yes, he'd left me a few steps away from his house. Still, I felt abandoned, which had everything to do with him driving off with America's favorite bear huntress. And he'd put me in charge of his grandfather! My throat tightened and I gulped hard. What if he took a turn for the worse? How would I help him? And even if he didn't. If tonight was just ordinary, what was I supposed to do with him until Walt got home? Tears pricked my eyes. "Walt Hitchpost, you shouldn't have left," I said, as if the wind could carry to him the message. I sighed. Walt and Shailene were gone, and there was no one to hear me but LeVan, who was still opening and closing the mailbox. So I hadn't expected him to say something, especially something that turned my skin to gooseflesh.

"That family likes to think they make the world go round," said LeVan, closing the mailbox again, but this time slower, with a sense of finality. He walked toward me. "Of course, they don't. The sun's gravitational pull is what accomplishes this, so every now and again someone needs to set them straight."

I looked to the left then right, hoping someone else was there to witness what was happening, but it was just LeVan and me on that cracked and narrow sidewalk. Just the two of us, and a string of well-constructed sentences. The thought occurred to me that his lucid-sounding response could have been a happy accident, sort of like two random lines of poetry coming together and making sense. Maybe he wasn't as aware as he'd just sounded. I decided to dig a little. "What do you mean, set them straight?"

"I mean, from time to time someone needs to let that family know they don't run the show," he said.

"I see," I said, and bit my lip. This didn't sound like a person with Alzheimer's either. I tried again. "So you've got a buyer for True Horseman. That's exciting."

"Never mind True Horseman," he said with a toss of his hand. "You came here to paint."

"Well, yeah,"

"Then let's get started."

I looked at my watch. It was nearly six. "Are you sure it's not too late?"

"Late?" he cried. "We may not get another chance."

"I'm sorry?"

LeVan thought for a moment. "I've become glacial chunks floating in the Antarctic."

I sighed, and felt the tension in my shoulders ease. LeVan hadn't made sense, and, oddly enough, this was comforting. He had Alzheimer's. Yes, it was sad, but at least I knew what to expect. "So you like glaciers," I said, my voice sweet, like I was talking to a small child.

LeVan smiled so wide the setting sun reflected on the gold rim of his tooth. "Not particularly," he said. "What I was trying to say is that since the onset of my illness, my mind has become segmented, like floating chunks of ice that keep drifting farther and farther away from each other," he said, his words heavy with sadness. LeVan thought for a moment, staring in the distance. "But lately, the last week, maybe two—it's hard for me to tell—the pieces of me have been coming together, and right now are fitting like a jigsaw puzzle." Walt shook his head. "It's the darndest thing! But there's no telling how long it will last, so as they say, there's no time like the present."

My mouth fell open. "Hang on a minute. You have Alzheimer's."

"I think so," he said, nodding.

"Just not right now," I said, screwing up my face.

"It appears I've been given a reprieve."

I let out a deep breath. "So, what do you want to do?"

"What you came here for!" he said, extending his hand toward me, his eyes sharp with intelligence. "I'm LeVan Hitchpost, by the way."

"Lana Huish," I said, shaking his hand.

LeVan hooked his thumbs around the straps of his suspenders and smiled a slightly mischievous smile. "Let's go paint."

Chapter Ten

I followed LeVan into the house, trying to hover close to him the way I'd seen Walt do. "Should we call Walt, and let him know what we're doing, and that you're . . . yourself again?"

LeVan let out a puff of air. "I've seen how he clucks about me. We wouldn't get anything done. He'd want me to lie down, as if a good spell were a dangerous thing. Now don't misunderstand me, Walt's a fine young man. I'm very proud of him, but he needs to learn how to relax, and I don't have the time to teach him. I appreciate all he does for me, though. Be sure to tell him that when I'm . . ." and he made a flitting motion with his hand to finish that sentence.

"I think he'd prefer hearing it from you."

LeVan fumbled as he reached for a set of keys hanging from a nail in the wall. "My dear, I've already said my good byes. No one must know. Can you promise me that?"

I nodded. "Of course," I said, though I didn't agree with his choice, not at all. He should have been shouting to the world, *I'm back! I'm myself again!* That's what I would have done. But instead, he wanted to keep secret the miracle that was happening, and go paint . . .It was puzzling, but, then again, he did have Alzheimer's. Maybe even on a good day he couldn't entirely think straight. That was the only logical explanation. "So," I said, watching him hobble over to the hall closet and grab his jacket, "what exactly are we doing?"

"We're going to my studio and rolling up our sleeves. Do you have your paints?"

"They'll be at Dogwood on Monday."

"What about any sketches?"

"Yes, of course," I said.

LeVan's wrinkled face split into a grin. "Always probing for material. Good girl. Bring them with us. They'll be our starting point, and, as for paints, we can use mine," he said. "I believe Walt has them stored in the garage. Would you mind helping me load them into the back of old Ruth?

"Of course not," I said, and followed LeVan. He shuffled outside and, with a bit of help from me, lifted the garage door. Inside were canvasses of every size and a large box filled with paint in cans and tubes.

"Walt must have brought these here when we moved," he said. "I assume he hoped that I'd feel inspired to pick up a brush. Probably thought it would be therapeutic for me, but who can paint in such a tiny kitchen?"

"That's what I told him!"

"Let's not be too hard on him, my dear," said LeVan. He's not an artist, and doesn't understand about such things." He pulled a can of paint out from the box. "Of course, some of these will have dried out," he said, "but we should be able to find enough that are still good to be productive for one evening. Grab that case over there, it's filled with my brushes."

I stowed everything in the back of old Ruth, and went inside to grab some snacks and my sketchpad. When I returned to the truck, LeVan was seated behind the wheel. "Whoa, whoa," I said, as if talking to an old horse instead of an old cowboy, "you can't drive!"

"That's certainly what wisdom would dictate, but Ruth's touchy. I'll need to show you how the old girl works. You've driven stick before," he said, sounding like he was stating a fact, not asking a question.

"Actually, no," I said, "and I'm not sure that driving up a winding road that, in places, hugs a cliffside is the best way for me to learn."

LeVan patted my arm. "The fear of imminent death will make you a quick study."

I bit my lip. "Maybe there's a coffee shop in town we could go to, find a corner for our easels, and—"

"You're forgetting that tomorrow I may not remember your name. While we can, we need to get to the studio and work."

I tried to gulp, but my mouth was suddenly dry. "This doesn't seem like a good idea," I said.

LeVan turned the key in the ignition and Ruth coughed to life. "True, but do you feel alive?"

"I can feel my heart pounding, if that's what you mean," I said, over the engine's roar.

LeVan grinned. "It's a start," he said, then gently released the clutch, pressed on the gas, and guided the old truck onto the street.

We weaved up and down the neighborhood as LeVan explained the basics of driving Ruth. "It takes a light touch." "She'll overheat if you're in a hurry." "She doesn't like to be rushed." "You can suggest she move, but she's the one who'll decide." "And don't be punchy with the brake, it tends to make her stall. So does idling too long, not topping off her gas, and thinking negative thoughts. It may sound crazy, but the old girl likes a positive attitude!"

Beads of sweat clung to LeVan's bony forehead as his withered arms struggled to shift Ruth and turn her stubborn steering wheel. Worried he was wearing himself out, I found myself saying, long before I was ready, "I'll give it a try." LeVan brought Ruth to a jerky stop, and slid across to the passenger seat.

I climbed behind the wheel. "You're sure you're ready?" asked LeVan.

A trickle of sweat slid down my back. "To be honest, no," I said, "so feel free to walk me through it."

81

"I'd be happy to," he said, "Now, you're going to want to gently release the clutch, nice and slow, like your foot's on a sleeping cobra . . ."

At first it seemed like Ruth was annoyed LeVan wasn't behind the wheel, and was practically refusing to go. But after a while, I got the hang of the delicate dance required to keep her moving, and we headed out of town and up the mountain to Dogwood Lane. I tried to focus entirely on driving, but it was impossible. Every bump in the road threw me into a panic. Was LeVan all right? Were the "glacial chunks" in his mind still floating together or had the truck's jostling sent them adrift? And, as the road got steeper, I tormented myself with worst case scenarios, like Ruth stalling, rolling backwards, and me confusing the brake for the gas and sending us flying over the cliff's edge. By the time we pulled into Seventy-Two Dogwood Lane, I was practically hyperventilating. "Here we are," said LeVan, rubbing his hands together. "Let's get to work."

"I'll be right there," I said, my eyes closed. "I just need a moment."

"Suit yourself," said LeVan, "but hand me the keys, I want to open the studio."

I gave LeVan the keys, and with light streaming from the headlights, watched him shuffle to the studio door. After a few failed attempts, he succeeded in getting the key in the lock, but didn't have the strength to pull it upward. I took a deep breath. "Calm down, Lana, you didn't die, even though it seemed like a strong possibility. So relax," I whispered to myself. "Pull yourself together, and get to work." After shaking like a wet dog, I went over and helped LeVan with the door.

LeVan flipped on the lights, which first flickered, then took their time growing brighter. "At my late wife's insistence, the house and my studio are powered by solar energy. She liked the idea of being self-sustaining."

"Smart lady."

"And not reading at night by candlelight. The power lines don't run this far out."

Worried LeVan might stumble in the dark, I brought in our supplies while he surveyed his unfinished panels. "Well, hello there, Sweetheart," I heard him say. "Aren't you a sight for sore eyes!"

I pulled out my phone. "Would you like some music?" I asked.

"Absolutely," said LeVan, his eyes still glued to his mural.

"What are you in the mood for?"

LeVan put a hand to his heart. "I'm a Sinatra man, but don't kowtow to me."

"I'll kowtow to you if I want," I said, teasing. "I can enjoy music any old day. But you . . ." I stopped, fearing I'd said too much.

LeVan nodded. "That's the unvarnished truth," he said, his voice matter of fact, not mournful.

I sighed with relief that he wasn't offended. "Then Sinatra it is?" I asked.

"Sinatra it is," he said.

"Well, Mr. Hitchpost—"

"LeVan," he said, his weathered hand pressed to his heart.

"LeVan, you're in luck. I have Sinatra in my playlist."

"Excellent," said LeVan.

"I can't call anyone," I said, turning on my phone. "I have zero reception up here. But I can listen to Old Blue Eyes." And after a few swipes across my screen, the rich sound of Frank Sinatra's baritone filled the studio.

LeVan smiled. "A good voice, like a good painting, feeds the soul," he said as he lowered himself into a chair next to the table. "Let's focus tonight on you. Where are your sketches?" he asked, pulling a pair of bifocals from his front pocket.

"I'll get them," I said, only remembering after I'd handed him the book about the sketches I'd done of Walt. I wanted to snatch them back, but it was too late. He was already cracking it open. My face burned with embarrassment as LeVan stared at Walt's likeness, but I told myself not to worry. Soon, perhaps even in the next hour, the "chunks" in LeVan's mind would begin to drift, and he would forget this.

As Frank Sinatra sang about flying to the moon, LeVan studied my sketches of Walt. "You've been busy," he said, turning to yet another one.

"Well, I couldn't sleep last night."

"And I understand why. You're in love with my grandson."

"Whoa!" I said, waving my hands in the air. "Talk about overstatements, I am not in love with your grandson."

LeVan smirked. "Well, at the very least, you find him cute."

"Isn't it possible I just consider him an interesting subject?" I asked.

"In this one he's surrounded by little hearts," he said, peering at me from over his bifocals.

"Those are stars!"

LeVan squinted. "I'll be darned," he said.

Calm down! The man has Alzheimer's! I reminded myself. *It doesn't matter what you tell him. You don't have to hold back.* "Okay," I said, and took a deep breath. "I'm going to level with you. I have a crush on your grandson."

"Forgive me if I don't act surprised. So far, I've counted twelve sketches."

I rested my elbows on the table and buried my head in my hands. "I couldn't get him out of my head last night."

"So it appears."

"But that's not important, what's important is art."

"Your talent is staggering." I was so focused on Walt, this compliment slid past me, almost unnoticed.

"Besides, from the looks of things, he and Shailene are a thing," I continued. "I wouldn't be so sure of that."

"Do you think she's right for him?" I probed.

"This is magnificent," he said, looking at one of my sketches of Ingrid.

84

"LeVan, I need information. Do you think Shailene is right for him?" I asked.

"Well, they do share the same faith. You see, we're what's called Mormon. Most in this town are. A few aren't. Hien Bao's Buddhist, Norm's Seventh Day Adventist, or is he Lutheran? They're all a good sort of people, but as Mormons, we believe in temples—"

"I'm-I'm a Mormon!" I spluttered, tapping my chest and berating myself for not wearing a CTR ring or an old EFY shirt—something that would have announced my faith.

LeVan gave me a long look "Well, I'll be," he said.

"So, tell me. Be honest. Are Shailene and Walt right for each other?"

LeVan crossed his arms. "I'm no good at this sort of thing, a relationship chat," He said. "For that, you need Rosemary." Fear gripped me like a hand at the back of my neck. Did he think Rosemary was alive? Was he already leaving me? I barely knew LeVan, but the thought of him slipping away made me feel cheated. "But," he continued, "as she is not with us, rest her soul, I suppose I'll have to do." *Rest her soul.* LeVan hadn't gone anywhere, and for that, I gave a silent prayer of thanks. "In my opinion, it doesn't matter if Shailene is right for Walt, the wrong people get together all the time. Certainly my parents' marriage was testament to that. The wrong people marry, have children, even grow old together."

"I think she's all wrong from him," I said.

"And she is all wrong for him, but that guarantees nothing."

I stood up. "Why do the wrong people end up together?" I groaned. "Why does it happen?"

"Because what's right is seldom easy."

"Are you trying to depress me?"

LeVan turned to a sketch I'd done of Ingrid. "This is really a conversation for another time."

"But there might not be another time," I said, giving LeVan a knowing look.

The corners of LeVan's mouth pulled downward as he thought. "Fair enough," he said, and closed my sketch book, "but only for a few minutes. We have other things to focus on, namely, your prodigious talent." I blushed a little and then nodded. LeVan settled back in his chair. "When I met Rosemary she was dating a boxer."

"Yikes."

"Ernie Snapp. The Bone Snapper, they called him. He had hands like steaks, thick and bloody."

"Bloody!" I cried.

"I may be embellishing for the sake of the story."

"Thank heavens," I said. "Go on."

"But you get my point, he was a tall, hulking man, and the easy thing would have been for me not to pursue Rosemary, but each time I didn't, each time I saw her and turned away, one thought would nag at me—*You're alive, aren't you? So live!* I tried to reason away this thought by telling myself that "living" would lead to me dying. Ernie's muscles had more peaks and valleys than the Grand Tetons."

"And you saying this for the sake of the story?"

LeVan winked. "You're catching on. But this much is true, he was intimidating. Still, that thought gnawed at me. If you're alive, you should live, and I knew that for me, that meant, trying, at least, to win the hand of Rosemary Willow."

"So how'd it go?"

LeVan let out a big breath, making his lips flap a little. "It was messy, but, in the end, Ernie accepted defeat, and Rosemary my hand in marriage." I opened my mouth to ask yet another question, but LeVan put up a hand to stop me. "Chew on that for now, and let's focus on your art."

I banged a fist (softly) on the table in protest and opened my mouth to protest.

LeVan raised an eyebrow. "I'll say one thing more, Walt is a good boy, and you should try and catch his eye."

"I never try to catch any guy's eye," I said, more to myself than LeVan.

"If Rosemary were here she'd ask why not."

"I'd tell her I don't know."

"She'd say that was nonsense. A girl who has the heart to sketch like you must know why she eludes attention." LeVan held up his hand again. "But my dear Rosemary has departed this life. We, on the other hand, haven't, and must get to work."

"True," I said.

"You should know that I nearly fell out of my chair when I opened your sketchbook. I stopped myself because my bones are brittle. At my age, one false move and we'd need all the king's horses," said LeVan while pulling a face. I laughed, which helped me forget Walt and Shailene for the moment. "Your work is magnificent," he said.

"Thank you," I said, but I guess, according to LeVan, his compliment deserved more.

LeVan frowned. "My dear, place your hand on the table, if you would," he said. I did and he placed his next to mine. Our two hands were so different. Mine was small and smooth; LeVan's didn't flatten entirely and his skin was mottled. "Old age, in my estimation, is like putting on a coat. Beneath, you're exactly who you've always been, but the coat is heavy and ill-fitting, and grows more so as time passes, until who you are—the person beneath the coat—is trapped inside. A simple thing, like holding a paintbrush or remembering that your wife has passed from this life . . . then becomes difficult." I slid my hand into my lap. I had just turned twenty-two, but such frank talk about growing old was hard to hear. "I don't mean to make you uncomfortable," said LeVan, "I just want to drive home a point."

"Which is?" I asked, though uncertain I wanted to hear what he had to say.

LeVan pointed an unsteady finger at me. "The number of paintings you will create in this lifetime is finite."

"Okay," I said, not knowing where he was going with this.

"Young as you are, the time you have to paint must seem like a path that winds into the distance with no end in sight. But it does end. For each artist, it's different. Picasso painted thousands, Vermeer just a handful."

"I don't know if I'm a Picasso, but I'm definitely not a Vermeer."

LeVan clasped his gnarled hands. "That's not important. However many you produce, understand your paintings are your—"

"Life's work," I said, parroting what I'd heard other artists say.

"Nonsense," said LeVan, his white eyebrows knit, "people, not paintings, will be your life's work. But your paintings are your *voice*, and if they're good, really good, they never stop speaking for you, saying what you wanted to say. And that, Lana Huish, is what I want you to consider, what do you want to say?"

I looked at the ceiling and pressed my lips together. What did I want to say? I had never thought of my paintings as my voice. "I don't know if I really say anything when I paint. I mostly do portraits."

LeVan held up a few of my sketches of Walt. "Portraits speak too. These say you're in love."

Instead of denying this, I gulped. "I've never fallen in love before," I said.

"It was bound to happen sooner or later."

"LeVan," I said, swallowing hard, "could you help me?"

"I am helping you."

"Not with painting. Well, yes with painting. I want to hear what you have to say about how my paintings are my voice. But I'm talking about Walt. Help me get to know him."

"You don't need my help with that."

"You have no idea how terrible I am at this. And I know this is really more Rosemary's thing—"

"You need to focus on your work."

"I will, I promise," I said, my hand to my heart. LeVan studied the table for a moment, then tossed his hands in the air. "Fine, I'll be your Cyrano, as long as when we're in the studio you paint with gusto."

I smiled. "You want gusto. I'll give you gusto," I said, and opened the box of paints.

Chapter Eleven

As Sinatra sang about doing things his way, I washed the poster-sized canvas in front of me with a thinned mixture of burnt umber and cad red. Doing so created a good background color and allowed me to use my finger, wrapped in an absorbent cloth, as a brush, and subtract paint as I created an image. Typically, after making a few sketches in my sketchbook, this was the way I liked to begin painting, but tonight I wanted to skip past sketching and dive right into painting. Just pick something worth saying and begin, but, so far, I'd etched nothing into the thin, wet paint. "I'm sorry," I said at last, "but thinking about a painting's message isn't a natural starting point for me."

LeVan flicked his wrist. "No matter," he said. "It will be something to consider as you work. So, how do you like to start?"

"With a gut feeling," I said, winding the small cloth tighter around my finger as I looked from LeVan to the canvas, and back again. "All I know at the beginning is who I'd like to paint."

"And what is your gut telling you tonight? Who do you want to paint?"

I chewed my lip. "Well, to be honest, you," I said.

LeVan arched one of his thin, white eyebrows as a hint of a smile played on his lips. "I just told you the number of paintings you'll create in this lifetime is finite and you want to squander one on me?" he said, feigning disappointment. "And without making a sketch or two first! Van Gogh said, sketching's the sowing, painting the reaping."

"I agree with Van Gogh, and, usually, I would," I said, beginning to make few broad strokes in the paint. "But tonight, I think I'm going to skip sketching.

LeVan rubbed his hands together. "She's going gangbusters, I like it! Where do you want me?" he asked, making as if about to stand.

I put up a hand to stop him. "I think I'd like you to stay seated," I said, as if for artistic reasons and not because I was afraid standing would make him tired.

"You say jump, I say how high," he said, and relaxed into his seat.

I worked swiftly, outlining what I saw in my mind—not a picture of LeVan, old and thin, sitting in his studio, but LeVan, perhaps fifteen years younger, looking stronger and standing outdoors. Where outdoors, I didn't know. The idea, or message of the picture, as LeVan would have put it, wasn't entirely clear to me yet. Like a flower beginning to bloom, it was still unfolding. All I knew was that it would be a picture of LeVan before Alzheimer's.

LeVan laced his bony fingers and placed them in his lap. "Let me know if you'd like me to strike a pose," he said, "my fist tucked under my chin, perhaps, or a rose between my teeth." I laughed at these suggestions. "You laugh but my first commissioned work was just such a pose. What was that woman's name? Anyway, she came from Montana and had more money than sense. I was not in a position to turn down the offer of work, so I did the painting, but I didn't sign it. I thought the job was beneath me, and so I told her my signature would have distracted from the painting's beauty. Luckily, she agreed.

I studied the cuff of his shirt and continued to outline in the paint. "So, was she happy with your work?"

"So happy she commissioned another," he mused.

"No!" I said.

"Yes," he said, solemnly. "She wanted a portrait of her aged beagle wearing a clown nose and four little clown shoes. Of course, the studio sessions were a nightmare. What beagle wants to wear clown shoes? And he ate every clown nose she put on him. Had to go to the vet and get his stomach pumped."

I stopped working and looked at LeVan, my eyes wide with surprise. "Had her dog worked in the circus?"

"No, she just adored clowns, and her beagle," said LeVan. "Smoochems, I believe was his name. Poor dog. I didn't sign that one either." He frowned. "Those were dark days. Little money, little children, and the agony of not yet succeeding gripping me like an iron fist, squeezing the hope, the enthusiasm, and the breath right out of me. I had graduated from Columbia. Despite long odds, I'd done it, and honed my craft further in France and Italy. I had worked alongside Turner Williams, for heaven's sake! Why shouldn't I be succeeding? My artist friends seemed to step from one success to another, exhibitions that sold out, commissions worth thousands, and I was painting a beagle dressed like a clown. Jealousy and frustration. Oh, how they tormented me, and kept me from enjoying the pitter pat of little feet in our home.

But, Rosemary, bless her heart, yanked me from my doldrums. "Recognition will come, she said, but that dog portrait has allowed us to stock our kitchen shelves. It's honest work, and you're painting, which is the work you were born to do! Don't lose sight of that, and be grateful." I was grateful, but most of all, for her. Her faith in me was my guiding star. I owe everything to her." LeVan stared off into the distance and was quiet for a moment, then slapped his knee. "But here I am yammering on while you're trying to work."

"It's not a distraction," I said, studying the dip in his nose as my finger moved across the canvas. "I'm enjoying it. So, please, keep yammering."

He did, starting with some questions about the painting. Had I considered standing it on its end? How long did I think this would take? Was I sure I wanted to go through with this? Why had I chosen to angle him looking into the painting? What was he looking at, and what else did I plan to put in the foreground? Had I considered that if this was a picture set in Bluegill there'd need to be a few mountains in the distance? Did I have a stick of gum? After I was finished outlining, and had started to paint, LeVan asked me to turn the canvas around so he could "take a gander," which, of course, brought forth more comments. "You're going for a younger me. Well, don't deify me in the process. Where are my faults? In my whole life I've never had such glorious biceps as the ones you've got there. Flaws, details! They make paintings interesting. Don't shy away from showing grit!"

In time, the conversation turned again to Walt. He spoke of the plane crash that took the lives of Walt's parents, and his wife. Hank had been twenty-two when the accident happened, and Walt ten. Walt had needed his grandfather in ways that Hank hadn't, and the two, though close, grew closer. My intention had been to paint LeVan, off set, looking at the sunset, the empty space beside him signifying Rosemary's absence. But as LeVan spoke, it occurred to me that a picture of LeVan in his sixties should be a picture of life after the accident—a picture of LeVan standing beside Walt, his hand resting on his grandson's shoulder, comforting him, despite his own grief.

I worked quickly, fixing what needed fixing, furthering on the canvas this image of LeVan and Walt that was unfolding in my mind. As I worked, LeVan told me more about Walt.

"He's always wanted to be farmer. Neither is the land without Walt, nor Walt without the land," he said with a smile. "Some girls find that off-putting. There was a lovely little girl from Chicago he met while studying Agriculture at Boise State who had great hopes of turning him into a dentist. That relationship didn't last long." LeVan stretched. "What would you turn him into?"

I glanced at LeVan and shrugged. "Nothing," I said, but wondered if I was being honest. I'd never had a boyfriend before. Would I push him to be what I envisioned? I had that sort of power over my paintings, but would I wield it over someone I cared for? I cleared my throat. "I'd want him to be whatever he wanted."

"And if he wanted to buy a doll museum, and spend his days making little doll hats, you'd be okay with that too?"

"Huh?"

"At some point your love's decisions shape your destiny. You wouldn't agree with anything and everything, no one would. So, could you see yourself as a farmer's wife?"

I thought of the dour faces of the farm couple in Grant Wood's painting, American Gothic, and a shiver went through me. "I need to get him to ask me out before I start thinking about that," I said, skirting the question.

He pointed at the canvas then twirled his finger. "Let's have a look," he said. I turned the canvas around. In the picture, LeVan and Walt stood side by side, looking at a plowed field that appeared to stretch to a distant mountain range. LeVan was silent.

"I know you're a painter, not a farmer," I said, as he studied the painting, his lips drawn tight, expressionless, "but it seemed right to place the two of you in a field, like the kind around here." LeVan said nothing so, I kept talking. "Metaphorically," I said, scratching the back of my head. "I suppose, the field could represent any kind of work. Or maybe the point is you're showing Walt how to be the type of man who could be a farmer." I sighed. "I don't know, maybe it's all wrong."

LeVan pulled from his pocket a folded handkerchief and dabbed his eyes. "A picture worth its salt should convey emotion. Just roughed in, this one already does that." He shook his head. "My dear, you paint like an old master."

"Thank you," I said, but, this time, with sincerity.

LeVan tutted and shook his head. "And you want to marry a farmer," he said.

I placed the canvas back on the easel. "*Date*," I corrected. "I want to date a farmer. And, don't forget, you said you'd help me."

"I haven't forgotten, not yet anyway," he said, knocking on the wooden table, "but whether you like it or not, the future is there, pressing its nose to the window like some busybody neighbor. You're an artist of the darndest talent, and Walt's a farmer. How would it ever work?"

"I don't know," I said, shrugging

LeVan smiled. "Like this painting you've started, I suppose you'll just have to figure things out as you go along."

"Follow my gut," I said, opening the box of paints and pulling out tubes of purple, white, blue, and brown.

"It will be interesting to see where it takes you," he said.

As I applied impasto (for texture) to the canvas and then color, we kept up our pattern of LeVan talking and me listening. Occasionally, I'd make a remark, but I didn't ask him about Walt, because that only led to us jumping on the, you-want-to-marry-a-farmer!-I-didn't-say-that!-merry-go-round. Time and our snacks disappeared. We laughed, argued about the color red (You need a dab, right there. I do not!) and forgot that at some point Walt would head home and wonder where we were. Not until we heard the crunch of tires on gravel did we remember.

"Land sakes, that must be Walt!" said LeVan.

I looked at my phone. "LeVan, it's past midnight! What are we going to tell him?"

LeVan's eyes darted to the glass door. "Quick!" he said, "help me to the cot!" Moving much faster than I expected, LeVan hurried to the cot and lied down.

"Why do you need to pretend to be sleeping?"

"Because I'm a coward."

"LeVan!"

"And a terrible actor. If I'm sleeping I don't have to say anything. Besides, I'm usually asleep by now," he said, crossing his arms over his chest like Dracula.

"You're supposed to be asleep, not dead! Turn on your side."

"Good idea," he said, and, with my help, turned on his side. What am I supposed to tell him?"

LeVan opened one eye. "That you're old enough to make up your mind. He's not the boss. Whatever you do, don't give in. We have to work here!"

There wasn't time to argue. Walt was striding to the door with quick steps that left no doubt he was mad.

"Oh boy," I mumbled, grabbing a paintbrush with shaky fingers and pretending to paint. LeVan, his face toward me, mouthed the words good luck, and then closed his eyes and began snoring a bit too loud.

With a burst of energy, Walt rolled the glass door upward, and then more softly brought it down. He took his time turning around, and even longer to look at me.

I made a big circle in the air like Pocahontas greeting John Smith. "Hello," I said, my heart pounding. Whether it was from fear or seeing Walt, I wasn't sure.

He took a few deep breaths. "Did it occur to you that I might be worried?" he asked.

"We were busy working," I said, pointing at LeVan, "and lost track of time."

A vein in his forehead bulged. "You drove Ruth here," he said, sounding like he was carefully choosing his words. I nodded. "Why?"

I cleared my throat, "You took your keys."

The vein in his forehead grew even fatter. "I told you not to come here."

"Well, you're not the boss of me," I said. For a moment, Walt said nothing, and in the ensuing silence, LeVan cringed.

Apparently, he hadn't expected me to say exactly what he'd said.

Walt took a step toward me; I took one back. "I'm not the boss of you," he said, calmly. "Well, be sure to tell whoever is the boss of you that you are never driving Ruth again."

"Fine" I said, as if annoyed, though all I felt was relief. I had no idea how I would've safely driven that truck down the mountain.

"And that you'll need to paint at the house in town," he added.

LeVan, subtly shook his head. "That's not possible," I said, my hands on my hips. "I have to paint here."

Walt clenched his jaw. "Be reasonable."

"I am being reasonable" I said. "We'll be fine. I can keep an eye on him."

LeVan discreetly gave me a thumbs up.

Walt shook his head. "That won't work. He needs me and I've got to be close to the fields and Stock Outfitters, in case they call."

"And I bet they call all the time!" I said, realizing too late I'd said it out loud.

"What's that supposed to mean?" he asked, throwing his hands in the air.

By the way, when trying to get a date with a guy, it's best not to sound crazy jealous. "Nothing," I said.

Walt took a step forward; I took one back. "I think it's something," he said.

"All I said was, I bet they do!"

"Yes, but you said it derisively."

"That's your opinion."

"Which should matter, since I'm the one who heard it! I bet they do," he said, imitating me, and doing a pretty good job of it.

Frustrated, tears stung my eyes, but I willed myself not to cry, a struggle, that didn't go unnoticed by Walt, and softened his expression, not with pity, but kindness. Ironically, this was so touching to me, I ended up bursting into tears all the same.

Walt took a step toward me; I took one back. "I'm sorry," he said. I should have said I was sorry too, but I was too busy crying to speak. "Look, we'll work it out. I promise you that. Please, don't cry. I know your introduction to Bluegill hasn't gone so smoothly, but things will get better. If you'd like, tomorrow I can drive you to Our Holy Mother cathedral. It won't be a problem. Mass starts at ten, and our church at ele—"

I sobbed harder. "You think I'm Catholic?"

"So you're Episcopalian?"

"No-o-o!" I croaked. "I'm Mor-or-mon!"

Walt put his hands on his hips. "Huh," he said.

"Why is that so hard to believe?"

"It's not hard to believe," he said, "It's just, not everyone you meet is Mormon."

"But sometimes you have a hunch. Like, hey, that girl looks Mormon. I bet she's Mormon. What is it? That I'm not wearing my young women's medallion? Well, I can't, I lost it in the Bahamas," I sniffed.

"I didn't say anything about a medallion."

"And my CTR ring turned my finger green."

"Also not necessary," he said.

"And just so you know, you don't seem Mormon either. You haven't once mentioned your mission!"

"Detroit," he said.

"Or road shows!"

"Oklahoma, tenth grade."

"Or Boy Scouts!"

"Eagles don't brag."

I pointed my brush at him. "Or home teaching."

"Gramps is my companion," he said, "and we usually teach on the last day of most months. I'm always grateful for the thirty-first."

Walt cracked a smile. He wanted this fight to be over, and so did I, but I didn't know how to do it, how to meet him half way, and so instead of saying something nice, I just repeated myself. "I'm going to work here!"

Walt's voice was soft. He held up his hands in surrender. "We'll figure it out," he said, walking to the door. "In fact, we'll leave everything here."

I blotted my eyes with my sleeve, and pointed at LeVan. "We have to take your grandfather," I sniffed.

"Except my grandfather."

LeVan was right, he was a terrible actor. Just then, he popped up and chirped, "Where am I?"

Perhaps overcome by my emotional outburst, his grandfather's behavior didn't strike him as odd. "At your studio, Gramps. We're going to take you home," he said, rolling up the glass door. "If you help Gramps to my truck, I'll drive Ruth around back. We can pick her up tomorrow."

I nodded.

I put the paintbrushes and the palette into a small box and placed it in the studio's small refrigerator, grabbed my sketch-book, and with LeVan holding onto my arm, headed for Walt's truck.

"So, how do you think it went?" he asked.

I sniffed. "It could've gone better."

"The good news is he seems to be warming to the idea of us working here."

"Yes, but the bad news is he thinks I'm a mess," I said.

"There, there," said LeVan. "One thing at a time."

Chapter Twelve

Crying saps my strength. I suppose that's true for everyone, but because I rarely allow myself to cry, a good sob does more than make me sleepy. It hits me like a tall glass of Nyquil. Add to that, and that it was well past midnight, and you've got a perfect storm for knocking me out cold. It took around twenty-five minutes to drive from Dogwood to Bluegill, and I was awake for none of it. All I could remember was buckling up, closing my eyes, pressing my cheek against the passenger window's cool glass, and the stern woman prying my fingers from my mother.

And then there it was, the stern woman's office, just as it had been—the peeling wallpaper, the metal desk, the pictures of past Russian leaders nailed to the wall. I knew I was dreaming, because in my dreams I often returned to the moment my mother left me. Knowing this didn't matter. Once again I felt the sadness and confusion of abandonment. Once again I pleaded, and once again I felt the slap.

Ne ostavlyay menya. Don't leave me, I said.

A gentle finger slid across my forehead and tucked my hair behind my ear. *Nikto ne pokidayet vas.* No one's leaving you, said my mother, her voice somehow huskier.

Ya obeshchayu, chto dudu khoroshim. I promise I'll be good.

No one's leaving you, she said again, scooping me in her arms, and, from the sound of it, shutting a car door. In my

100

dreams, my mother always fled from the stern woman's office, her face buried in her hands, but not this time. This time, she stayed, reassuring me in Russian, *You don't have to worry, everything is fine, you're safe*, her voice lower and her accent, for lack of a better word, wonky. Instead of reminding me of clear water rushing over stones, it sounded like a tin can falling down a flight of stairs.

Slowly, like light piercing thick fog, it occurred to me I should open my eyes. At first, I resisted the idea. It was late, and though I was getting a kink in my neck, it was nice to be carried, especially when I was so tired. All I wanted to do was drift deeper to sleep in my mother's arms, feeling her warm breath against my cheek as she whispered, *She's so light. It's like carrying a ten-year-old, but this one is doing a number on my heart.*

In the distance a train whistled, coaxing me awake. I opened my eyes, realized I was in Walt's arms, and jumped out of them, then instantly wished I could jump back in, and let him carry me to my room and kiss me good night. But no. I had to freak out, and what's awful about freaking out is that you feel like you have to defend yourself. Or, at least, I do.

My feet hit the sidewalk in front of the Hitchpost house with a thud. "Oh my gosh! What are you doing?" I asked.

The porch light made it easy to see Walt. "You were asleep," he said. "I thought I'd—"

"You could have woken me up," I said, my voice a bit snappish. A few strands of my hair fell in front of my eyes. I blew out a puff of air to move them. They lifted just lifted, and settled back where they'd been.

He pressed his hands to his eyes, then dropped them to his sides and took a deep breath. "I didn't want to disturb you," he said, kindness and frustration tinging his words.

I should have said, *Thank you*, and left it at that. But instead I put my hands on my hips. "You don't pick up a fully grown person, and—"

"What if there's a fire?" asked Walt, cutting in, a hint of a smile curling his mouth.

He was trying to get me to smile, but I pretended not to notice. "Other than when there's a fire," I said, "you do not pick up a . . . Hey, wait a minute, did you compare me to a ten-year-old?" I asked.

Walt scratched the back of his neck. "I might have said you're lighter than a ten-year-old, which—He put his hand to his heart—in my defense, a lot of women would consider a compliment."

"So you think I'm a child," I said, trying to glare at him.

"No," he said, shaking his head. "I think you're built like a gymnast. There's a difference."

A chilly canyon breeze rushed between us. "What's that supposed to mean?" I asked, thinking how nice it would be to have his arms around me to shield me from the wind.

Walt hooked his thumbs on his belt loops and shifted his weight. "That means you're no harder to carry than a sack of feed. I take that back. A sack of feed doesn't give me a piece of its mind when I carry it," he said, his teeth flashing white as he grinned.

I folded my arms. "You should have asked," I said, my teeth chattering.

He placed his hand on my forearm, heat against ice. "You're cold," he said, and then something occurred to me; he'd said it in Russian.

Yabyl kholodneye. I've been colder, I said, in Russian, my voice softer now. Maybe it was the hour, or his lingering touch, but I was through with arguing.

"Ne ostavlyay menya. Don't leave me. You said that in your sleep. What happened to you?" he asked.

"I don't want to get into it," I said, but without an edge.

Walt nodded. "Fair enough," he said.

His hand was warm against my chilly skin. "It's just that if life were a book—"

102

"Shh. You just said you didn't want to talk about it," he said, interlocking his fingers with mine.

"True," I whispered.

"Then don't talk about it," he whispered back.

"You speak Russian well," he said reaching out and holding my other hand.

"Yours is terrible," I said.

Walt smiled. "That might have something to do with learning it in Detroit," he said. "I take it you didn't learn Russian in Detroit."

"I did not," I said, blinking slowly. My mind, which usually was constantly observing, darting here and there like a squirrel, was now as relaxed as a well-fed puppy

Walt squeezed my hands. "It's late, Lana Huish," he said, his voice a whisper.

I yawned. "Yes, it is."

He tucked a few strands of my hair behind my ear. "You should get to bed."

"But your grandfather."

"Already taken care of him."

"Oh . . . well, in that case . . ." I said, stalling, because, how exactly did you end holding hands with a guy? I was twenty-two and didn't know. I opted for a solid handshake before slipping my hand from his. Talk about embarrassing.

Walt grinned. "Good night," he said. And, no longer holding hands, we walked inside.

I had held hands with Walt Hitchpost. That thought, and brushing my teeth, woke me up just enough for me to check my phone. And it was a good thing I did. Ingrid had been waiting hours for a reply.

Lanaahhhhh! Text me now!

Are you up?

Of course I'm up! I'm in college!

Sorry I didn't text you sooner. I take it your date with Riley went well.

So well! We talked until three in the morning!

And by talked you mean talked?

Mostly

Ing, don't be that girl

I'm trying!

There's no trying! When it comes to The Plan, there's only doing . . . or not doing, depending how you look at it.

104

This is true, but Riley is so sweet, and we're so good together. We already finish each other's sentences

Wow

And he bought me flowers!

That's nice. Flowers cost twenty bucks, the cost of your virginity is marrying you.

But he's so cute!

Ingrid! Snap out of it! More than that, you pinkie promised. Don't forget.

I won't. Besides, I won't be seeing him for a week. So, how's Bluegill?

I'm falling for a guy in work boots.

As if. So there aren't any cute guys in that town?

Only ruggedly handsome ones.

Funny. Well, keep me posted!

I will.

And don't forget! You have to call me if, by some miracle, you find some guy to kiss out there.

I won't forget. And you don't forget what you shouldn't forget.

I won't! Bye! Love you!

Love you too.

Chapter Thirteen

It's a good thing I wasn't trying to make it to Holy Mother Cathedral for mass because I slept past ten. Stretching, I looked at my phone, and slowly remembered the events of the night before. First, LeVan had been lucid. This man who talked about his dead wife like she was out shopping, and opened and closed the mailbox more than necessary—this man had given me a crash course (almost literally) in how to drive a stick shift and had shared sound advice about being an artist. And, what's more, he had agreed to help me catch Walt's eye. Sure, so far, his advice hadn't helped. Still, he had been *all there* while giving it.

Then there was the studio. I loved working there, its rustic, spare feel. And though I was still groggy from waking up, I hungered to return there, to finish the painting I'd started, and begin others. Yes, arriving in Idaho, hadn't gone smoothly. Like stepping off a twirling carnival ride, I'd felt disoriented, but now the spinning was slowing, and my perspective shifting. And wasn't that Lefty's point? I smiled. Just two days in Bluegill and I was agreeing with Lefty. Well, not quite. Still, my outlook had brightened, which, I'm not going to lie, had something to do with Walt Hitchpost. We had held hands, and my heart warmed with happiness at the thought.

But the happy bubble I felt wrapped inside popped as one thought occurred to me: How was I supposed to act around

Walt now that we'd held hands? It was a question for middle schoolers, not college graduates. But even award-winning artists can be late bloomers, and there was no denying the truth—I had never before held the hand of a boy I liked. What to do next was all I thought about as I showered and got dressed, and would have been the first question I asked LeVan, but, of course, the first had to be, "How is your wife today?"

Wearing a freshly ironed white button-down shirt, striped tie, and dark pants held up by suspenders, LeVan folded his newspaper in half and looked at me. "She is a spirit," he said, a sad smile creasing his weathered face, "awaiting the glorious day of resurrection."

I sat in the chair next to him, and leaned in, conspiratorially close. "So, you're still here?" I asked, my voice low.

"For now, but I think we both know, I'm a house of cards," he said, "and all it would take is just the right breeze." LeVan rubbed his hands together. "So, we need to make the most of the time we have," He checked his wrist, in search of the time, "head back to the studio and get to work."

"But, LeVan," I said, "it's Sunday."

He fingered his tie, as if making sure it was real. "So it is," he said, smiling, despite the flicker of worry in his eyes. "Forgetting the Lord's Day. It's like I'm nine and the circus is in town."

I tossed my hand. "It's nothing. I'm sure you're fine," I said, because kindness sometimes makes me lie.

LeVan gave an almost indiscernible shake of the head. "If there's one thing we know it's that I am not fine, but, while I can, I want to teach you a thing or two about painting, take care of some unfinished business of my own, and, his face split into an impish grin, "help you ensnare my grandson."

My eyes darted, scanning the kitchen. "Is he here?" I asked.

"No, he's at ward council, which makes sense now that it's Sunday."

I sighed with relief, then narrowed my eyes on LeVan. "Ensnare your grandson? Don't you think that's a little strong?"

"Capture then."

"Now you're just trying to bother me," I said.

LeVan's eyes flickered as if lit by an inner fire. "Well, do you want some other girl to get her hooks into him?"

I sat up. "Of course not."

"Then quit your moaning and let's get to work!"

"You're right," I said.

"And the first order of business is you singing him a love song at karaoke night. Something flowery."

I folded my arms. "That's the best you've got, me singing him something flowery?" I asked.

"It'll work wonders."

"LeVan, I'm tone deaf."

"There's got to be a Helen Reddy tune you could stay in line with."

"There is no way I'm singing to him."

He tapped his chest. "You need to trust me. Remember, I'm your Cyrano," he said.

"Well, guess what, Cyrano," I said, my hands on my hips, "Walt held my hand last night."

"Did he kiss you?" Walt asked.

"No!"

"If you'd sung to him maybe he would have."

I pointed a finger at him as I collected my thoughts. "You're persistent, I'll give you that," I said. "Well, let me tell you something, you don't save a city from turning into a lake without having a little gumption."

"Bluegill nearly turned into a lake?"

"Never mind that. Right now we're talking about you beguiling Walt."

I closed my eyes and exhaled sharply. "No one's trying to beguile Walt, except for possibly Shailene." LeVan clucked his tongue. "I think Shailene's about as romantically interested in Walt as Hank is."

"She's always touching him."

"Always," he said, lowering his gaze.

"Sometimes," I admitted.

"Walt's not the Mona Lisa," said LeVan. "He can be touched."

I groaned. "I hate that I'm sounding petty. Great. She's gorgeous and I'm petty. I don't stand a chance."

"He held your hand last night, didn't he?" I didn't answer. "Well, didn't he?"

I gave a slight nod.

"I know my boy, and he wouldn't have done that if he were already sold on Shailene."

I frowned. "I don't know why I think we'd be right together. So far, all we've done is argue."

"That's not true. You've held hands."

"Maybe that's not a big deal to him. He might hold hands with all the girls. In fact, he's probably in ward council holding hands with some girl right now."

LeVan psshawed. "Nonsense." He shook his clenched fist. "You need to show Walt that you're the one who should be his gal!"

"LeVan, I am not singing to him."

"Tell you what," said LeVan, crossing one knee over the other, and swinging his foot, "bake him cookies."

"It needs to be something bigger. Like, whoa! Really get his attention. Something that says, *Hello! I'm awesome! Take me out!*

"What about soup?"

I let out a long breath. "LeVan, if his stomach were the way to his heart he'd be crushing on the fry cook at Faye's Luncheonette."

"That would be Min Tso, Hien Bao's uncle."

"Well, you know what I mean." I bit my lip and thought for a moment. "What if I finished his sentences?"

"Come again?" he asked, cupping his ear.

"Finish his sentences. Apparently, it's something in sync couples do."

"You want to be his sweetheart, not a side show magician. Who told you this?"

"My girlfriend."

"And she's an expert at this sort of thing?"

"I wouldn't say that."

"You could just be yourself and see where it leads?"

"I know where it leads—nowhere. I'll watch him fall in love with Shailene, or some other girl, and not say a word. I've got to push myself, LeVan."

LeVan wagged his finger. "Don't finish Walt's sentences."

"Do you have any better ideas?"

"A casserole."

I picked up a banana from the bowl on the kitchen table and started peeling. "I'm terrified," I said, my mouth full of banana. I took a moment and swallowed. "What scares me most is never risking, and never falling in love."

LeVan raised an eyebrow. "Never falling in love? You really think that will never happen?"

Emotion tightened my throat. Here it was, the fear I kept tucked away, hidden from view, and now I was going to share it with LeVan. I braved a smile. "Me falling in love, yes, that will happen; someone falling in love with me, probably not." I swiped at a lone tear.

LeVan slapped the table. "What in the Sam hill are you talking about! Who could help but love a horrible singer, like yourself!" he said with just enough humor to make me laugh. LeVan placed his hand over mine, its tremble slight, but constant. "Now you remember something, even behind the thickest clouds, the stars continue to shine, and when they part do you know what you'll see?"

"Stars?"

"Yes, but I'm speaking allegorically."

"Your Alzheimer's is seriously on hold."

"Stay focused. I don't want you to miss my point."

"Okay, when the clouds part, I'll see the stars, and what do they represent?"

"What's been there all along."

"Which is?"

"This simple truth: you" He paused, his voice warbling with emotion, "are worthy of love."

His words seared the ice inside me, creating fissures and cracks, causing great chunks of what held me emotionally bound to fall away. I tilted my head upward to try and keep tears from spilling, but there were too many. "You think so?" I asked.

"Since getting my marbles together, have I been honest with you?"

I sniffed and laughed at the same time. "I suppose."

"As long as I'm able, I'll tell you like it is, that's a promise." LeVan squinted, reading the kitchen clock. "Good heavens, it's time to start walking to church."

With my help, LeVan stood. I grabbed his hat and coat off the hook and opened the front door. "Let me know if anything else comes to mind."

LeVan put on his hat. "Make him peanut brittle."

"I'm glad you're off karaoke, but why now are your suggestions revolving around food?" I asked, helping him across the threshold and shutting the door.

LeVan pulled a key from his pocket, and, after a few tries, slid it into the keyhole. "I have no idea," he said, twisting the key. "Food didn't matter to me in the slightest when I was courting. Had Rosemary offered me a stale cracker it would have been enough to win my love."

I pushed open the front door. "So, you're easy to please."

"No, just in love with her from the first moment I saw her."

"You're a lucky man," I said, extending my arm to him as we walked down the path to the sidewalk, and joined the others in their Sunday best heading to church.

LeVan kindly declined my offer of help. "You say luck, I say blessed." he said as we turned left with the others, heading toward a steeple peeking over rooftops.

Poplars lined the street, their branches dappling the pavement with bits of light. "She must have loved that you were willing to fight for her," I said as a boy in a white shirt and tie rushed passed us, his little sister, though in heels, close behind.

"If I'd have let it come to blows, I'd just now be waking up from a coma."

"But you did something!"

"True."

"Well, I have to do something."

LeVan snapped his fingers. "Baklava!"

"How about I take him to an all-you-can-eat buffet and call it a day?"

"That might not be a bad idea."

Smiling, I rolled my eyes. "You say it like you see it."

LeVan nodded. "And what I've got to say is this: Blessed is the mostly honest man, for no dress ever made his wife look fat."

"Amen to that," said a father walking nearby, carrying his toddler on his shoulders. "Amen to that."

Chapter Fourteen

I tried to tell myself that, in general, holding hands wasn't a big deal. That on a scale of one to ten, one being unimportant and ten through-the-roof important, holding hands was a one, two, tops—barely a blip on the radar. So why wouldn't my heart stop hammering, and, when I saw Walt, why did my tongue twist itself into a knot?

I didn't say a word to Walt during church. I take that back, when he passed me the sacrament tray, like an idiot, I whispered, *Thanks*, then, embarrassed, melted into the pew. I was equally unchatty as we drove to Flintlock, Shailene's parents' house, but, once there, who could blame me for not talking, since that place left me speechless. Flintlock looked like it was meant for rock royalty or CEOs wanting to give the outdoors a try. At night, it had been impressive, but in the middle of the afternoon, it loomed massive and intimidating, like an alien warship (made of logs), ready to take over the world.

I wanted to dislike Clint and Patsy Stock, Shailene's parents, but that was hard to do when Patsy kept rushing across the family room's bear skin rug to refresh my lemonade.

Clint Stock loosened his tie. "So, you're in town to paint?" he asked, his eyebrow tilted, showing, I suppose, he considered art a serious subject.

"I am," I said, then sipped my lemonade greedily. The weather had turned hot, and before joining the others inside, the Stocks had insisted on first giving me a tour of the grounds (think Versailles's American cousin.)

"How lovely!" said Patsy who was so weighed down with diamonds it was a miracle she could lift a finger, but she somehow managed.

"I'm looking forward to it," I said, sinking into their leather couch.

"And how long will you be staying in Bluegill?" she asked, sitting in a leather chair across from me, her eyes bright with kindness and sparkly mascara.

"She's here for six weeks," said Shailene, emphasizing, I thought, the number six as if to say, *and not a day more.*

"That's right," I said, stopping myself from giving her a sideways glance. Patsy's eyes were filled with sympathy. "And you're here to learn from Bishop Hitchpost?" She asked, glancing at LeVan who was standing at the back of the room, staring out the wall of windows.

"LeVan is fine," said LeVan, which I understood to mean he preferred not to be called Bishop, but everyone else seemed to think he was referring to himself in the third person, and was having just another Alzheimer's moment.

I gripped my glass of lemonade, wet from condensation, and gathered my courage. Clint's arched eyebrow, Shailene's smile, and Walt's piercing stare had me rattled. But LeVan was listening, and I didn't want what I said to disappoint him. "The Wilmington Trust is progressive in the way it approaches its mentoring opportunities," I said. "I'm not here just to learn from LeVan. We're here to help each other as artists."

"That's so sweet," said Patsy, a diamond-laden finger touching her short, black, perfectly teased hair.

Clint's eyebrow was tilting so far it was practically standing on end. "Does the Wilmington board of trustees *know*," he said, gesturing at LeVan who was watching a deer walking across the lawn.

"All considered, shouldn't they have sent you somewhere else?" asked Shailene like she cared. I sipped my lemonade, then smiled. "Lefty Zaugg wanted—"

"You know Lefty Zaugg, that graffiti artist who's big on Instagram?" asked Shailene, sounding stunned, as if the world, as she understood it to be organized, didn't allow for Lefty Zaugg crossing paths with me.

"Lefty?" asked Patsy.

"Sounds like a pitcher," said Clint.

"Yes, I know him," I said, debating whether to add, *we go way back*, but I decided against it. "Lefty is the one who designed this experience. He's the reason I'm here. Well, I'm the reason I'm here. It's a bit of both. But, I know, Alzheimer's or not, he wants me to stay in Bluegill, and see how my time here influences my art." *He's crazy like that*, was on the tip of my tongue.

"So, you'll be painting at the Dogwood studio?" asked Clint.

I looked at Walt. "We're working out the details," he said, rubbing his index finger above his upper lip, which I was beginning to understand meant he was uncomfortable, "but yes, they'll be painting at Gramps's studio."

"Clint nodded, his eyebrow still doing a hand stand. "If I had a nickel for every time I've offered to buy that property . . . During season, the house could be rented to hunters. You could turn the studio into a meat room. Just buy a commercial refrigerator, a stainless-steel table, and add some hooks on pulleys and—"

"It's an art studio, not a slaughterhouse," I interjected, then embarrassed to have said anything, I drained my glass.

Lemonade pitcher in hand, Patsy Stock hurried across the bear skin rug and poured me another glass of the sweetest tartest tastiest lemonade I'd ever had. "Oh, it's just wishful thinking, honey," she said.

"It's not for sale," said Walt, managing to sound both kind and firm.

"What's not for sale?" asked a man, walking into the Stock's family room, who looked to be Hank, Walt's older brother. Hank was a squatter, older version of Walt Hitchpost. Same thick crop of sandy hair, same brown eyes, but gone was the intense look that had kept me up all night sketching. With him was his wife, Britney, and a little girl who looked to be about five years old. Everyone, except LeVan, went to greet them. I'd heard a little about Britney and the mental picture I'd drawn wasn't entirely off—another Shailene, which made sense since they were cousins. But unlike Shailene, Britney seemed intent on perfection—her hair, her nails, her biceps, her teeth, her abs, her clothes—all were perfect, making her daughter's glasses, and the way she sucked her thumb, contrast sharply.

"Walt says Gramps's house isn't for sale," said Shailene, pulling her lower lip into a pout. I didn't know what bothered me more, her pout, or the way she referred to LeVan as Gramps, like she was already a part of the family. I looked away in frustration and to my surprise saw LeVan, his hand at his side, motioning for me to come to him."

Now? I mouthed when LeVan glanced at me. Wasn't it obvious I was about to be introduced to Walt's brother and his family?"

LeVan, stared out the window and nodded.

Can it wait a minute? I told him with a wide-eyed look when he looked my way again. LeVan snorted his disapproval, so while

everyone else hugged the newcomers I walked over to LeVan.

"What's so important?" I whispered.

"They have True Horseman," LeVan said, looking out window.

"*Your* True Horseman?" I asked.

"Yes, I caught a glimpse of it as we walked in. Ask them why it's hanging in their monstrosity of a home rather than in the Wyoming state capitol where it belongs."

"Okay."

"Patsy's daddy bought several of my paintings. Find out if she has them, or any other works of mine."

"Sure."

"And inquire as to why they thought they should change the True Horseman frame. I designed that frame for that painting, and now they've got it in a baroque number."

"That's going to be kind of complicated to slide in, but I'll—"

"And be sure to tell them the new frame doesn't match the tone of the painting. Tell them it makes about as much sense as a beagle in a clown suit."

"Would you also like me to bring you a Sprite, easy on the ice?"

LeVan brought his head a little closer to mine. "Why are you asking that?"

"Because you're making a lot of demands right now! Just relax, I'll ask them during lunch."

LeVan touched my sleeve. "I can't wait," he said. "We don't know when I'm going to slip away again. I want to know. Do it now."

I exhaled sharply and walked across the bear skin rug, just as Hank let out a low whistle, and said, "I don't know, Walt's seems as attached to that old house as he was to his man bun in high school."

"Everyone on the football team let their hair grow," said Walt, shoving Hank.

"But they cut it after the season. Like your man bun, it's time to let Dogwood go, bro," said Hank, shoving Walt back, then resting his hand on his daughter's head. She stood next to him, clinging to his pant leg.

"It's beyond time," said Britney, taking a section of Shailene's hair between her fingers and inspecting the ends.

"I'll tell you what it's beyond time to do," said Walt, sounding good-natured, "and that's introduce you guys to Lana." He motioned at me. "Lana, this is my brother, Hank, his wife, Britney, and their daughter, Kylie."

"Nice to meet you," I said, glancing at LeVan who was rolling his wrist, no doubt, to tell me to hurry.

"Lana is an artist," said Patsy.

"Nice to meet you," said Hank, shaking my hand, then placing his hand again on his daughter's head. "By the way, sorry about the mix up, you getting dropped off at Dogwood," he said.

From the corner of my eye, I watched Walt's jaw tighten.

"It all worked out, I said with a shrug.

"Walt nearly ran over her," said Shailene, folding her arms.

"Let's talk about something else," Walt and I both said, our synchronicity taking us by surprise.

"I, for one, am glad you'll be working at Dogwood. I adore that studio," said Patsy.

Shailene gave Walt a playful nudge. "One day," she said, her voice babyish, "Daddy and I we'll figure out how to get you to turn Dogwood into a hunting lodge.

"We just visited Watsadon, a fantastic hunting lodge in Zimbabwe," said Clint, apropos to nothing, his eyebrow tilting again. "The hunt, of course, wasn't bear . . ."

Everyone sat down, and as Clint talked of hunting in Zimbabwe, I thought of Shailene. How had she done it, switch so effortlessly from girl to flirty girl? She possessed a gift, not a rare one, but one I didn't share. When I tried to flirt I felt like an actress reading a terrible script—nothing flowed. Maybe flirting was like a muscle, and the more you worked it, the stronger it got. I'd just begun wondering if there were flirting tutorials online when LeVan snapped his fingers, telling me to get with it.

"We'd been hunting African buffalo all day," said Clint, "and finally we spotted one. Gently, I placed my finger on the trigger, and—" "Sorry to interrupt," I said.

"Daddy was just getting to the good part," said Shailene.

I ignored her. "I was wondering if you've collected any of LeVan Hitchpost's work?"

Patsy's eyes lit up. "Heaven's yes. My daddy was a big fan. He started the collection, and since then, we've been able to acquire more than our fair share," she said.

LeVan appeared to be studying a deer out on the lawn, watching its slow, graceful movements. "I bet you have," he muttered, though no one appeared to notice but me.

"Am I mistaken or was that True Horseman that I saw as I walked in."

"Of course it was!" said Patsy.

"Of course it was," grumbled LeVan, again without attracting attention.

"I thought it was in Wyoming," I said.

"Me too," said Walt, not giving away whether this bothered him or not.

"Wyoming is a fantastic state," said Clint.

Patsy's smile grew wider. "It was, but when we offered the powers that be what we did we were able to come to an agreement."

"Keep going," said LeVan, and for a brief moment him sliding back into Alzheimer's didn't seem like such a bad idea.

"Interesting," I said, "Is it in the original frame?"

"Heavens no. My art consultant advised me to not remove it. He said it was worth more if I didn't, but it didn't look right with our tile. Do you like it?"

I put my hand to my heart. "I, for one, like it. I suppose there are those who might think it's a monstrosity, but the world is full of opinions. Variety's the spice of life. And so while someone might think putting it in a baroque frame makes about as much sense as dressing a medium sized dog like a clown, in the end, you gotta do you."

Walt scrunched his eyebrows together.

Patsy tilted her head and smiled. "I'd be happy to show you our collection after we eat."

LeVan cleared his throat.

"Is there any way I could see them now?" I asked

"Of course, Shailene why don't you take everyone into the dining room and, Daddy and I will take our guest to—"

LeVan didn't need to coax me. "Would it be all right if LeVan came with us. It might spark something inside him. You never know."

Again, Patsy's glittery eyes softened with sadness. "Yes, if only it could. He was Daddy's greatest friend." LeVan scoffed at this, but did his best to hide it with a cough. "Let's start with True Horseman. It's just around the corner."

Chapter Fifteen

As it turned out, Clint and Patsy Stock had collected seven of LeVan's paintings, and in that seven, his four most important works. They had purchased Saddling Whiskey from a lasso museum that had fallen on hard times, Lambing Season from the grandchildren of Leslie and Winona Carmichael, True Horseman from the state of Wyoming, because as Clint pointed out, everyone has their price. And lastly, they had acquired Wind and Willow from Hank and Britney. "It was their wedding present."

"And they didn't want to keep it?" I asked.

"Not when they heard what we were willing to pay for it," said Patsy with a laugh.

"Money talks," said Clint and his eyebrow.

LeVan stood before Wind and Willow, a picture of his late wife, Rosemary Willow Hitchpost.

Patsy looked wistfully at LeVan. "He was a great artist," she said, which was true, but I had expected her to say, *He was a great husband*. Who could look at *Wind and Willow* and not see how much he loved her?

Clint glanced at LeVan and then shook his head solemnly. "Indeed, he was a great artist, and a great person," he said, using the past tense even though LeVan stood beside him.

"Daddy thought of him like a brother." LeVan blew a raspberry. "It's so sad what's happened to him." Clint put his hand on his wife's shoulder. "Life is sometimes cruel," she said.

"Yeah," I said, agreeing, but it seemed odd for Patsy to be talking about the unfairness of life, not with her lavish jewelry and log cabin mansion.

From somewhere in the house, Shailene shouted for her mother. "Heavens, the roast must be done," she said. "Clint, come with me. You two meet us in the dining room in a few minutes."

I considered briefly asking her if she had a map. "Okay," I said, then waited until I was sure we were alone before I walked to where LeVan stood, studying Wind and Willow, as if remembering every brushstroke, how he had managed to create the appearance of movement, his wife hurrying, the wind rushing across the lawn, catching her skirt, and—were she not pressing her hand to it—blowing the hat off her head. His color choices, the blues and oranges, added another layer of movement, creating in the finished piece energy and vibrancy, action and reaction, chaos swirling all around, yet in the center of the storm, Rosemary's calm expression. This painting said as clearly as if it were a love letter, *she is the love of my life.*

How had Hank and Britney ever parted with it? Yes, the painting was large. A young couple probably wouldn't have had room for it. And they, no doubt, had needed the money. But still, it was a beautiful work of art, and a beautiful gift.

"Your brushwork is incredible."

"Professor Saul didn't suffer fools."

"I'm sorry?" I asked, fear prickling my skin. Was he slipping away?

"He taught me my junior year at Columbia. He was an alcoholic and bad tempered, but he pushed my technique, and demanded I push myself. I said as little as I could to him back then, but now, looking at this painting, I wish I would have thanked him. He's long dead, but he deserved a thank you. My goodness she's magnificent!"

"She really is."

He tapped the side of his head. "You know it's all in here," he said, "everything Saul taught me—attacking the canvas, submitting it to your will, going big, not compromising, probing for depth, infusing the painting with your voice. It's all here, at least for now. Professor Saul, Professor Meeks. Not Professor Gordon, he was boring, but a lifetime of learning is inside me. I'm being chased by a tiger, to be sure, but he hasn't caught me yet, and I want to paint. What time I have left, I want to be painting."

"Okay," I said.

"All day into the night, barely sleeping or eating, sometimes forgetting to breathe, just painting until the brush falls from my fingers."

"That's fine," I said, "but I don't think Walt is going to go for that kind of schedule. I mean, we'd be leaving Dogwood pretty late, and—"

"Tell him we won't be leaving Dogwood."

"Excuse me?"

"Tell him we have to stay there. Time is too precious. We need to be at the studio."

"No."

"Yes."

"He is going to think I'm weird, calling the shots like that!"

"And tell him not to come to the studio."

I raised a finger. "Have you forgotten you're my Cyrano? Yes, I want to paint, but how am I supposed to ever go on a date with Walt if we never see him?"

"You need to trust me."

"And you need to not trust me! What if something happens to you while we're up there? I am not a nurse! I'm not even certified at CPR!"

"I can't do anything about my work ending up at Flintlock en masse. It's irritating, certainly not what I wanted, but they had the money, and, as Patsy said, money talks."

"Clint said that not Patsy."

"Doesn't matter. Two heads, same monster."

"LeVan!" I hissed, my eyes darting to the doorway to make sure no one was there; they weren't.

"I shouldn't have said that," he said. "They're good people, even if they stoop to buying wedding presents off young couples."

I looked at Wind and Willow, and gave him a sad look. "I'm sorry."

"Well," he said, "the Stocks couldn't have bought it if it weren't for sale." He shook his head. "Should have given those two a toaster, but that's in the past. What matters now is if you meant what you said."

"What did I say?" I asked.

"That we're here to help each other as artists."

"Of course!"

"Then help me now," he said, and the longing in his eyes was too much.

I let out a conciliatory sigh. "Fine, but you are ruining my chances with your grandson," I said

"You're helping me, I'm helping you. I haven't forgotten that."

"And we might have been good together, you know. I speak Russian."

"Interesting."

"And he speaks Russian."

"Now you're stretching it."

"He sort of speaks Russian." LeVan nodded, accepting this description. "But after I tell him everything you want me to, he's going to think I'm crazy."

"Are you okay," said Shailene standing in the doorway.

I jumped. "Woah! I didn't see you there. Yes, I'm fine. Why?"

Shailene gestured toward LeVan. "You were talking to Gramps."

Fear prickled the back of my neck. How much had she heard? "That's right," I said, acting calm.

Shailene frowned. "It just never gets easy, you know, him being this way. He was a great man, and now, he's here, but he's not here." She sighed.

"Anyway, it's time to eat," she said. LeVan gave me a knowing look. "A tiger's coming," he said, "that I can't outrun or outsmart."

"A tiger's not coming, Gramps," she said, "and if it were, we've got fire power." Shailene turned to leave, then stopped. "Does he need help?"

"Yes," I said with a sigh, "he does."

"Then what are you waiting for?" she asked, walking away.

"Indeed, Miss Huish," said LeVan, shuffling toward the door, his eyes bright with intelligence and something resembling mischief, "what are you waiting for?"

Chapter Sixteen

"You want to do what!" cried Walt, gripping the steering wheel hard, probably wishing it were my neck.

"Would you like me to explain ag—"

"No, I heard you," he said, whipping his truck around a corner and onto a dirt road. We were on our way to get Ruth, which was still parked at Dogwood, but first Walt had needed to check on the irrigation in field six. The air was cool, our windows down, and though I was completely freaked out about having just dropped the, your-grandfather-and-I-are-moving-to-Dogwood-without-you bomb, I was watching the dust clouds kicked up by our tires, and moving my finger across my palm, imagining how I would paint them.

Walt sped down a dirt path, lined on either side by rows of plants. From the corner of my eye I saw him grit his teeth. Not a good sign, but, what had I expected? I'd just told him I wanted to commandeer his sick grandfather, the man who had raised him, who he now cared for. All considered, that he hadn't pulled the truck over and told me to get out, was a small victory.

In the field up ahead sat a giant metal structure on wheels. Part erector set, part predatory bird, the machine sprayed the crop beneath it with an even mist, heightening the smell of earth. It was a sweet smell, one I would have liked to have taken in in giant gulps had Walt not jerked the truck into park, gotten out, and slammed the door behind him.

"Oh boy," I said, under my breath as I watched him storm toward the gangly machine. I knew nothing about farm equipment, but when he kicked one of the tires over and over, I thought it safe to assume, that not only was he mad at me, but something with the machine wasn't working.

I got out of the truck and walked over to Walt who, enveloped in mist, was adjusting a valve. "Can I help?" I asked, bracing myself for an angry outburst while simultaneously reveling in the colors that surrounded us.

Walt pressed his hands to his head. "I'm trying to make this work, Lana!" he cried.

I stepped closer, mist tickling my face, "Does it come with an instruction manual?"

The wheels of the machine edged forward. Walt took me by the arm, moving me out of its slow, but certain path, his touch making my heart flip. "I'm talking about you!" said Walt. "You and Gramps working together!" He pinched the bridge of his nose and thought for a moment. Water droplets clung to his hair, glistening in the afternoon sun. "Why are you making this so complicated?" he asked.

It's not me it's your grandfather! That's what I wanted to say, but, of course, I couldn't, not with LeVan counting on me. "It's really not that complicated," I said. "We need to be at the studio."

"I get that, but why day and night?"

I shielded my eyes from the sun with my hand, but there was no shielding myself from the mist. It clung to my clothes, my face and neck. "It's complicated," I said, realizing as I said it, that I should have used a different word.

"You see!" he cried.

"What I mean is, as an artist speaking to a non-artist, it's difficult to explain the importance of staying there. But it's important, really important."

Walt shifted his weight. "I was just wrapping my head around the two of you working there in the afternoons for a few hours, and now you want to turn it into some sort of marathon studio session. Why? And don't say it's complicated!"

"I have work to do," I said, "and," I bit my lip, deciding how much to say, "I think your grandfather does too."

"He's done painting!"

"Then why do you have his easel set up in your kitchen?"

"You know what I mean. His days in the studio are over!" he cried, throwing his hands in the air. "Don't you get it? He's marking time! His career is over, his life is over!"

"You're the one who said he's not dead yet!" I said, my fists clenched.

"And I'm trying to keep it that way!" Walt shook his head. "You take him there, and help won't be close by."

"I'll have help!" I said, just going for it and lying big time.

"Who?"

"Carl," I said, rubbing my nose as if to see if it were growing. "He's a healthcare worker. The Wilmingtons set it up."

Walt thought for a moment. "But *I* won't be close by!" he finally said.

It was time to start winning this argument; LeVan was counting on me. "You're not close by as it is."

Walt tensed at my words. "I'm still working the kinks out of his schedule," he said.

A canyon breeze whooshed by, making my wet skin turn to goose flesh. "He's alone part of the day," I said, folding my arms tight to my chest.

"Well, he wouldn't be if Britney would help," he said, bitterly. As the machine continued to creep along, Walt slid open a panel near one of its legs, revealing a computer screen. He punched in some numbers and closed it. "Her salon is downtown. It would be the perfect solution."

"Except that he doesn't want to be around her."

"He has Alzheimer's!"

I forced myself to focus on the argument, not how I would mix blue with red and yellow to create his skin tone. "Are you saying he no longer has an opinion, because I think he does."

"I'm saying he needs supervision"

"Which is what I'm saying! Look, even with your friends in town keeping an eye out for LeVan, he's still spends time alone." Walt bent down, touching the soil with two fingers. "It doesn't take much to see that Britney doesn't want the added responsibility."

"You can say that again," he mumbled.

"I'm here for the next six weeks, and I'm *supposed* to spend time with him. So instead of having him sort nails with Norm at Ace Hardware, let him paint with me at the studio—his studio. You can trust me."

"I've known you three days!"

He was right. He hadn't known me long, and I was asking him to trust me. It all came down to whether he thought he could. Sure, he could run a background check, but allowing LeVan to do what I was asking was going to require a leap of faith. I decided to try a different tack. "If he were well," I said, "where would he want to be?" Walt didn't answer, but I knew what he was thinking: he would want to be in his studio. "Let him be there, one last time."

Walt rubbed above his upper lip.

"But without me; you don't want me around," he said, his hurt little boy look making me melt.

I swallowed hard. "You take good care of your grandfather. Consider this a chance to rest, recharge your battery," I said, thinking of how much time this arrangement would free up in Walt's schedule to spend with Shailene. An image of them driving in his truck, and her sliding closer to him came to mind, and made stomach churn. "We'll, of course, see you on Sunday."

Walt looked off into the distance. "That's fantastic. You're awarding me supervised visitation," he said, his voice flat.

"What's that supposed to mean?"

"Nothing," he said, slapping his hands together, trying to remove the moist dirt sticking to them. "We're done here. Let's go."

I got in the truck, slumped against the truck door, and, in my mind, watched Shailene, rest her head on Walt's shoulder

We drove in silence up the canyon, Walt's frustration thickening the air, making the truck's cabin uncomfortable. Walt was stewing, which, obviously, isn't healthy in a relationship, not that we were *in* a relationship. We were not, which wasn't surprising, considering how short we'd known each other and how rocky our start. But rocky or not, I wanted to keep trying, and see what was around the corner. It might be heartache, I realized that, but that didn't make me slink away. I thought of LeVan's words, *You're alive, aren't you? So live!* I wanted to live. Walt placed his hand on the seat. I watched it there, his hand, callused from working outdoors, curled against the cracked leather seat, and felt my fingers twitch. Usually this meant I wanted to sketch, but not this time. This time I just wanted to reach out and hold his hand. It was an irrational impulse, one that, of course, I didn't act on, but it crashed in on me with such force that, even though I was sitting, my knees wobbled. *Living* was going to take some getting used to.

The truck climbed the winding road to Seventy-Two Dogwood Lane, and as it did, I found myself wishing the road would stretch, and Walt would ease up on the gas so that our time together would last longer. Yes, the silence was agonizing, but on the flip side, I could smell through the open window the evergreens, and Walt Hitchpost was sitting just one seat over.

I wanted to say something, break the ice, move us past the silence that held us captive, and show him that, despite occasionally not seeing eye-to-eye, we clicked

I adjusted the shoulder harness on my seat belt and went for it. "So!" I said.

Walt turned to look at me.

"So . . . ?"

"What's your favorite color?"

Walt gave me a sideways glance before guiding the truck around yet another bend in the road. "I'd have to say, bl—"

"Blue!" I said.

"Black," he said.

"Seriously? No one ever likes black, except me."

"Why would I lie? I really do like black. It's so—"

"Sophisticated!" I said, jabbing the air with my index finger.

"I guess, but I was going to say soothing."

"Oh."

"Why do you keep trying to finish what I'm saying?"

My face burned with embarrassment. This was one of the dumbest things I'd ever done to try and impress a guy. "I don't know, trying to be helpful," I muttered.

Walt laughed.

"You're an interesting one, Lana," he said, and though I generally hated to be laughed at, I didn't mind it this time, because his laughter swept away the tension between us.

"That's not something I hear every day," I said.

Walt rested his arm on the edge of the seat, his fingers inches from my neck. "What do people usually say about you?"

"That I'm quiet, hard to get to know," I said, aware that his fingers were close enough to brush against my skin.

"Quiet!" he said, shaking his head. "That doesn't seem very accurate."

"Why?'

"Because you've been giving me a piece of your mind since you got here," he said with a smile.

"I wouldn't put it that way," I said, turning to look at him.

"And how would you put it?" he asked, glancing at me.

"That we've had our share of disagreements."

"Like right now. We're disagreeing about our disagreements," he said as the truck passed over a bump in the road.

"I'd have to agree with you on that," I said.

Walt smiled. "Which now blows our streak. What do you think that means?"

"Just like your grandfather," I said, "you're looking for meaning," I said, more to myself than to him.

"Did he talk to you about that, the meaning he wanted to convey in his paintings?" asked Walt, his voice rising with hope.

"No, no! Of course not," I said, trying to sound casual. "How could he? I, uh, did some research."

"Oh," he said, his voice trailing off. "When you've been with him, he hasn't had moments of lucidity?" Walt's eyes searched mine, trying to find some sign of encouragement. "Because, call me crazy, but sometimes it's felt like he's all there, but is holding back."

I cleared my throat. "Just the same old, same old," I said. *Quick! Change the subject before you break!* "So, you learned Russian on your mission," I said.

"I did. How about you?" he asked, and when I didn't respond added, "or is this the time you start getting hard to know?"

My fingers curled around the edge of the seat as I forced myself to not dodge his question. "I learned in—"

"Russia," he said with a snap.

"Yes," I said.

"What brought you to the States?" he asked.

I looked out the passenger window, seeing wild flowers, but thinking of dark memories. "I was—"

"Adopted," he said.

"Yes," I said, my voice soft. "I came from—"

"Let me guess, a miserable place like Siberia, where jobs are scarce and inflation high. Child abandonment is a big problem there, parents turning over their children to the state because they can't afford to take care of them. Social orphans. I saw a documentary about it."

I knew he hadn't meant it, but it didn't change the fact that the questions he'd asked me, and the way he'd guessed at their answers stung. He had reduced that part of my life that I hid to a common social problem instead of something singularly hurtful.

"Is this some sort of joke to you?" I asked.

He gave me a quick glance, his eyes wide with surprise. "What do you mean?"

"Nothing," I said, feeling myself grow cold toward him.

"I was just trying to help," he said. His tone sincere, but his words mocking me all the same.

Fresh sleet blanketed my heart. I stared straight ahead. In the distance, I could see Seventy-Two Dogwood Lane, its white clap board exterior glowing in the late afternoon sun. And from the corner of my eye, Walt, alternating his glances between me and the road.

"Lana," he said, his voice soft, "I didn't mean to offend you."

"I know," I said, my tone flat, emotionless. Why had I tried? Maybe it was better to accept that I wasn't capable of connecting with people, not deeply, anyway. Even those closest to me, Ingrid and my parents, whether they knew it or not, I kept at a distance. It was always winter inside me, a side effect, perhaps, of my childhood, but perhaps not. Maybe it was just who I was, not something I could shake. Maybe this was just me.

"Lana," he said, the pleading in his voice, like fire against my ice.

I studied the windshield, determined not to crack.

Ne Serdites. Don't be angry, he said. Hearing him speak Russian shouldn't have mattered. Millions of people spoke Russian, most of them much better than Walt! But it did matter, and, with a speed and force I found frustrating, turned big chunks of my ice to slush.

YA ne zylus. I'm not angry, I said, like a robot giving a programmed response.

We pulled up to the house, the gravel crunching beneath the tires. Walt put the truck in park, and turned to me, both hands still on the steering wheel, making me long for him to reach for me, to simply place his hand over mine.

"*Prosti*. I'm sorry," he said.

I looked him at him. There were flecks of gold in his eyes.

I took a breath. "You don't need to apologize," I said, "I'm here for just six weeks to work with your grandfather in his studio."

"And nothing more?" he asked.

"Nothing more," I said, even though I knew that when it came to not falling in love with Walt Hitchpost, I was skating on thin ice.

Chapter Seventeen

Sketching takes focus, so does regret, and, so far, regret was winning. That night, after my conversation with Walt, I lay awake, my hands pressed to my face, as the things I'd said to Walt paraded through my mind, frustration flying at me like tennis balls served rapid-fire from a machine. I should have handled things better, not gotten upset when he peered into my soul and declared it a cliché. I still felt hurt at the thought. Probably not a good sign.

What was it about Walt that robbed me of sleep? I'd never lost sleep over a guy before, but then again, I'd never *tried* with a guy before. It's easy to stay detached when you don't return a guy's calls. If I hadn't been, as Ingrid put it, such an *artful dodger*, maybe I would have endured restless nights over someone else. It was possible, but I doubted it. I tried to pinpoint what it was about him that I found so irresistible. In truth, it wasn't just one, but a combination of things: his loyalty, his goodness, that he had served a mission and could speak (sort of) Russian. And it didn't hurt that he was as fit as Captain America.

My stomach growled. I looked at the clock; it was almost six. Most likely, Walt would soon be leaving for work. I felt a ping of sadness knowing he wouldn't be down the hall. It was a silly ping, but the truth was, I liked when he was near, even after the way I'd handled things last night. I cringed at the memory. Frustration with myself pressed in on me, and, so discomfited, I sat up in bed.

I took a deep breath. The adult thing to do would be to go to the kitchen, and talk to him. I swung my feet onto the floor where they stayed, as if trapped by the shag carpet. Why was this hard for me? I'd smoothed things over after disagreements before. I did it all the time with Ingrid. It was easy, so what was holding me back? The truth stung like the stern woman's slap, and made me feel foolish. There was no reason why he should have known that his casually guessing at my past would bother me, and yet a part of me was frustrated he hadn't. We'd only known each other a few days and yet I felt connected to him. I shook my head. It was stupid. *I* was stupid! But still, I felt connected to him.

I dug my toes into the carpet's thick pile. *Go talk to him*, I told myself, but still, I resisted. What was I waiting for? I wiggled my toes. I wanted things to feel right between us, and that wasn't going to happen while I sat on this bed. Me continuing to sit was emblematic of my entire approach to guys—I avoided, stayed on the sideline, did nothing. It would be just like me to lay low the rest of my time in Bluegill, only talk to Walt about the weather or his grandfather's medication schedule. Just like me. And later if life, if by some miracle we ever saw each other again, like in our thirties, I would be alone, and he would be holding the hands of his toddler twins, each wearing a t-shirt that said, *Grizzlies Are For Shooting*, and each with Shailene's impossibly brilliant blue eyes. Shailene, appearing from around a corner, would then slip her hand in Walt's, and together they'd walk away, a happy family. I leaned forward, pressing my palms into the mattress. This was ridiculous. I wanted to see Walt and there was no reason why I shouldn't. I stood up. It was time to quit stalling. What was I afraid of?

He was out there. I could hear cupboards banging shut and the scraping of a chair across the floor.

I threw on my sweatshirt and tousled my hair. I didn't have to say much, just *Hi, how are you? Sorry I was emotional last night. Please don't think I'm always like that.* I cringed. Maybe I'd stick with *Hi.* I could handle that. I stood up, opened my bedroom door, and walked the short distance to the kitchen, expecting to see Walt, but he wasn't there. Instead I found LeVan, sitting at the table, struggling to open a new bag of cereal.

I looked around, then put my hand my forehead as if trying to remember where I'd placed something.

"Is everything all right?" asked LeVan, attempting to grip a pair of scissors between his fingers. They fell with a thud onto the table, but not before nicking the skin between his thumb and forefinger. "Confound it," he grumbled.

I rushed to get him a napkin from off the counter. "Where's Walt?" I asked without wondering first whether he was clear-headed enough to answer my question.

"Already gone to work," said LeVan. He shook his head, and pressed the napkin to his wound. "Growing old wouldn't be so bad if everything didn't stop working, even your skin."

I don't know what I'd expected. A knock on my bedroom door? Pebbles thrown at my window? He had to get to work! There was no reason why he should have said good bye before leaving. No reason at all, except that I would have liked it. "So, he's already at work," I said, my eyes fixed for no reason on the refrigerator magnets, seeing but not seeing.

"He's not one to miss," he said

"Good for him," I said.

"You don't sound convinced of that," said LeVan, his blue eyes looking deep into mine.

"Let's talk about something else," I said, my expression sullen.

LeVan gestured to the refrigerator. "We can start by me telling you that he left a note. It's folded over, with your name on it, and I'll be honest, it's been difficult not to pry."

A note from Walt! I'd looked right at it but hadn't seen it! I unfolded it. *The keys to my truck and Gramps's studio are on the hook. See you Sunday.*

LeVan licked his lips. "So what'd it say?"

"Well, you got what you wanted. We can stay at Dogwood," I said, wishing it had said *I'll miss you.*

"Hot spit! Where's my hat?" he asked, letting the napkin fall to the ground.

I found a box of Band-Aids in a cupboard. "It's still dark outside," I said, tearing open one of the larger ones and covering his cut. "You want to go now?"

Gripping the table, LeVan rose to his feet. "Yes, I want to go now. Now I've got all my marbles, but who can say about later? There's a hole in the bag, so to speak, and I don't want to waste a minute."

And we didn't. We gathered the supplies we needed, both from the garage and the grocery store, and headed up the mountain to Seventy-Two Dogwood Lane. Driving Walt's truck required no coaching from LeVan, which should have meant that we were free to talk about other things, but my thoughts held my tongue captive and we drove in silence to the house. In fact, it wasn't until we had been painting in the studio for close to an hour that a conversation crept in between us.

"You seem preoccupied," said LeVan, standing on the scaffolding and pointing the tip of his brush at me. Rather than finish painting the first two panels, he'd decided to begin by outlining his vision for the third, and this required working on the scaffolding, which, despite his claims of being more at home up there than anywhere else, didn't seem like a good idea to me.

I shrugged my shoulders. "Of course I'm preoccupied, you're all the way up there."

"No, something else is worrying you," he said, squinting. "Trust me, you're worrying me."

"Maybe so, but something else is on your mind, and whatever it is has got you peeved," he said, making small movements in the air with his brush as if rendering my perturbed look.

I stared at the canvas in front of me. "I don't want to talk about it."

LeVan squinted harder, narrowing his eyes to two slits. "What's more, you look flushed, like you've swapped hearts with a jackrabbit."

I gave him a long look. "Stop," I said.

He didn't.

"And," He thought for a moment, "there's a touch of doom and gloom in your eyes, as if the whole world—"

I tossed my brush on to the long wooden table, and threw my hands in the air. "Fine, okay! I admit it. Right now, I'm a bit all those things, except for the doom part of doom and gloom. That's overkill.

LeVan put his thumb out in front of himself and squinted, an artist's trick for measuring depth, or in my case, doom. "From where I sit, I see it differently"

"Okay!" I said. "I'm doom *and* gloom, all thanks to . . . never mind."

LeVan set aside his brush, walked to the scaffold's ladder, and took a wobbly step down. "Is there something you'd like to run past me? I've lived a long life, learned a thing or two. Why the long face, missy?"

I took a deep breath. "We're *here*, LeVan," I said, gesturing at the studio, "and, don't get me wrong, I'm glad—"

LeVan took another step down, this one a little more sure-footed. "You bet your last dollar you're glad! We're artists, we have work to do, and this is the place to do it!"

I glanced at the three panels on the wall, three panels that, for LeVan, were a last chance to paint. A last chance to be, LeVan Hitchpost, the muralist. "I know," I said, "this is a great place to work, but—" My cheeks burned with that admission— that there was a *but*. There shouldn't have been. Working in LeVan's studio *with* LeVan while he was still in possession of all his marbles was an opportunity scarcely to be believed, and I was wasting it worrying over a guy.

LeVan stepped onto the floor, allowing me to breathe easier. "But what?" he asked.

Like a just shaken bottle of soda, I opened up, and didn't hold back. "You and your demands!" I pressed a hand to my forehead and started to pace.

"My demands?"

"Yes, your demands. You want to be here."

"So we can work."

"And you don't want Walt here."

"So we can work."

I folded my arms. "Well, maybe I don't want to work. Maybe I want to stare at your grandson all day."

LeVan's face split into a grin, revealing strong, yet dingy teeth. "I'd forgotten you had Cupid's arrow lodged in your heart. Well, no wonder you're distracted."

I continued to pace. "I've always been able to work. Always. Even when I haven't had anything to work with. But now, I can't focus. I keep thinking about Walt."

LeVan sat down, and I sat next to him and buried my face in my hands. "Oh my gosh, I'm turning into Ingrid."

LeVan patted my shoulder. "Blessed are the infatuated, for they will receive their first kiss."

I looked up at LeVan, my eyes wide with astonishment. "How did you know I haven't been kissed before?"

"It was just a guess, but you do take everything to heart."

"And a kissed woman wouldn't?"

LeVan shrugged. "She would be more decorous."

"I bet Shailene is plenty decorous."

"Now, now."

I stood up and grabbed my palette. "It doesn't matter," I said. "It's like you said, we've got work to do."

"My advice is leave it alone. Let him—"

"Be with Shailene?"

LeVan shook his head. "For heaven sake, let him miss you."

I bit my lip. "Absence makes the heart grow fonder?"

LeVan's mouth pulled downward as he considered this. "Sometimes," he said, "And sometimes it just makes you forget somebody's name."

I squeezed a tube of yellow a little too hard, creating a blob on my palette. "Not encouraging, LeVan."

LeVan chuckled, making his thin body shake. "You need to wait and see what happens. Give it a week. See if he misses you too."

Careful this time not to overdo it, I squeezed black onto my palette as well. "You're making this easy for yourself," I said, giving him a sideways glance. "You're supposed to be my Cyrano and you tell me not to speak to him."

"There's a method to my madness," he said, rummaging through a drawer filled with odds and ends."

"Yeah, it's called avoidance."

"Have a little faith."

"I need information, LeVan. I need to know if he likes me?"

LeVan pulled from the drawer a few pencils and slid them into the front pocket of his overalls, and started for the ladder. "You need to paint," he said. "Don't take this the wrong way, but I'm tired of talking about my grandson."

"Okay," I said, watching him study his mural, "instead we could talk about how you going up and down that ladder doesn't seem like a good idea."

LeVan stepped onto the ladder. "I'm a muralist, my dear. This is what I do, when I *can* do it. Just be grateful I'm not a trapeze artist."

"Very funny," I said just as he momentarily lost his balance, sending my heart into my throat. "You certainly are giving me something else to think about."

LeVan grinned. He was always grinning, especially now that we were at his studio, but this time, at the corners of his mouth, I saw Walt in his grin, and it made me melt a little. "I'll take that as a compliment," he said, then climbed higher up the ladder and got back to work.

Chapter Eighteen

Despite missing Walt, the week passed quickly at Dogwood studio. We worked from morning to night, talking or not talking, our silence as comfortable as our conversation. When we did talk, we talked about everything. My life, his life, art, politics, whatever came to mind. Now and then, LeVan would nap on the cot, his breathing peaceful and easy, until waking with a start, he'd complain about time slipping through his fingers, and return to work. That moment—LeVan summoning the strength to paint more—fascinated me, and each time I saw it, I stopped what I was doing and sketched him. Determination, excitement, and a sense of urgency—it was all there, in the glint of his eye, and the set of his jaw.

You're worse than the paparazzi, he'd say with a hint of a smile.

LeVan had been right, of course. Without outside distractions we were getting a lot done. I was working on my portrait of LeVan with Walt as a young boy, and LeVan was hard at work making progress on the three panels that comprised his mural. At first glance, the panels seemed simply to be a series of pictures about a man in a field. Whatever crop was planted has grown, and reaches the knee of the man's pleated trousers. The man isn't dressed for farming, but his tie, which has caught the wind, is loose at his neck, as if he's beginning to adapt to the environment. In the first panel, his eyes are fixed on something lying in the thick of the crop; in the second panel, he is on his knees, gazing awestruck at whatever it is he's discovered, and in the third, his head is bent, and, overcome with joy, he is weeping.

"So, you're paintings are about farming?" I asked one day, glancing up at the top of the scaffolding as he made corrections to his sketches.

LeVan turned to give me a look of consternation. "This is my swan song. Why would I paint about farming?" he spat.

"Maybe you were a farmer?" I asked, shrugging.

"I've never farmed a day in my life," he said, jutting his brush in my direction "If I had, that grandson of mine you're so fond of would most likely have some land of his own."

"If he marries Shailene, he'll have plenty of land," I said, pleasantly, like I was looking on the bright side of things.

"Don't worry about Shailene. She's a good girl."

"Said no bear, ever."

"You need to focus," he said, a hand on his hip as he assessed his work. "Now where were we? What was it we were talking about?" LeVan looked at me and scratched his head.

A cold prickle tip toed down my spine. When it came to LeVan's clear-headedness, I didn't know what to expect. Would it leave as quickly as it came, or would it fade gradually, a minor forgetfulness that would grow until, like a thick fog, it blanketed every memory? I cleared my throat. "We were talking about your mural, and what you wanted it to say."

"That's right," he said, his index finger jutting upward. "Which brings me to an important point. *There is no new thing under the sun*, Ecclesiastes 10:9. Not to sound smug, but this would be a good time for you to take notes."

I grabbed a pencil and sketchbook as relief flooded over me. LeVan was okay if he could quote scripture, at least for now. "Ready when you are," I said.

LeVan sketched as he spoke. "Now I suppose you could make a case against it, but the way I see it, it's true—there is no new thing under the sun. Everything that can be said, has been said, and so the question to ask is not just what do I want to say, but what do I want to *resay*, keeping in mind that how I go about doing so will be what makes it uniquely mine.

I looked up from my notes. "And so what is it you want to resay?"

"Well, I'd rather not say."

"Come on, LeVan," I coaxed, bringing my fist down softly to the table. "There shouldn't be any secrets between us, especially when I'm curious."

LeVan smiled. "Just give it some time. Soon enough these paintings will tell you themselves."

"Fair enough," I said, gathering my hair into a twist and sticking it through with my pencil. "But could you at least tell me *who* you're borrowing from?

"Only the greatest."

"Velasquez?"

"Greater."

"Picasso?"

"Still greater."

"Greater than Picasso? Wow, LeVan, you don't fool around."

Gripping the ladder with one hand, he tapped the side of his head. "Not with this right here held together with shoe laces."

"It's been close to a week since you've been *all here*. So far, so good," I said, and knocked on the table.

"It won't last," said LeVan.

"You don't know that," I said. "Maybe it will."

"It won't," he said, without remorse, "but today's not that day." LeVan studied his work. He swallowed hard, the scarf knotted at his neck moving with his Adam's apple. "Time to get back to work."

"One last question," I said as LeVan sketched. "Why? why did you pick what you picked to paint, whatever it happens to be."

"Because it shares the secret to a happy a life."

"The secret to a happy life," I said, looking again at LeVan's sketches. "Are you trying to kill me with curiosity?"

"Just chew on that for now, missy."

I watched LeVan step higher, his movements both confident and shaky, like a tipsy sailor climbing the mast. "If I said I was used to you going up and down that thing, I'd be lying," I said, watching him reach out with his arm to create the movement of the grass in the wind.

"Me up here? Why that's old hat. Don't give it a moment's thought. If I tumble to my death, I suppose you could take comfort knowing I died doing what I loved."

"And I suppose you could come down and not die. Maybe work on a miniature."

"A miniature! Over my dead body," he said.

"I know that's a figure of speech, but it's still totally inappropriate."

"My apologies," said LeVan.

"Just don't stay up there too long. It's about time you got some sleep."

"I'll sleep when I'm dead."

"Okay, new rule," I said, my eyes squeezed shut from a sudden burst of frustration, "no referring to death or dying or your time on this planet nearly being up, while you're up there."

"Fair enough," he said as he continued to work. "Tell you what, give me a half an hour more, and then we'll call it a night."

I briefly considered also getting back to work, when it occurred to me that it felt nice to sit, and so ignoring my paintbrushes, and my embarrassment for calling it quits before an octogenarian, I sat there watching LeVan. He was so certain about what he wanted to do, what he wanted to say, or rather, resay, with his art, and it made me wonder Why was I painting portraits? I was creating art, finding the beauty in things like a gap-tooth smile or a weathered face, which in the past, had been enough, but LeVan had me thinking. What message did I want my work to carry? People's reactions to my work had nearly always been positive, and it had humored me when they would offer an interpretation of my work, the message behind it. If that's what they thought it meant, then that's what it meant, had been my approach. But I had never stopped to ask myself, what it meant for me.

Of course, everything had already been said, wasn't that what that scripture LeVan had quoted had stated? There was no new thing under the sun? I looked at my notes. Ecclesiastes 10:9. I may not have known what I wanted to say as an artist, but I did know I wanted to mark that scripture. Leaning across the table, I grabbed my scriptures. Instead of underlining verses, I liked to sketch images in the margins to help me remember what was being said. I turned to Ecclesiastes 10:9 and was about to draw LeVan (since he was no new thing) standing under a sun, when my eye caught the verse, and my heart climbed into my throat.

Whosoever removeth stones shall be hurt therewith; and he that cleaveth wood shall be endangered thereby. I checked my notes and read it again, hoping that perhaps I'd made a mistake, but I hadn't. I had gotten it right. It was LeVan who had gotten it wrong.

Chapter Nineteen

Lana! How's it been? Any cute boys?

Just cute farmers.

That's an oxymoron. Ask me how things are going!

How are things going?

Amazing! Riley is the best!

And you picked this up over the phone?

No, he came to Tallahassee for the weekend!

Ahem . . . and where did he sleep?

Here, but I promise we didn't do anything . . .

You've known him a few weeks and you let him sleep on your couch!

We were up practically all night. I'm telling you, we click!

Ing, you need to take a deep breath and pace yourself.

You have no idea how much I've paced myself. My sorority sisters can't believe how much I've paced myself.

150

Okay, I'm just going to say it. Do not sleep with this boy!

I'm not . . .

Ing! Stick to the plan! Remember your sister, how mad she made you!

I know . . . but maybe I was being judgmental.

Ing!

Don't panic, I've stuck to the plan so far. But you need to do something about your phone. I'm tired of texting, and only when you're in town

I'll try, but I can't make any promises.

Me too.

Ing!!

Lan!!

I love you.

Love you too.

"You didn't say two words to Walt at church," whispered LeVan as we sat down for lunch in Flintlock's dining room, a dining room that though western in design, was still grand enough to satisfy the Queen of England.

My eyes darted to Walt, sitting across the enormous dining room table, and then to my lap. "Shh! Now's not the time," I whispered to LeVan, though I knew, as big as the table was no one had heard us.

Clint and Patsy Stock had, once again, invited us over for Sunday lunch, which meant, once again, I was forced to chat politely while Shailene did things like poke Walt, tease Walt, and snag the seat next to him. After a short speech from Clint, welcoming us to their "humble" home, and Patsy had offered the blessing on the food, LeVan leaned toward me again, his hand cupped to his mouth. "Why are you not talking to him?" he asked.

Because, LeVan," I whispered, "that's what I do when a guy is cute. I clam up and watch other girls date him. Now shh!"

"You can tell me the secret," whispered Kylie, leaning across LeVan to talk to me. "I promise I won't tell," she said, her voice raspy, and her little face earnest.

"There isn't a secret," I whispered.

"Of course there is," whispered LeVan, his paint-stained cuticle brushing across her golden head "And I'm sure you are an excellent secret keeper,"

"There's plenty to eat, so don't be shy," said Patsy as her guests helped themselves to the barbecue and trimmings.

"What are you three talking about?" asked Britney, making me jump in my seat.

Kylie put her finger to her lips. "We can't tell you, Mom. It's a secret."

Secrets didn't interest Britney, and she said nothing to this, but rather, turned to her aunt, and announced, "I'm desperate for a sparkling water."

Patsy pressed her napkin to her mouth. "They're in the outside fridge, I'll go get you one," she said, starting to get up, but Britney was already on her feet.

"Don't worry," she said, "I'll find it."

"Seventy percent of the human brain is water," said Clint, eyebrow tilted, addressing no one in particular.

"Be sure and make yourself at home," said Patsy, smiling brightly as she passed the buttermilk biscuits.

"That would involve me walking around in my underwear," LeVan whispered to me.

"Shh!" I warned, which made Kylie shush him as well. Embarrassment had just started to engulf me when I noticed that the sight of the three of us huddled together like a team of game show contestants was making Walt smile, and so instead of wallowing in agony, I shushed them both again, making Kylie giggle.

Patsy broke up the party by handing me the corn casserole. "So how did things go up at Dogwood this week with Bishop Hitchpost," she said, almost squeaking with delight.

"If she insists on calling me bishop, I'm going to leave," LeVan whispered, his hands cupped around his mouth.

"It's been two years since the Mayor worked at his studio," said Clint, his voice, low and serious. "Does he seem to recognize the place?"

"Although I wouldn't mind Mayor Bishop," mused LeVan, this time speaking a little louder. "That has a certain ring to it."

I kicked LeVan (softly) under the table. "It's hard to say what he thinks of his studio," I said, because it was hard to say. I had been sworn to silence.

"So wonderful, Bishop Hitchpost is back at Dogwood," she said, "although it must make it difficult for you to work, taking care of his needs," said Patsy, just as Britney sat back down, a slender bottle in her hand. Patsy hadn't meant to make Britney or Hank squirm, but taking care of LeVan seemed to be a sensitive subject for them.

"He's no trouble," I said.

"Thankfully, she has help," said Walt.

"Who's that?" I asked.

"Carl," said Walt, his tone saying, *You should know this.*

"Oh yes, Carl," I said, smiling weakly. "Silly me."

Patsy leaned forward, a look of excitement in her eyes. "I'd love to pop over and take a peek at what you're painting," said Patsy, rubbing her hands together.

"When pigs fly," whispered LeVan.

"I thought Shailene said you were a sculptor," said Britney, looking me over.

"You wanted to know what she looked like, and I said she wears black, but without skulls," said Shailene, sounding annoyed.

"She never listens, unless you're a customer, sitting in her salon chair," whispered LeVan.

I cleared my throat and elbowed LeVan. "I'm here to paint."

"Hmm," she said, cupping her hand to her chin.

"During the summer, Daddy used to sometimes pop in at Dogwood," said Patsy, passing the honey butter.

"Drove me half mad," whispered LeVan.

I turned slightly toward him, my expression saying, *Be quiet!*

"There were always visitors there when the weather was fine," said Patsy, "other artists, buyers from places like New York and San Fransisco, Bishop's friends from town, and sometimes Daddy." Patsy paused for a moment, staring at her goblet, then shook her head softly and mustered a smile. "Sometimes during a hard winter, the Hitchposts would spend a few months living with Rosemary's parents in town, and Bishop would use the back of Schumaker's Deli as his studio, its walls being tall enough to handle his work. Of course, as a little girl, I never went to Dogwood, but during the time Bishop was in town, I'd sneak behind a pickle barrel and watch him work.

"Peeking Patsy, I used to call her," whispered LeVan, just loud enough to be shushed by his great granddaughter.

"It was fascinating to watch him. One day he turned dabs of color into a sparrow so real I thought it might fly off the canvas, and all while arguing politics with my father."

I remembered what LeVan had said about Patsy's father wanting to turn Bluegill into a lake. Was this what she'd heard them arguing about? I was about to ask when Walt spoke.

"Sorry, Patsy," he said, "but you can't pop in at Dogwood. No visitors are allowed."

"No visitors? said Clint, his eyebrow tipping on end, "sounds serious."

"Not serious," I said, poking a green bean on my plate, "just trying to get a lot done."

"So, what kind of painting do you do?" asked Britney. "Do you fling paint onto a canvas? I just read about a little girl getting paid thousands for her pictures, and, honestly, they looked like splattered drop cloths. Is that the sort of art you do?" she asked.

I thought of my first picture, the one I drew of my mother on the airplane napkin, and the awes it had produced. "No," I said, "that's not the sort of art I do."

"You can say that again!" whispered LeVan.

"Thousands of dollars!" said Hank. "Kylie, do you want to paint?"

"I want to paint unicorns," she said, her voice heartbreakingly sweet.

Hank put his hand to his chest. "That's crazy, because I want to make thousands of dollars selling unicorn paintings!" he said, making his daughter giggle. "We should go into business together!"

"Daddy!" giggled Kylie.

Britney looked at her husband, then turned her attention back to me. "So what kind of art do you do?" she asked, her sudden interest surprising me.

"I gravitate toward representational art," I said. Confused, Britney tilted her head. "And by that," I continued, "I mean art that is a more faithful representation of its subject matter.

"You don't paint people with three eyes," she said, her hands pressed to the table as she clarified this.

"Not unless they have three eyes," I said.

Britney bit her lip and smiled.

"I once did a macaroni collage of General Custer," stated Clint, adding after a short pause, "at a scout jamboree."

"It would be fascinating to watch you work," sighed Patsy.

"Quit trying to weasel—" muttered LeVan.

I bumped his knee. "We really are busy," I said.

Patsy leaned forward. "*We?* And what does Bishop do while you work?" she asked, managing to sound both sweet and nosy.

"Is he painting?" asked Walt, his eyes widening ever so slightly with hope.

"What I'd pay to see Gramps at it again," said Hank, surprising me. Their selling *Wind and Willow* had made me think he wasn't interested in his grandfather's art.

I felt like a spot light—its heat and expectations for the interesting—had landed on me, and I squirmed in my chair. "Yes, he's painting," I said, making Patsy gasp. "But, he also sleeps a lot on the studio cot," I added, snuffing out the hope in Walt's eyes.

"You're up there all week alone? Well, nearly alone," Patsy said, giving LeVan a weak smile

"Yes, but I stay busy," I said.

"Could be busier if you weren't gaga for my grandson," LeVan whispered.

I pressed my lips into a thin line.

"That studio's in a plumb spot," said Clint, again not speaking to anyone in particular.

"Did you see any shooting stars?" asked Hank. "Remember, Brit, when we used to go up there and watch the shooting stars?" There was something in Hank's voice that said he missed those times, and something in the way Britney nodded while checking her phone that said she had other things to think about.

"I love shooting stars!" cried Kylie.

"More importantly, did you see any bears?" asked Shailene.

"I do not love bears," said Kylie, fear lacing her words.

A chill entered Flintlock's majestic dining room, or maybe just into my bones. Bears at Dogwood? I hadn't thought about the possibility, but there was Shailene, looking at me across that monster of a dining room table in a way that said, *You better be thinking about bears at Dogwood.*

Chapter Twenty

"Oh please," said Walt, stabbing his baked potato with his fork. "There aren't any bears at Dogwood."

Shailene shoved his arm. "How would you know? You never hunt! Every time I invite you, you say you're busy."

A wispy butterfly of happiness, flitted through me as I thought of Walt turning down an invitation from Shailene, but then I remembered what we were talking about—bears at Dogwood studio, and that butterfly fluttered away.

"I'm too busy to hunt," muttered Walt.

"Jell-O?" asked Patsy, her smile growing stiff.

"And too busy to pay attention to the feeding patterns up the canyon."

Walt rolled his eyes. "Feeding patterns," he said. "I spent every summer during my childhood roaming around that canyon and never saw anything more threatening than a family of quail."

Shailene pointed the tip of her fork at Walt as she swallowed. "Consider yourself lucky," she said, her tone deadly serious.

Walt waved this away.

Shailene tore open a biscuit. "The snow caps have shifted the mating and feeding patterns," said Shailene.

"Snow caps. You've personally measured the snow caps?" he challenged.

"I certainly hope not," said Patsy, looking startled.

"I do not love bears," said Kylie, her voice soft.

"I've always wanted my portrait done," mused Britney.

Shailene poked Walt, in frustration, not flirtation. "They're measured by satellites, you idiot," she said. Walt shrugged dismissively. "And it's not just the snow caps, hunters are setting traps—"

"No one is setting traps near Dogwood," said Walt.

There was no denying I had a major crush on the guy. There was also no denying his know-it-all tone was beginning to bother me.

"How can you be so sure?" I asked.

"Traps or not, Dogwood's six acres is now in the heart of bear country," said Shailene.

"A plum spot for a hunting lodge," said Clint.

"Amen to that," said Hank.

LeVan grumbled. Shailene looked at me, her expression all business. "Do you know what to do if you encounter a bear?"

"Shailene, come on," Walt said, his tone asking her to drop it.

"What do you mean, come on?" she said, her voice rising with irritation.

"You're trying to scare Lana," he said.

"She's not the only one you're scaring," said Hank, motioning to Kylie who was sucking her lower lip.

"Living here, in my opinion, you're never too young to learn about bears."

"You're blowing this way out of proportion," said Walt, as Kylie sniffed and Patsy passed the buttered peas.

"This coming from a river guide," said Shailene.

"I'm a farmer," said Walt, resolutely.

"Well, you moonlight as a river guide and you know that nine times out of ten nothing out of the ordinary happens going down the river—the rafts don't flip, no one falls out, but we still have to go through the safety drill. Whether you like it or not Dogwood is smack in the middle of bear country." Shailene looked at me. "Where are you from?"

I gulped. "Florida."

"And this girl from Florida, not to mention your niece, should know what to do when face to face with a bear."

Walt opened his mouth to protest, but I spoke first. "So what do I need to know?"

"If it is smaller than you, which would be a black bear, stand tall, punch it in the muzzle if you have to, but scare it away if you can. If it's bigger than you, which would be a grizzly, freeze, and pray he can't smell peanut butter on your breath."

My mouth went dry. "So maybe buy chewing gum?"

Shailene shrugged. "Wouldn't be a bad idea."

Walt rolled his eyes.

Shailene speared a potato wedge and pointed it at me. "And never leave any garbage out."

"Okay," I said, my voice almost as raspy as Kylie's.

"EVER."

"Got it," I croaked.

As Shailene and Walt continued to bicker about bears at Dogwood, LeVan leaned close to me, and whispered, "These two will never back down. Announce that you're going up Novia Spring to paint."

"Why?"

"Just say it."

"I don't even know where Novia Spring is!"

"Am I your Cyrano or not?" he exclaimed.

I bit my lip. "You got the scripture wrong, the one you quoted from Ecclesiastes. It's not chapter ten verse nine."

"What does that have to do with anything?"

"I don't know if I can trust what you tell me."

LeVan gave a nod. "Looks like you're in a pickle," he said.

"Shh," said Kylie, her finger pressed to her lips.

For a moment, we were silent, picking at our food and listening to Walt and Shailene have at it. Then LeVan leaned toward me. "But the scripture was in Ecclesiastes?"

"Yes," I whispered.

"Well, I was in the ball park. I think I should get credit for that," he said. I sighed, not knowing what to do. "I realize it's a leap of faith," he continued. "But trust me. Announce you're going to Novia Spring. At the very least it will get those two to quit arguing. Poor Patsy is covering her eyes."

I closed my eyes as if summoning the courage to jump from the high dive. And then I went for it. "Did I mention I'm going to Novia Spring?" I blurted, louder than necessary.

Walt stopped arguing with Shailene and looked at me. "Why are you going there?" he asked.

LeVan rolled his wrist, his subtle way of saying, *Keep talking.* "To paint," I said.

"That's why you're at the studio—to paint," he said.

"You just said you paint portraits," said Britney.

"That's true, but sometimes it's nice to switch things up," I said.

"I don't know what you're worried about," said Shailene, lifting her glass, "the worst she'll encounter there is a squirrel."

"So Gramps is going with you?" Walt stated more than asked.

"Yes," I said.

"No," whispered LeVan. "I've work to do."

"I mean, no," I said, my face hot with embarrassment, "but I'm going Tuesday."

"Wednesday," whispered LeVan.

"Or rather, Wednesday. Yes, that's it," I said, "Wednesday. Definitely Wednesday. Don't know why I said Tuesday," and then stuffed half a roll in my mouth to keep from saying more.

Britney tried to spear an elusive cherry tomato in her salad. "I'm busy all day at the salon," she said, stabbing again and again at the little red orb. "Gramps can't stay with me."

Hank kept his eyes on the napkin he was twisting, which, I guess, was his way of saying, *He can't stay with me, either.*

"Not a problem," said Walt. "Gramps will stay at the studio with Carl."

"Carl?" I cleared my throat. "Who's Carl?"

"The healthcare worker provided by the Wilmington Trust," said Shailene, her eyebrow arched. Why can't you remember him?"

I bumped my head with the palm of my hand. "Oh yes, Carl," I said, my voice trailing off as panic began to overtake me.

"Good, then I'll plan on taking you," said Walt.

Shailene threw her hands in the air. "Take her to Novia Spring! That's like her needing an escort to Faye's Luncheonette."

"I'm sure I'll be fine," I said, because something told me (more precisely, LeVan's elbow digging into mine) that Walt would insist on coming. And he did.

"I'm taking you, and that's all there is to it," he said.

I shrugged. "Suit yourself."

Shailene glared at Walt. "We've got two busloads coming in the morning to float the river," she said. "We're going to need you."

"The other guys can cover it."

"We don't want to be shorthanded," said Clint, this time his serious tone sounding appropriate.

"The customer is always right," said Patsy softly.

"Mom," said, Shailene, her fingers pressed to her temples as if trying to hold off a headache, "that doesn't have anything to do with it. Mountain man Walt here thinks Dogwood is safe and Novia Spring isn't, which is absurd."

"I'm entitled to my opinions," said Walt.

"Well, you're a dunderhead," she said, and for some reason I liked her a little more for it.

We stayed at Flintlock until early evening, Britney scrolling through her phone, LeVan wandering off to stare at his paintings and the rest of us playing Monopoly. Shailene was back to shoving Walt, and, by the end of the game, everyone was shamelessly cheating to increase Kylie's odds of winning.

The game made me forget my nervousness around Walt, making it easier for me to talk to him, even if all I was mostly saying was something like, go to jail. When it was finally time to head back to Dogwood, Walt followed us out, his hand hovering below his grandfather's elbow.

"Wednesday, I'll have to check the fields in the morning, so what if I came by to get you around noon?"

"That will work," I said, trying to sound casual.

With Walt's help, LeVan climbed into the truck. "So," said Walt, once LeVan was buckled in, "are you doing okay?" he asked.

I rocked on my heels. "Yes," I said, "and what about you?"

"Fine, I guess, but it's too quiet at the house," he said, staring down and kicking the stone path, before turning his gaze toward me. "Look," he said, his voice, softer, "about the other day . . ." but before he could say more, Shailene shouted my name, allowing my hammering heart to take five.

"Lana!" she said, running toward me.

"I'll see you Wednesday," he said.

"See you then," I said, and he headed further down the stone path to where Ruth was parked.

I watched Shailene race toward me, her raven hair flying about, framed by a purple twilight sky. It was a beautiful sight, the kind I loved to paint, and so, it didn't matter whether I liked her or not, my finger itched to sketch her.

"Hey," she said, slightly winded, "I have something for you," and she handed me a canister.

"You're giving me hair spray?" I asked.

"Bear mace."

"That makes a little more sense," I said, sheepishly.

"Have you ever used it?" she asked, her blue eyes narrowing.

"No," I said.

"It works, but only for six seconds."

"Six seconds?"

"That's all you got. So don't spray too soon, and don't spray too late."

"Okay," I said, my heart climbing into my throat. "And thanks."

She tapped the can of bear mace in my hand. "You're welcome. Keep it with you at all times. Get a holster. They sell them online."

"Okay," I said.

Shailene started to leave, then stopped. "Don't forget the holster," she said.

"I won't," I said with images of wild west shoot-outs moving across my mind.

Shailene gave me a long look, then headed up the path to Flintlock. My hands trembled, making the little metal ball in the can roll across the bottom. Bears scared me, but then another thought occurred to me—maybe Walt was right. Maybe there were no bears up at Dogwood and she just wanted me to look ridiculous with bear mace continually holstered at my hip. I could see her smile, hear her shared giggles with Britney, and suddenly I felt silly.

"What was that about?" Asked LeVan as I climbed into the truck.

I tossed the canister into the back. "Nothing," I said as I started the truck, "Right now, we've got more important things to think about, like getting in touch with a guy named Carl." Then, putting the truck in drive, we drove down the stone path and back up the winding canyon road to Seventy-Two Dogwood Lane.

Chapter
Twenty-One

Hello Our Darling Girl!

Just wanted to send you this care package to let you know that Daddy and I are thinking of you. Hope you're having a magnificent time. Let me know if you need me to knit anything!

Love and kisses and more kisses!

Mom and Dad.

"You want me to do what?" asked Carl when he arrived at Dogwood on Wednesday, just before noon, looking far less menacing than he had the other day. Yes, he was still pierced and inked, but there was a kindness in his eyes that I hadn't noticed, a kindness that made me feel that though what I was proposing was crazy, it wasn't dangerous.

"I know this is an unusual request, but, like I said, I need you to stay here with Mr. Hitchpost until I get back."

"Just call me LeVan," said LeVan, shaking Carl's hand.

Carl looked at me and scratched the back of his head. "So you don't want me to drive?" he asked.

"Actually, a drive up the canyon would be nice when I need a break," suggested LeVan.

"No!" I said, my fingers flared. "You two stay here until I get back." I pointed at the three panels attached to the wall. "You've got a lot of work left to do."

Carl let out a long whistle. "Yowza, even unfinished, it's stunning."

"Well, I don't know about that, but I'm on the right path at any rate," said LeVan, clearly pleased with this compliment.

Carl patted his chest. "As it turns out, I'm a bit of an art enthusiast. I delivered mail for twenty-five years in West Harlem. Rent is cheap there, so my route was filled with artists. I liked it. The artists gave the neighborhood vibrancy. That's something I miss about New York, not the traffic, or the garbage."

"I loved New York while I was there," said LeVan. "I lived in a tiny Soho studio. Used to share my brown bag lunch with Jackson Smith when we were both working in Queens. He was forgetful of food, so I'd pack extra."

"You shared your lunch with Smith!" cried Carl, eyes wide with amazement.

"What can I say, he liked salami," said LeVan with a shrug.

I looked at my watch and felt my heart race. Walt would be here any minute. "So, Carl, you're okay staying here?"

"Of course I'm okay. It's like spending time with a living, breathing museum." Carl turned to LeVan. "Who else did you spend time with?"

"The list is long."

"Which is great, you two can discuss all of that while I'm gone," I said.

"Not that I have anything else going on today, but for curiosity's sake, how long do you think that will be?" asked Carl.

"Two hours," I said, though I knew, once you factored in how long it took to drive to Novia Spring, that wouldn't give me any time to work. But that was okay. I shouldn't have been leaving LeVan in the first place.

"You should plan on four," said LeVan

Carl pulled out his phone. "Okay, so if we go with my usual rate that's going to be . . . 672. 25." I gulped. "No, I'm sorry, 672.35. My screen's a little smudgy." Carl paused, just long enough for panic to sprint through me, and then he said. "I'm joking! Look, I'm new here, and looking to make friends. The way I see it, you're giving me an opportunity, so reimburse me for gas, and we'll call it square."

I breathed a sigh of relief. "That sounds perfect. I made a list of some things you should know," I said, and handed him a paper, covered, front to back, with my writing.

"Step-by-step instructions for the Heimlich maneuver?" said Carl, reading number four on list.

"I wanted to be thorough," I said.

Carl placed the paper on the long table, putting an empty jar on one of its corners, as if to prevent it from walking off. "I'll read through this, follow it step by step, I promise. I'm in no rush. I'm retired. Delivered mail for twenty-five years in West Harlem, but I already told you that."

"I don't mind hearing things twice," said LeVan. "I have Alzheimer's."

"Alzheimer's?" asked Carl.

"Just not right now. I'm experiencing a bit of a break."

"This a lot to take in," said Carl, pulling out a chair and sitting down.

"It is a lot, and, I'm sure, completely unheard of, at least to the level I'm experiencing. If others knew, my doctors and my family would want to run tests, have me fill out paperwork, and be a guest on a morning news show, perhaps. But there's one thing I know, one thing I sense, and it's that I don't have time for that. The sand is slipping through the hourglass, and so while I can, while I am *me*, I want to work in my studio."

"Incredible," said Carl, running a hand over his bald head.

"Even more incredible," said LeVan, "is that you being here is allowing this young lady here to go on a date."

"Whoa, whoa, whoa. It's not a date," I said.

"Is it just the two of you?" asked LeVan.

"Well, yes," I admitted.

"Then it's a date," said LeVan.

"If there's one thing I love, it's love. You should see my Netflix line up," Carl said.

"We are not in love," I said.

"It's in the beginning stages, to be sure; it's a possibility," said LeVan to Carl, "and, what's more, she's never been kissed."

"You're going to make me cry. Stop it," said Carl, waving his hands.

"Both of you stop it," I said.

"So, really, we should be having *the* talk," said Carl.

"Not what I ever expected to hear from an Uber driver," I said, dryly. "Thank you, but, no, we do not need to be having *the* talk."

"Then let me offer you some friendly advice," said Carl, leaning back in his chair and crossing his legs.

"What kind of advice?"

"Kissing advice," said Carl.

"I think I'm going to be sick," I said, clutching my stomach, which both LeVan and Carl ignored.

"When kissing," explained Carl, "what you're looking for is cushion, just enough pucker so that his lips land on yours like a soft pillow." Carl rolled his wrists. "Let me see you pucker."

Hesitantly, I obliged.

"That's too much. More like this," he said, and demonstrated what he considered puckering perfection. "And what do you think, LeVan, eyes open or not?"

"We close our eyes when things are too wonderful," said LeVan.

"That's nice," I said, my heart melting a little.

"Or too terrible," he added.

The melting stopped. "And that's not nice," I said.

"So I hope you close your eyes, and that the reason is happiness."

"Fair enough," I said.

Outside, a horn honked.

I grabbed my supplies. "That's him," I said, my breath catching.

"He's not coming in to get you?" asked Carl, his voice rising with irritation.

"He can't," I said, pointing at the three panels. "No visitors are allowed in the studio."

Carl nodded. "That's right, that's right. Well, you go and have a good time. Don't worry about us."

"Not possible," I said as I walked to the door.

"And one last thing," said LeVan.

"Have fun?" I asked.

"Lay your cards on the table."

"Excuse me?"

"Don't waste time," said LeVan. "Tell him how you really feel. Be up front.

He's guarded, you're guarded. It's the only way to break down those walls."

I shook my head. "LeVan, I can't."

"Then bat your eyes a little," suggested Carl.

The horn honked again.

"And while you're batting your eyes," said LeVan, "think of Shailene all snuggled up with the man you love."

"Quit saying love," I said. "I *like* your grandson."

"Does your heart race when you're near him?" asked LeVan.

"Yes," I said timidly.

"And do you fall asleep thinking about him?"

"Yes," I croaked.

Carl opened his mouth, then slowly said, "That sounds like, pardon the expression, *love.*"

"Be honest," said LeVan.

"LeVan, come on!" I said.

"I'm your Cyrano!"

"I'm starting to hate it when you say that," I muttered. "It makes you sound like a know-it-all."

"And when it comes to Walt, I am. I knew if you announced that you were going to Novia Spring, he would come with you."

"How?"

"Because it's his favorite place, and has been since he was a little boy."

"You took a shot in the dark," I said, refusing to accept LeVan's window into his grandson's soul. He wanted me to be honest? What kind of crazy advice was that?

"A chance to take the girl he's falling for to the place he loves? Of course he'd insist on coming with you." I steeled myself against the temptation to smile. "Now go," said LeVan, "enjoy your day."

"And Lana," said LeVan as I swung the door upward. "Blessed are the up front, for they shall kiss my grandson."

I rolled my eyes at this. "How do I look?" I asked.

"Honestly," said Carl, "like you're in an orchestra. Why so much black?"

"AAAHHHH!" I cried, shouting in frustration from the bottom of my lungs, sending a white-hot heat coursing through me. Then I smiled (stiffly) at Carl and LeVan whose eyes were wide with surprise, rolled the door shut, took a deep breath, and walked down the gravel path toward Walt.

Chapter Twenty-Two

"Is everything okay?" asked Walt, looking more handsome than ever in a plaid button down and Levi's as he helped me put my supplies in his truck. He had driven up the canyon in Ruth, but apparently didn't want to risk taking her to Novia Spring.

I smiled brightly. "Everything is fine," I said as the LeVan that resided in my head shook his finger and said, *Be honest!*

Walt opened the passenger door. "Really," said Walt, one eyebrow raised, "because I just heard you shouting." I cleared my throat. "I had to," I said, as I climbed in the truck.

"Why?" asked Walt, leaning into the truck to see me, his arm pressing against the top of the doorframe.

It was time to lie, and lie big. "I have asthma. Shouting . . . clears my lungs," I said, causing the in-my-head LeVan to throw his hands in the air and walk away.

"Well," said Walt, "it sounded like you'd just won the lottery."

"Oh," I said perkily.

He held up a hand. "While simultaneously chopping off a finger."

"Wow," I said, no longer perky, "that's a very precise description."

Walt straightened up. "Just being honest," he said, and shut my door, but not before raising his eyebrow and smiling.

I slumped in my seat, convinced that, like the slightly bug-speckled windshield before us, Walt could see through my lies—that not only did I not have asthma, I had hired an Uber driver to take care of his grandfather, and that, at the moment, his grandfather was clear-minded, painting beautifully, and making unreasonable demands. Guilt, though it had never before had such an effect on me, made me start to hiccup.

Walt slid behind the wheel and started his truck. "So, did you sleep all right?" he asked, looking in the rear view mirror as he backed his truck out of the driveway.

"Like [hiccup] a log," I said, covering my mouth a little too late. Truth be told, I hadn't slept well the night before, or the night before that. Since arriving at Dogwood, LeVan had insisted, though the house had two bedrooms, on sleeping in the studio so that he could wake whenever he had the strength and continue working. It didn't seem to me that this arrangement helped him work faster. If anything, it assured him taking a long mid-morning nap, but he insisted on working this way, and though I didn't feel the same sense of urgency, I knew if he was up I needed to be as well, and so I kept the same schedule, working at odd hours through the night.

When LeVan did sleep, it was on the cot. I had insisted on this much. He had tried to get me to take the cot, but I was unwavering on this point. He would sleep on the cot, and I would sleep on a thin mattress dragged over to the studio from the house, and the pillows that I, despite his complaints, surrounded his scaffolding with while he worked. He could grumble all he wanted, but as soon as he ascended the ladder, I put them in place, ready to soften a fall, if ever one happened.

Walt turned his truck onto Dogwood Lane. Heading down to the fork in the road, he veered right, the same way when I had gone the night I'd ended up hopelessly lost. Walt had been the one to find me. I thought of him that night, so tall and strong, his eyes wild with a mixture of fury and worry. I had felt emotion then like never before—an instant connection to someone I'd just met, someone, who though towered over me, I wasn't afraid to stand up to in an argument. We had met here, on this tucked-away country road, and though I still stopped short of admitting I loved Walt, this place was special to me.

My hiccupping, as we winded down to the valley floor, grew only more frequent and forceful, each one jarring my body like a punch from inside, but I was optimistic that the bumpiness of the road was masking these outbursts.

"We could have taken the interstate to Novia, but I like the back roads," he said.

"It's [hiccup] lovely," I said as it occurred to me that this was the first honest thing I'd said so far. And it was lovely. The jagged mountains were so awash in a green that in splotches turned neon, making the cliffs pulse with color. The valley floor was dotted with wild flowers of every color, the reds and pinks appearing to compete for who could be the most brilliant, while the pale yellow and purple blooms clung to the roadside as if wanting to steer clear of their sassier siblings. And the mountaintops and the clouds above them were both so intensely white it seemed that some clouds were resting on the peaks, taking a breather from the hard work of scudding by.

I reached for my sketchbook and pencil pouch, then remembering they were in the back of the truck along with the rest of the supplies, moved my finger across my palm, forgetting as I did, my hiccuping or Walt sitting one seat over from me.

"So, I assume you brought your swimsuit," said Walt, pulling my focus away from the stream that like a silky ribbon fallen from a little girl's hair, curved and snaked along the valley floor.

"Swimsuit?" [hiccup] I asked. "Was I supposed to bring one?" [hiccup] Walt shrugged and rested one hand on the top of the steering wheel. "Doesn't matter. You don't need one."

My finger stopped its movements against my palm. "Then [hiccup] why'd you ask?"

"Well, you can always count on finding people at the first spring. It's pretty popular."

Walt took a corner faster than I was expecting and I let out a hiccuppy shriek. "Okay," I said.

"But farther down is another spring. It's a secret. No one will be there, so if you want to swim, I promise I won't look."

"You can look all you want!"

"So you're a hippy chick."

"What I mean is I am not going swimming! And to be honest, it's weird that you suggested it."

"That may be, but—"

"But what?" I snapped,

"You're not hiccupping anymore."

Embarrassment singed my ears, but I was unable to keep from smiling, not with Walt's chuckling making his shoulders shake. I thought about nudging him, but instead I folded my arms, trying to look grave. "Very funny," I said.

Walt rested his arm on the edge of the bench seat, his fingers almost brushing my neck. "Sorry," he said, flashing me an enormous and unrepentant grin, "but you can't argue with success."

"I suppose not," I said, his hand, so close, turning me to melted wax, soft and pliable, making me want to lean back, relax, and allow his palm to cup the nape of my neck. Ingrid would have done it . . . in grade school, but that wasn't me. I was careful about such things. Okay, too careful, some might even say emotionally frozen, but despite that, I liked me, I liked Walt, and I liked his hand so close. So I stayed there, stock still, cherishing that closeness, the sun warm against my cheek, and the sweet smell of pine, as the road turned up a hillside, and climbed into another valley.

Close to an hour later, a wooden sign, constructed by Boy Scout Troop 797, welcomed us to Novia Spring, and indicated that parking could be found to the right. The clouds, which had been garishly white, now looked tinged here and there with ashen gray. Still, the sun shone brightly, the breeze was soft, and in every way it seemed the perfect day for an outing.

"This is one of my favorite places," said Walt, putting the truck in park.

"I know," I said, too busy taking in the beauty around me to carefully consider my words.

"How?" he asked. It was a simple question, but uttered with hope—hope that I was obliged to quash.

"Um, just watching you, uh, your facial cues, like your forehead. Your forehead is practically screaming, *This is one of my favorite places!*"

"You can tell that by looking at my forehead?" he asked, his tone playful.

I leaned back, feeling relief soften my shoulders. "Yep."

Walt pulled the truck into a shady spot. "You've got incredible powers of perception," he said.

I shrugged. "I'm an artist. It's part of the job."

"So what does my elbow tell you?" he asked putting the truck into park and killing the engine.

"That you were late filing your taxes."

Laughing, Walt walked around to open my door. "I apologize for my forehead making such a racket back there," he said as a breeze sent a whiff of musky aftershave toward me, making me feel a rush of absurd happiness.

I looked into his brown eyes as I stood up, noticing that in them were flecks of gold. Walt had a lot of good qualities, and among them, it must be said, was that he was a hottie. "Yes, your forehead was making quite an uproar," I said, my voice softer than usual.

A strand of my hair caught the breeze, wandering in front of my eyes. Walt hooked it with his finger and tucked it behind my ear. "I'll try to control myself," he said, his voice also softer than usual.

Walls can be impenetrable things. Certainly, the one that fortressed my heart seemed so. I didn't want to be distant, always keeping people at arm's length, but a breakthrough was easier said than done. Still, watching Walt pulling our gear out of the truck as shafts of light sliced through the gathering clouds, my heart felt light—warm and light.

We hiked past an egg-shaped indigo spring ringed with soft grass and a few large, smooth stones the perfect size for lounging on after a swim. "That's the tourist trap part of Novia," said Walt, gesturing toward the handful of bathers, mostly young mothers with small children, lolling in or near the water. "It's not crowded now, but it will be on the weekend, unless the owners decide to close it. Novia's on private property."

The climb beyond Novia was long, but not arduous (especially since Walt was carrying everything). The trail meandered on and on, and just when it appeared like it might zigzag forever, Walt, first looking to see if anyone was watching, chucked his backpack over a boulder the size of a Volkswagen bus that was sandwiched between two canyon walls. Then, with my backpack strapped to his back, he climbed to the top and disappeared behind it. "Do you need help?" he asked, hoisting himself high enough to look at me.

I wedged my tennis shoe into a chink in the boulder and reached up, trying to find a place to grip the cool, immovable stone. "I think I got it," I said, before losing my grip and slipping down. "Or maybe not." By the time I looked up, Walt was on top of the boulder. "How did you do that?"

"Do what?"

"Climb up there so fast," I said, dusting off my black t-shirt. "It's like you're part mountain goat."

"Dunno," he said with a shrug. "Seems like I've always been able to. How do you draw like you do?" he asked, extending to me his arm.

I grabbed Walt's hand, and he moved our grip to the wrist. "Pictures of angry guys are easy," I said, thinking he was referring to the picture of him I sketched my first night in Bluegill. Walt shook his head.

"I'm not talking about that," he said, pulling me to the top of the boulder. "I looked you up online," he said, his face reddening either from lifting me or embarrassment. "How do you do it?"

I sat down on the boulder, Walt still gripping me, as if I were a balloon that might fly away. "Dunno," I said as my heart hurled itself repeatedly into my ribs, "seems like I've always been able to." And for a perfect moment we sat there, the well-worn path to one side, and a less traveled path to the other, the two of us close enough to kiss . . . until I looked away. Why did I look away? Simply because I always did. I was the artful dodger, looking away when a guy wanted to kiss me. And, in the past, that was okay, but this was different. I wanted Walt to kiss me! I began to worry. Would he think I didn't like him? The sun slipped behind a cloud, darkening the sky as if to match my mood, until, that is, I looked at Walt and saw his smile.

Walt nudged me with his shoulder. "Are you ready?" he asked, and pointed at the ground below, which seemed farther away now, as if the boulder, like Jack's beanstalk, was climbing heavenward.

"Maybe we should just stay up here," I said. "I could sketch and, you could, what were you going to do?

"Fish."

"Well, you could try," I said, smiling weakly.

Walt nudged me again. "Come on, Lana," he said, channeling his inner mountain goat and scrambling down the boulder's face, "quit stalling. It's time you made your move."

"You're right," I said, then muttered under my breath, "You don't know how right." Turning onto my stomach, I splayed my legs in search of a toe hold. "There doesn't seem to be a ladylike way to do this," I said.

"That's okay," said Walt, standing below me, his hands above his head, "you're an artist, not a lady."

"Hey!" I said as I tried to find a place for my hand to grip.

"What I mean is you are no corset-wearing, parasol-toting girly girl who can't climb down a rock," said Walt. "You are strong—" Walt had to cut his pep talk short to catch corset-free, strong me as I lost my grip and fell backward. Falling is one of those fast/slow events in life—fast enough to take you by surprise, and slow enough for thoughts to race through your mind, thoughts like, *This is embarrassing. You're going to get a concussion. No girl ever looked cute getting a concussion. You should have kissed him on the boulder!*

"Heads up," said Walt as I fell into his arms and he let out a tremendous groan.

"Are you okay?" I asked, jumping out of his arms. As girls go, I was petite. Still, catching even a petite girl couldn't have been easy on the back.

Walt bent over, resting his hands on his knees and catching his breath. Still hunched over, he held up a finger as if about to say something, then put his hand back on his knee, took a few gasping breaths, and keeled over.

"Walt! I'm so sorry!" I cried, kneeling beside him, brainstorming ways to save his life, until I noticed he was shaking, not from a seizure, but from laughter. I stood up. "You are the worst," I said, trying and failing to sound mad. "I thought I'd killed you."

Walt sprung to his feet, a wicked smile playing on his lips. "You almost did. I swear I saw a long tunnel and a light."

"Very funny."

"Come on," he said, putting on our gear, "there's something I want to show you."

"If it involves anymore obstacles like that one, I'm out," I said.

"No more obstacles, I promise," he said.

We walked down a lightly worn path through a dense patch of woodland into a clearing where an elm tree stood, providing plenty of shade by the bank of a meandering stream. "Welcome to Pirate's Cove," said Walt.

"Pirates Cove?"

"That's what I named it when Gramps showed it to me as a kid."

I looked around, soaking in the beauty before me. "It fits," I said, "even if we're nowhere near a coastline."

Walt spread out a blanket for me beneath the tree, pulled his telescopic fishing rod from his backpack, and walked further down the stream to fish. Leaning against the elm's trunk, pencil and sketchbook in hand, and Walt Hitchpost fishing close by, I sighed with happiness. This was a perfect moment, a truth made all the sweeter because of the many imperfect moments I had known.

I thought of me as a little girl, cold and unloved in Siberia, and it seemed impossible *that* me and *this* me were the same person. I had seen beauty then, uncovered it in unexpected places. Finding it had lifted my heart, and Lois Huish finding me had saved it. Art, family, and friends had all helped to heal me. Without them, where would I be? Probably not Novia Spring with Walt Hitchpost. And I was glad to be at this place with Walt, so glad. My heart burned with a happiness that seemed to me both irrational and wonderful, and I wanted to stay there forever, sketching while Walt fished nearby. But mostly, I thought as I covered my mouth and yawned, I wanted to sleep.

Chapter
Twenty-Three

"Hey," said Walt, shaking me gently, but also with a sense of urgency. "I've been watching the sky, and I think we should go," he said.

I rubbed my eyes and looked into a sky still bright with sunshine. "Is something wrong?"

In the distance, thunder rumbled. "Dark clouds have been gathering by Whitney Peak." said Walt, pulling me to my feet and stuffing the blanket and my sketchbook into his bag, "It feels like we need to get to higher ground."

"Higher ground?" I asked as, taking me by the hand, he hurried me along the trail we'd walked, casting a wary eye every few seconds behind us. "What's going on?"

"Sweetheart," he said, like he'd done it a thousand times before. "I don't want to startle you, but I need you to run. Can you do that?"

I nodded as a loud crack and then another filled the air. Not the crack of lightning, but the distinct sound of large branches tearing from their trunk.

We took off. "As fast as you can," said Walt.

I flew down the soft dirt trail, running faster than I had since high school. My lungs burned, my heart pounded, spots blurred my vision, and still I ran, harder and harder as another

crack and another sounded behind us. My legs felt like noo-
dles, but I sprinted faster still, giving my all as Walt, running
beside me, encouraged and calmed me. There was no room for
any other thought except running, and yet still one niggled its
way in—I was slowing Walt down.

"Walt, go ahead!"

"Just keep running!" he said as the cracking sound drew
near and a rush of thick, brown water sped past us, quickly
climbing to our ankles.

"Walt!" I screamed.

"Don't look back! Just keep going! Almost there!"

The water, a nasty stew of mud and debris, slowed my pace.
I tried to go fast, tried to dig deep like Walt was asking, but my
legs wouldn't obey. I was moving, just not fast enough. Fear
can have a way of paralyzing you, or at the very least dulling
your senses, and so I'm not really sure when the mud sucked off
my shoes, or the water, rushing faster, climbed to my knees. My
recollection of Walt dropping our backpacks and picking me
up is hazy at best. I remember climbing when he asked me to
climb, grabbing branches and rocks that he pointed out for me
to grab, but that memory is blurry. Not until we were, at last,
huddled together on a ledge near the Volkswagen bus boulder
did life, once again, sharpen into focus: water was crashing
violently beneath us, it was beginning to rain, the ledge was
barely big enough for the two of us, and yet with Walt sitting
beside me, I felt safe.

Leaning back and catching his breath, Walt laced his fingers through mine, too softly for it to just be a preemptive to
keep me from falling. "How are you doing?" he asked.

"Good," I said, aware that having passed through something terrifying, I was now experiencing an almost luxurious
calm, a calm that worked on stubborn Siberian ice like gusts
from an Arabian desert. Holding Walt's hand, I watched the
lightning crack, and felt the rain on my face.

"Sorry about your stuff," he said.

"You lost your stuff too," I said as he caressed the top of my hand with his thumb. "We're down to just us."

"And my keys," said Walt, touching my cheek. "They're in my pocket."

"I don't have a pocket," I said, not because I wanted to talk about pockets I was just hit with a sudden surge of nervousness; Walt was leaning in.

"Ya khochu potselovat' Tebya," *I want to kiss you,* he said, running his hand softly across my hair

Hearing this, my heart burned with inexpressible joy . . . and nervousness, and so though I had just heard exactly what I wanted to hear, I covered my mouth.

Walt laughed. "Long shot, here, but I'm going to guess that you're not wanting a kiss right now." Walt looked up at the rain, then down at the raging water. "And I see your point."

"That's not it," I said with my mouth covered.

"Lana," said Walt, "I won't steal a kiss. You don't have to do that."

Cautiously, I let my hand drop. "Walt, I want to kiss you. It's just that—"

"Lana, I get it," he said, speaking in the sweetest of tones. "We're here," He gestured around just as a bolt of lightning momentarily turned the sky from dark to light. "And I probably need a breath mint."

"It's not that," I said, turning to look at him. "It's just that . . . I have—"

"Chapped lips?"

"No."

"A cold sore?"

"No."

"Two cold sores?"

"Walt, be serious!" Walt tilted one eyebrow a-la-Clint. "This is a serious subject." He somehow tilted it further, making me laugh. "You don't understand! This is easy for you, all considered. The way girls fall for you."

"Are you calling me a player?" He asked, pretending to be offended.

"You know how to ask for a kiss in Russian! It's not a phrase most missionaries learn. Just sayin'."

"I never said that on my mission!" he cried. "I mean, had the Russian girls in Philly been cute, that would have been another thing."

I giggled, though below us roared a situation that was no laughing matter. We had made a narrow escape, cheated death, even, and we should have been soberly obsessing over how things might have turned out. But instead, Walt was making the moves on me. Thinking of this, I giggled some more, and then whether from exhaustion or familiarity, I put my head on Walt's shoulder and watched the rain fade to a misty sprinkle.

"Sunday," he said as the rushing water snapped another tree in two.

"Sunday what?" I asked, turning to look at him.

"That's when I learned how to say that line in Russian. As soon as I knew we were coming here," he said, his sandy hair clinging to his face.

"Walt Hitchpost," I said, as he smoothed his hair out of his eyes, "we are experiencing a natural disaster of the first order and you want to kiss me."

"That's exactly right."

I bit my lip and heard LeVan whispering to me, *Tell him the truth—your truth.*

"Walt," I started, sounding serious.

"Lana," he said, sounding serious *and* silly, making it hard for me to not laugh.

"I have something to tell you."

"Then say it," he said, touching my cheek.

I exhaled sharply. "It's so hard . . . I've put this off for so long, and built it up in my head, and then there's Ingrid, making me feel like it's going to be some spectacular event."

"Spectacular event?" he asked, clearly not following what I

was trying to say, which was understandable, a helicopter was approaching. "I think that's for us!" he cried, pointing up.

"I want to kiss you!" I shouted, sitting up straight and looking at him. "But I'm freaking out!"

"Why are you freaking out?" He shouted over the helicopter's whirring.

The rain fell harder. "I'm good at observing life, but terrified of living it!!" I shouted, my hair flying about in the Helicopter's windstorm. "It involves questions like, How do you feel about me? Will you want to kiss me again?"

"Crazy for you, and yes!" cried Walt, raising his thumb and index finger while counting off his answers to my questions.

"WALT!" I cried, trying to be heard as the helicopter lowered. "I HAVE NEVER KISSED A BOY BEFORE!"

Walt waved to the guy in the helicopter's open door. "THAT'S OKAY," shouted Walt close to my ear, "NEITHER HAVE I!"

"WALT!" I cried, my eyes imploring him to take this seriously.

"LANA, WHY WOULD I WANT OTHER GUYS TO HAVE KISSED YOU?" He asked, looking me in the eye despite the wind and the noise.

"BECAUSE IT'S THE NORM, WALT! YOU HAVE KISSED OTHER GIRLS!" Walt didn't deny this.

The roar of the helicopter was almost deafening; Walt spoke directly in my ear. "YOU'RE OVERTHINKING THIS, SORT OF LIKE TEN-YEAR-OLD- ME ON THE PITCHER'S MOUND."

"WHAT'S THAT SUPPOSED TO MEAN?" I asked.

Walt took a moment to look at the rescue worker, hovering above, preparing to drop down to us. "YOUR MENTAL GAME IS ROBBING YOU OF YOUR KNUCKLE BALL!"

"HUH?"

The rescue worker wearing a waterproof orange jumpsuit and a helmet, descended to us in what looked like an oversized lobster crate. "RELAX, LANA. FORGET ABOUT KISSING. NOW'S NOT THE RIGHT TIME, BUT WHEN THE RIGHT TIME COMES ALONG—"

I held up my hand. "DON'T GIVE ME KISSING ADVICE," I cried." I'VE HAD ENOUGH OF THAT FOR ONE DAY!"

"IS THAT SO," he said smiling.

"JUST BEING HONEST," to which I thought I heard LeVan shout over all the noise, *Thank the heavens above!*

"JUST BEING HONEST, I'D LIKE TO ASK IF YOU'D COME WITH ME TO THE BARN DANCE THIS FRIDAY," said Walt as he helped me inside the crate. "OF COURSE, WE'LL HAVE TO BRING MY GRANDFATHER, BUT—"

"I'D LIKE THAT," I shouted.

"IT'S A DATE THEN."

"WALT!" I shouted as the rescue worker secured a strap across my lap, "NOW IS THE RIGHT TIME!"

Walt didn't hesitate. He leaned in and kissed me, and before the rescue worker gave the signal we were good to go, he kissed me again. Then the cable attached to the crate tugged upward and, in more ways than one, I felt like I was flying.

Chapter
Twenty-Four

Ing!! We need to talk!!!

Ing!! Where are you? Call me!!!

What is taking you so long??

Ing!! Text me when you get a chance!!

Getting kissed for the first time, not to mention, heli-rescued, can make it difficult to settle back into regular life, but settle back in I did, painting day and night along with LeVan. However, "regular life" at Dogwood studio was changing, and not for reasons I'd expected. LeVan was fine. He was making steady progress on the panels, and, as far as I could tell, still himself. The change at Dogwood was Carl. Since Novia Spring, Carl had become our friend, and, when he could, stopped by to chat, read us the local paper, and watch us work.

"It says here," said Carl, Friday afternoon while sitting at the long table, his bifocals perched on his nose and the Bluegill Bugle before him, "that barn dance you're heading to tonight is a fundraiser for the Bluegill Art museum."

"Okay, that makes so much more sense," I said.

"What do you mean?" asked Carl.

"Expecting me to say something at the barn dance in front of everyone. I thought it was some sort of weird Idaho tradition, but the dance is benefitting the town's art museum. I totally get it. I didn't know Bluegill had an art gallery," I said, watching LeVan climb down the ladder and kick a pillow out of his way.

"I hate to disappoint you, but there isn't a Bluegill art museum," grumbled LeVan as he stood back and looked at his work. "There might have been if Old Love hadn't tried to turn the town into a lake."

"And by Old Love you mean Patsy's father, Phil Love?"

"I do indeed."

"He seriously tried to turn Bluegill into a lake. Why?"

"Love owned the upper valley and envisioned Bluegill as a tourism spot, a place for boaters and fishermen, all coming to rent the lodges he and his cronies planned to build. He told me about it one day while pestering me with a visit to my studio. At the time, he was a powerful senator. He had the clout to make it happen, especially with Idaho Energy hungry for another dam. Never mind the many people, including my Rosemary, who called Bluegill home."

"So what did you do?" I asked.

Turning to look at me, LeVan folded his arms. "I ran for Mayor. Never would have had to if that blockhead wasn't about to destroy the town. Of course, for me, Love getting his way would have been almost welcome—a reason to leave Bluegill.

We could have moved to New York, but it was unthinkable. Rosemary loved this town, and so there was nothing left to do but set aside painting and run for mayor.

"That's so sweet," I said.

LeVan picked up a wet paintbrush and started drying its bristles with a rag. "Sacrifice is easier when it's for someone you love."

"It's true," said Carl, "I had a schnauzer named Millicent I had to walk down five flights of stairs every night at midnight so she could do her business, but did I mind? No. I loved that dog. But you're wrong about there not being a Bluegill art museum. Well, wrong and right. It's in the works."

LeVan's mouth fell open and his lower lip quivered. "I feel like Rip Van Winkle, waking up to a changed world. Bluegill art museum is in the works! Who's funding it?"

"Says here," said Carl as he read the paper, "The Friends of LeVan Hitchpost."

LeVan's mouth fell open further still. "Does it say who these friends of mine are?"

"No," said Carl, it says, and I quote, *During renovations to city hall two years ago a file marked LeVan's Vision was discovered in a desk that was slated to be thrown out. The current mayor, John Ledbetter—*

"Never met him," mumbled LeVan.

"*—read the file and was deeply moved. I felt inspired to act, said Ledbetter. Here was a man who had saved this town from destruction, said the Mayor, referring to the well-known story of former Senator Love's attempt to turn Bluegill into a lake and LeVan Hitchpost's subsequent fight to keep that from happening. Bluegill, back then, was hit hard economically, folks were leaving, but Mayor Hitchpost had a vision for what this town could be, and I felt it was our turn to help him, and bring this art museum to life in the way he outlined.*

Mayor Hitchpost, having fought against well-monied power during his term as mayor had no interest in a town art museum

funded by large donations that came with strings attached. Large,
Lovely sums, he stipulated, most likely a reference to the wealthy
senator, must not be accepted. This will be an art museum for the
community, which all help build and feel justly proud.

LeVan sat down and stared at his paint-speckled hands.
"Well, I'll be," he said. I had no idea. Lana, you'll have to say
something."

"That's what people keep telling me," I said.

"And when you do, say a little something for me as well."

I walked over to where LeVan stood and caught his gaze.
"LeVan, you should say something," I said, a hint of pleading
in my voice.

"That would be nice," said Carl, folding the paper and
setting it aside.

"No," he said, his eyes on his work, "I'll never finish if I
do."

"LeVan," I said, "you'd be talking to The Friends of LeVan
Hitchpost—people who care about you. After you tell them
you've miraculously bounced back, just let them know you're
busy at the studio and can't be bothered."

"Sounds like a good plan," said Carl, sipping his tea.

"Time," he said, rubbing his fingers together as if adding
a pinch of salt to a dish, "it slips from you, and its leaving gets
you thinking—if you're lucky and still can think—about that
thing you intended to get done. You thought you would do
it, thought you had plenty of time, so you set it aside to run
the town, the ward, and raise a boy broken by grief, not just
because it's the right thing to do, but because in the midst of
your own grief, you can feel her close, hear her, almost as if
from another room, helping you parent him, and you love the
sound of that voice. Love it." LeVan pressed his sleeve to his
eyes. "I don't regret my choices, but I have a chance now to
do that *thing* I intended to get done," he said, pointing a bent
finger at his mural, "and it sure would be a help if most everyone thinks I'm still out to lunch."

I folded my arms, trying to muster the umph to continue to argue, but it was pointless. Resolve was draining from me.

"I don't know why I have resumed my life," said LeVan, taking his bony hand in mine. "Whether the result of others' prayers or the disjointed ones I prayed while my mind was in pieces, I haven't a clue, but this much I know—this is my last work, and to complete it, I need you, Lana. So please, let me do what I want to do, and, if you don't mind, say something for me tonight."

Out of the corner of my eye, I noticed Carl, hands clasped to his heart, mouth the word, *Please*. "Fine, I'll say a few words for you, but just a few. I'm not a fan of public speaking," I said, giving Carl's soft clapping an irritated look.

"And there's just one more thing," said LeVan. "Of course there is," I said, sounding tired.

"Ask Britney if Kylie could come up to the studio some afternoon. Carl could pick her up from day care."

"LeVan, she's five and he's a total stranger to her!" I cried.

"He's a good driver," said LeVan.

"Thank you," said Carl, crossing one leg over the other and swinging it.

I put my hands on my hips. "How do you know that?" I asked.

Carl's leg swinging turned into a nervous-looking shake. "Uh, LeVan," he said.

LeVan smiled and waved a hand in the air, indicating that the alarm in my voice was unfounded. "We took a short ride into town for a double-chocolate shake at Faye's. Carl had never had one, and it'd been years since I had, as far as I can remember anyway.

"It was delicious, but I should probably get going," said Carl, his eyes on his tea as he slowly stood.

That's fine, you can go," said LeVan.

"It is not fine. You need to stay!"

Carl sank into his chair. "Sadly, this is reminding me of my childhood,"

I threw my hands in the air. "You went to Faye's! You said you were going to stay put!"

LeVan shrugged. "I also said I'd vote for Nixon."

I ran a hand over my head. "LeVan, please tell Walt! Everyone else can think you're out to lunch, but if you don't tell him, he's going to think you don't love him."

"You'll have to tell him that's not true."

"He is going to be mad at me for not saying anything!"

"Well, he won't stay mad for long."

"Why is that?"

"Because he loves you."

I put my hands over my ears. "Don't say that. It's like you're going to jinx it before it has a chance to happen."

"I don't have time to quibble. He loves you, and I need you to—"

"You need me to do something else!"

"Yes," said LeVan, a wry smile spreading on his face, "I need you to keep kissing my grandson." I blushed. "No use trying to deny it. I can spot a kissed girl easily enough."

Carl shot out of his seat. "You two kissed? That's wonderful!" he cried. "Tell us about it!"

"Well, no offense, Carl—"

"None taken," he said, in that blinkless way of his.

"But it's the sort of thing you tell your girlfriend."

Carl sighed with happiness. "That's true, that's true, but just tell me this. Was it everything you hoped it would be?"

The heat in my cheeks spread to the tips of my ears. "Yes," I said.

"Then be sure to kiss him again tonight. In the meantime, I've got to get back to work," said LeVan, rising out of his chair and heading back up the ladder

I let out a sigh of surrender. "Fine," I said, "but I am still surrounding you with pillows. I don't care what you say, LeVan Hitchpost."

"Suit yourself," he said, climbing higher.

Chapter
Twenty-Five

Lana! Lefty here! Just landed in Tokyo and wanted to check in. How's tiny town Idaho?

It's going great!

I've got good news! You're loved!

You know about Walt?

Walt? Who's Walt? I'm talking about Helsinki! They loved you there! Your list of future buyers is long, even a few requests for commissioned works.

Serious?

And that's just my first stop! But I can tell you right now you're going to burn it up in Berlin. So, what are you doing tonight?

Going to a barn dance

Girl, we've got to get you out of there!

No, it's going to be great, and it's a fundraiser for the town art museum.

194

Idaho art. The thought makes me shiver. Have a good time hoofing it up, eating corn on the cob, and apple pie. In the meantime, I'm going to make you an art superstar!

You do that!

You'll be hearing from me soon!

With the truck windows down, and crisp twilight air caressing my cheek, LeVan and I wound our way to the barn dance, heading down the canyon, through downtown Bluegill, and past Flintlock to a sturdy, yet weathered barn with Hinckley Dairy written on the side in faded lettering. LeVan marveled at the traffic and having to pay ten dollars to park. With wide-eyed wonder, he looked at the gathering, the café lights and food trucks, the children tossing bean bags in a game of corn hole. "All this for art," he said, shaking his head in disbelief.

Walt insisted on coming up the canyon to get us, but I had told him that wasn't necessary. It was out of his way, not to mention, asking a lot of Ruth. And since he was trying to finish an enterprise, as he called it, that was taking longer than he expected, it made sense for us to meet at the barn dance. The sky was a lovely bronzy plum scattered with tufty clouds that glowed in the slipping sunlight. It was a sight that normally would have had me reaching for a pencil, but not tonight. Tonight, all I wanted was to see Walt.

I hadn't seen him since Novia Spring, partly because we were both busy, and partly because I was terrified. Yes, I was twenty-two and a college graduate, but the truth was, I was nervous about where we went from here. We had kissed, and dodged a flash flood together—two events that tend to bring people together. And yet, were we together? What exactly were we? Was it too early to ask? Of course it was. I had watched more than one roommate come up empty by asking the guy they were dating to define their relationship.

The smart money was on being chill—friendly but not needy, interested but not invested, available and yet swamped with other options. I took a deep breath as we walked into the barn, and tried to focus on being the ideal date, but it felt false, like I was a pretender, and that all I was or would ever be was a lost little girl from Siberia. And where do lost little girls from Siberia go when they're at a barn dance to meet up with an incredibly good-looking Idaho farm boy? To the bathroom to hide.

"Hey," said Britney as, breathless, I rushed inside the bathroom.

"Hello," I said, sounding jumpy, like I was on the run from the police.

"I see you're wearing black again," she said, leaning in close to the vanity mirror as she applied mascara. She pointed at my white tank top that I wore with a long-sleeve black shirt. "At least you're breaking it up with a bit of white."

My skin prickled. "I would call this a soft charcoal," I said.

"Britney shut her mascara as she turned to look at me. ""Doesn't matter," she said. "You're a grown woman you can wear what you want."

I nodded slowly. "Thank you for that, Britney."

She studied me for a moment. "Have you ever thought about a smoky eye?" she asked.

"A what?" I asked.

"It's a way of wearing your eyeshadow," she said, stepping closer. "Dark shadow on the eye lid, and smudging the upper and lower lashes with eyeliner."

"I don't wear a lot of makeup," I said, trying to politely decline her offer.

She patted the counter. "Here, let me," she said, "you need a little something."

I considered bolting from the bathroom. As much as I loved to paint, painting my face wasn't my thing. And besides, I hadn't gotten the feeling that Britney liked me. She was pleasant enough to her wealthy aunt and uncle, Patsy and Clint, but other than that seemed aloof. Bolting seemed the right choice, except doing so meant seeing Walt, and as much as I wanted to see him, my heart was hammering, and I needed a moment to calm down. "Sure," I said, sitting on the counter, "smoke away. Well, you know what I mean."

Britney pulled from her Louis Vuitton tote a bulging zippered makeup pouch.

"Do you take that with you everywhere?" I asked.

"Only where I take my vital organs," she said, but without that hint of humor that might have softened things between us.

"I see," I said.

"Eyes closed," she said before dabbing something cool on my cheeks. Not expecting this, I flinched. "Some primer," Britney explained, "Thought we might as well start by evening you out. "So how long have you dyed your hair black?" she asked in that tone that I imagine doctors ask their patients how long they've been smoking.

"Since high school," I said,

"It's like turning off a light."

"I'm sorry?"

"It makes you look like a spy, or an assassin. Someone who doesn't want to attract attention. But maybe that's your thing. I've seen weirder. Stop opening your eyes."

I squeezed my eyes shut and thought about what Britney had said, trying to decide if it bothered me that, according to her, I looked like worked for the secret service.

Britney cupped my chin and, after applying several shades to my upper lid, took a dark eyeliner to my lower. "I'd like to ask a favor. Eyes closed," she reminded.

"Is the favor keeping my eyes closed?"

Britney clucked her tongue. "No, I'd like you to paint my portrait." Surprised, I opened my eyes. "Eyes closed!" she ordered.

I snapped them shut. "Sorry," I said, although what I wanted to say was, *I don't want to paint your portrait. Yes, you're pretty, but in a pretentious way.* With her finger, Britney rubbed my lower lids. "Have you even seen my work?" I asked.

"Eyes open," she said, a brush gripped between her teeth. "No, I haven't seen your work." She took the brush from her mouth and gave me a hard look. "Why, is it awful?"

"I don't think I'm awful," I said.

"Hmm," she said, appearing to wonder if what she had before her was an awful artist who didn't have the smarts to recognize her own glaring lack of talent. Britney shrugged. "As long as you don't make me look bad, I'm willing to give it a shot," she said, dabbing my chin and forehead with a bit more powder.

"Are you—"

"Pucker," demanded Britney, cutting me off. I puckered and Britney slid a thick gloss over my lips. "Now press." She pressed her lips together to demonstrate. "Am I what, expecting you'll work for free? Of course not. I'll pay you."

I blinked. "Pay me?"

"Eyes, mouth closed," she said, and almost before I'd had a chance to comply, she misted my face with what she referred to as, her favorite finishing touch.

I was about to say, *you don't need to pay me because I'm not painting your portrait* when it occurred to me that this odd stylist/client intimacy was presenting me with an opportunity to accomplish what before had seemed to me impossible.

"Rather than pay me, there's a favor I'd like to ask of you," I said.

"Yes, I'll take you back to blonde!" she said, almost breathless with relief.

"That's not it," I said, my voice flat.

"Oh. Then what?" she asked, sounding puzzled.

"Allow Kylie to visit us at the studio," I said. "But don't mention it to anyone."

"Are you kidding me?"

"I know it's a strange request, but that's the way—"

"Save money on daycare *and* get my portrait done? Deal! And, don't worry, I won't say a word."

"Then it's a deal," I said, though I doubted whether I could trust her. Still, it had gone easier than I'd expected.

Shailene swung the bathroom door open and said, "There you are! Everyone's been looking for y—" She pointed at me. "Britney, what have you done? She looks like Gao Gao."

Britney, who had been giving my face yet another layer of powder, stood back. "She does not," Britney insisted, but her heavily penciled brow wrinkled with worry.

"Who's Gao Gao?" I asked.

Shailene didn't sugarcoat. "A panda at the San Diego Zoo."

"I look like a panda?" I asked, my voice cracking.

Britney stood in front of me and examined her work. "With a smoky eye you have to smudge the lower lid," she said, smoothing and tucking my hair.

"Not while making her as pale as a geisha," said Shailene.

"That's her skin tone!" Britney studied my face. "She looks like a trend-setter."

"I'm not seeing it," said Shailene. She shook her head. "It doesn't matter, they need her on stage right now."

I looked at Shailene, tears threatening to fill my eyes. "How am I supposed to go on stage looking like Gao Gao?" I asked as honestly as if I were speaking to Ingrid.

"You're an artist," she said, pushing me toward the door, "people expect weird, so just go out there and own it. And hurry, Hien Bao's the MC, and he's stressed. He's grumbling in Vietnamese."

I opened the bathroom door and weaved my way through the crowd. Though the barn doors on either end were open wide, with so many people inside, the barn felt hot and stuffy. Tiny beads of sweat popped up on my forehead, and I rubbed my face before remembering Britney's makeup job. Now, I looked like a smudged Gao Gao. Fantastic.

Hien Bao's eyes opened wide when he saw me, reminding me of the exaggerated surprise of silent movie actors. "Holy cow!" he said. More than any other time in my life, I wanted to run, to dodge the situation, avoid it entirely. But there was LeVan, sitting on the stand, a smile crinkling his tired eyes, and his speech—the one he wanted me to give—in his hand. And so slowly, dreading each step, I climbed up to the stage.

After a few words from the mayor and other members of the community, it was my turn to speak. A rustle of whispers spread across the barn as I walked to the microphone. Own *it,* I told myself. *Own it!* Smiling, I looked out at the crowd, grateful the lights blinded me a little. *Just get through this and then hide. Forever.*

"Hello," I said, standing too close to the microphone and making it squeal. Covering the mic with my hand, I stepped back, pushed passed my embarrassment, and started again. "For those of you who don't know me, I'm Lana Huish, and I'm here in Bluegill as an artist through the Wilmington Trust." I had expected to hear a ripple of applause, recognition for the Wilmington Trust and its generous support of things like PBS, but all I heard was an elderly man near the stage shout to his wife, *An artist! That explains why she looks like she looks!* And his wife shouting back, *What?* I cleared my throat, willed my hands to stop trembling, and continued. "Through the Wilmington Trust, I've been given the privilege of working with the man some of you have called Bishop, others Mayor, and who the art

world calls one of the finest western muralists of our time—
LeVan Hitchpost."

The barn erupted in applause and shouts of, *We Love You,
LeVan!* Waiting for the cheering to die down, I searched the
room for Walt, and when I couldn't find him felt both relief and
disappointment. Shailene and Britney were there, easy enough
to spot, in the back, whispering instead of applauding, which got
me thinking. Maybe they had wanted me to look ridiculous. Had
they worked together, one doing my makeup, the other planting
in my mind the idea that I looked like a panda? *Well, it's not
going to work,* I thought. Standing taller, and speaking directly
into the microphone, I continued. "Despite the health challenges
LeVan faces, I think it's safe to say that he's enjoying being back
at his studio with a paintbrush in hand." This brought forth even
more applause, and I turned to smile at LeVan, giving him just
enough time to point discreetly at the paper he'd pressed into my
palm when I'd sat next to him on stage.

I unfolded the paper and noticed he had written, in scratchy
penmanship, additional lines at the top of what he'd already prepared to say. "And if he could," I continued, "I think he'd like
to say something like this:" I cleared my throat. "Oh my, you're
a beautiful sight! I wish Rosemary were here to see this—her
hometown rallying together for the sake of art. If she were here,
she'd nudge me and tell me, 'I told you Bluegill had potential,'
and I would nudge her and say, 'Quit gloating.'" Laughter filled
the room, and I paused for a moment. "But you're a good group.
As fine an assemblage as ever was, and I know just looking at you
that Bluegill is in good hands, which means everything to me,
because it meant everything to her. Also, thank you, for your
friendship, your kindness, especially these last few years when I
haven't been myself. Now let's get down to brass tacks . . ." I said,
and moved on to the part he'd prepared before coming.

"A town that appreciates art," I continued, "has a soul that
enlivens everything around it. I came to Bluegill intending to
stay a year, maybe two. Just long enough to let Rosemary get

I

Bluegill out of her system. I didn't expect Bluegill to work its way into mine. How could it? All anyone wanted to talk about here was the price of hay! Calling Bluegill the pearl of Idaho seemed absurd to me, unless you were saying it tongue in cheek."

The crowd laughed and so I waited a moment. "But that's the thing about pearls," I said, reading on, "they're hard to spot, especially the precious ones. And finding them's a cinch compared to keeping them. For that, you must do all you can—give all you have. For Rosemary, Bluegill was a pearl beyond price. I didn't always agree with her on that point, but she was, *is* my pearl, and so what mattered to her mattered to me. Bluegill matters to me. Bless you all for working toward this worthy goal—an art museum in Bluegill. And remember, time sprints more than it drags, so, while you can, seek after pearls, my friends. And when you find them, give all you have to keep them. Thank you and good bye."

The room grew quiet, a hollowness filling it. It had been a long while since any of them had heard LeVan's voice, not the fractured version to which they had grown accustomed, but LeVan's true voice, and hearing it again intensified their missing it. I wanted to say, *Wait! Don't be sad! He's back!* And with that in mind, I turned to LeVan, pleading with my eyes for him to say something. Softly, almost imperceptibly, he shook his head, making my heart sink.

Hien Bao stood, wiped his eyes, then after making a few announcements regarding the silent auction, turned it over to the band who, seemingly on mission to switch the mood from funeral to fun, got things going with Cotton-Eyed Joe. I wasn't ready for fun. Stepping down from the stage, I threaded my way through the crowd, and walked out into the cool night air toward the dark stretch of land. Why was he so obstinate! So determined to live as he wanted! My frustration made me forget about meeting up with Walt, until, appearing out of the darkness, he walked toward me. This was both romantic and terrifying, and, startled, I let out a scream of joy and fright, which made Walt scream.

Chapter
Twenty-Six

Walt placed his hands on my shoulders. "Geez, what'd you scream for?" he asked, his white teeth flashing in the darkness as he dissolved into laughter.

My face reddened with embarrassment. *Great,* I thought, *now I look like a sunburned, smudgy panda. Thank heavens it's dark.* "I thought you were . . . I don't know . . . a ghost," I said, my mouth curling into a smile despite my mortification. A thought flitted through my mind like a shooting star flashing across an inky sky—*you're with a guy, you're embarrassed, but you're not planning your escape. This is progress.*

Walt's hands slid from the slope of my shoulder, down my arms, to my hands. "A ghost in a potato field," he said, his voice droll as he interlocked his fingers with mine.

Sometimes it feels like a hummingbird lives inside me. Most of the time it sleeps, but when I like a guy, it takes flight, and each beat of its wings fuels my fear and anxiety, until, overwhelmed, I bolt. But that was before. Standing in the semi-darkness with Walt as a few children zigged and zagged around us playing tag, I didn't want to run. The hummingbird had stilled its wings.

"Have you never seen a ghost in a potato field?" I asked, the playful hint in my voice feeling new and exciting to me. I was flirting!

"I've seen Hank shirtless in a potato field, which is pretty much the same thing," he said, pulling me a little closer toward him.

"Then you can understand my surprise," I said, shyly tilting my head upward and looking into his eyes. We were close enough to kiss, and we did. It was more a peck than a kiss, and that filled my heart with happiness. I'd seen plenty of kissing in college that had nothing to do with actually caring for the other person, but I had never seen a you-use-me-I'll-use-you peck. Pecks were sweet, the stuff of couples, and the thought of becoming one with Walt made me dizzy with happiness.

Walt gently pulled me in the direction of the field. "There's something I want to show you," he said, his excitement sweet.

"You want me to walk into the potato field with you, at night, while wearing heels?" I asked, laughing a little at this unexpected suggestion.

"Tell you what," he said, scooping me off my feet and making me laugh harder, "I'll do the walking."

"My farmer in shining armor," I said, putting my arms around his neck.

"At your service," he said just as I spotted a ghostly glow in the distance.

"Walt," I said, a prickle of worry working its way up my spine, "what is that?"

"Something I've been working on for you," he said, his voice unstrained, as if he were carrying a bag of groceries, and not a full-grown woman.

"Walt," I said, as, closer now, I saw that the glowing was coming from candles placed in mason jars. They were set on the ground in a ring around a low wooden platform that was no bigger than a picnic blanket. "This is beautiful," I said.

Walt tipped me onto the platform, then jumped up there too. "All week," he said, clasping my hands in his, "I've been looking forward to seeing you at the barn dance."

"Me too," I said.

"And then it occurred to me that if, until recently, you'd never been kissed, there was a chance that you've never danced a slow dance."

"You think you know me."

"Am I right?"

"Do girlfriends and grandfathers count?" I asked as, in sync, we went from holding hands to pressing our palms together—his rough from working outdoors, and mine smooth.

"They do not," he said.

"Then, no, Mr. Hitchpost, I have never slow danced."

There was enough moonlight, starlight, and candlelight for me to see Walt smile. "I was hoping you'd say that," he said.

I laughed. "Why?" I asked as we interlocked fingers again and he kissed the top of my hand.

"I wanted your first dance to be memorable."

"As memorable as my first kiss?" I asked, teasingly.

"I have not hired a helicopter, if that's what you're wondering."

"Life's full of disappointments."

Walt poked me in the side, making me squeal with laughter. "I asked myself, where would be the perfect place for Lana's first slow dance—and though it may sound crazy, which it did, particularly to Ed Hinckley who farms this land—I thought the perfect place would be here, surrounded by—"

"Potatoes," I said, looking into his eyes.

"I was going to say stars," he said, his hands on my waist now, pulling me toward him.

"And so I built this dance floor, which took longer than I expected."

"Your enterprise?" I asked.

"My enterprise," he said, "Sorry I missed your speech. How'd it go?"

"You would have found it fascinating."

"Girl's got confidence."

"Just stating a fact."

"Now it's my turn to state a fact," he said, taking one of my hands in both of his. "I would very much like to dance with you."

"That's was statement, not a question."

"You're splitting hairs."

"This will be my first slow dance. You've got to do it right."

In high school all it took was snapping my fingers. I laughed. "How gentlemanly."

"But this isn't high school," he said, his voice softer as he took my hands in his, "so Miss Huish, could I please have this dance?"

"You may," I said. Walt jumped off the dancefloor and turned on a boom box "Thank you," I said as, returning, he took my hand and pulled me close.

"For what?"

"My dance floor under the stars."

"You're welcome," he said, pulling me in a little closer.

I rested my hands on his shoulders and, together, we swayed to a slow, twangy country song about a kiss that went on and on, longer than Grandma sayin' Grace. Walt cleared his throat. "Never let Hank make you a mix tape, unless you want it to be terrible."

"I like it."

"What are older brother's for, except sabotage and humiliation."

"Speaking of terrible, never let Britney do your makeup," I said.

Walt stopped dancing to scrutinize me, and though somehow not feeling self-conscious, I still covered my face with my hands.

Gently, Walt peeled them away. "You don't look terrible," said Walt, bringing me closer and swaying again with me to the music.

I could tell he meant it. Still, I said, "You're right. Pandas look cute, not terrible."

"You do not look like a panda," he said, pulling away and sending me into a slow spin.

"You say that because it's dark," I said, resting my hands on his upper arms since his shoulders were a bit too high.

"I can see you well enough."

"Then what do I look like?"

"I was going to say that you look like my girlfriend." I couldn't speak. Hearing exactly what I wanted to hear took my breath away. Walt, however, mistook my silence for me trying to figure out how to let him down softly. "Unless you don't want to look like my girlfriend," he added, his sudden lack of confidence melting my heart.

On tip toe, and jumping just a bit, I kissed him on the cheek, making him break into a slow grin. "I want to be your girlfriend, Walt!" Walt lifted me off the floor and spun me around or two, then gently placed in back down. We stood there, looking into each other's eyes as ice seemed to break from me. As it turns out, joy is pretty good dynamite. But even in the midst of happiness, worry can weasel its way inside me. "Not to doubt your sincerity," I said, "Well, okay I'm doubting your sincerity, but only because this is kind of scary for me."

"You've never had a boyfriend before?"

"You guessed it."

Walt bent down and gave me another peck. "Awesome, fewer guys for me to beat up."

"Walt, I'm being serious."

"Lana, you're the one I want to be with, the one I want to get to know."

This made me smile, which I tried to conceal. "What do you want to know?" I asked, taking on a mock serious tone.

"What's your favorite color?"

"I'm an artist," I said as Walt sent me into a twirl. "That's like asking a mother who her favorite child is."

"Then why do you wear black so much?" He asked, but without judgement, which made me want to give him an honest answer, but in Russian, because somehow I was too timid for such honesty in English.

Ischezut, I said, my voice soft. To disappear.

Ne ischezayut, he said. "Don't disappear." His accent was terrible. "You look pretty in anything, but I'd like to see you in bright yellow."

"Bright yellow!"

"You'd look cute."

"I'd look like a banana," I said, only vaguely aware that one twangy slow song had ended and another had started. *Twenty-two and dancing my second slow song with my boyfriend,* I mused. *Things in my life are picking up!*

"This may surprise you, but I know more about farming than fashion," said Walt.

"Shocking. Just when you think you've got someone figured out," I said as a guy with a reedy voice sang in a slow, gushy way, *Goin' get you a big ol' ring. Rustle up a preacher and a ding a ling a ling them weddin' bells will ring.*

"It's unfortunate," said Walt, "but I'm going to have to kill my brother.

He went out of his way to find the worst country songs ever written."

"Never mind Hank," I said.

"Good point," he said, "I don't want to waste time talking about my brother. I want to get to know you."

I smiled. "What else can I tell you?" I asked as we continued to sway to the sappy song.

"What do you like to do?"

"Besides slow dance with you?"

Walt kissed the crown of my head. "Yes," he said.

209

"Lots of things—horseback riding, playing the guitar, traveling, sketching, and painting."

"And what does Gramps do while you're painting?"

For a moment, it felt as if everything stood still. My mind was racing about how to best lie to my boyfriend. "It depends," I said.

"Is he painting much?"

"He's painting." *Every waking moment,* I thought.

"I'd like to see it."

"See what?"

"What you two are working on. Would you mind if I came up, maybe at the end of the day when you're done? We could sit out on the front steps of the house. I could kiss you good night a dozen times, and take a peek at the studio. A quick, harmless peek."

A shooting star flashed across the dark sky and disappeared. Disappear. I was good at doing that around guys, but I didn't want to disappear, not now, even though answering Walt's question was going to be tricky. I wanted to stay here, slow dancing on *my* dance floor with *my* boyfriend. That was all I wanted to think about. I didn't even want to sketch the moment; I just wanted to live it. And so, like a pesky fly, I shooed away Walt's question. "I'll think about it," I said.

Chapter Twenty-Seven

Ing! Even bigger
news!!! But I'm not
telling until you
text me back!!!
Hurry!!!!

Whoever said that artists need to be miserable to work never spent any time around happy artists. All I had to do was think, *Ahem, Lana Huish, you are Walt Hitchpost's girlfriend,* and it felt like I could paint forever—ideas, enthusiasm, and energy almost overwhelming me. And remembering Hien Bao's expression as we walked into barn dance holding hands didn't slow me down either. Inside me, winter hadn't entirely ended, but the sun was shining and there were more traces of spring.

Weeks become days when you're blissfully happy, and things that would normally upset you, like your best friend still not responding to your texts, or having to continually lie to your boyfriend and put off his requests to visit you at work— those types of things get placed on the back burner. There are so many other happier thoughts to occupy your mind. And they did. They kept me so busy that it felt like I blinked and I had been in Bluegill a month—long enough to have created ten good paintings, and for Bluegill to feel like home.

A pattern emerged as the days whipped by. Every day, except Sunday, we worked, but Wednesdays and Fridays we slowed things down a bit in the afternoon to enjoy Kylie's visits. Around lunch time LeVan and I would drive down to Little Darlings Daycare where we would find Kylie waiting for us by the front window. After telling us in a tremulous voice, *I was afraid you forgot!* we'd climb in the truck and head back to the studio with Kylie giving us a breathless account of her day.

She was true to her word. She wanted to paint unicorns, and so while we worked that's what she did. Well, that and talk. But when something was troubling her, the chatter and singing stopped, and she'd lower her gaze and raise her eyebrows in a pitiful expression, which is how she looked one afternoon while Carl read LeVan the paper, and I spread out on the long table my sketches of Britney.

"What's the matter?" I asked, patting her head.

Kylie looked at my sketches of her mother, and then at me. "Will I be beautiful one day?" she asked, pushing up her glasses.

"Well, as it happens," I said, "I am an expert at spotting beauty."

"Why is that?" she asked, tilting her head.

"Because I'm an artist."

"So, what do you think," she said, taking off her glasses and leaning toward me. "Will I be beautiful?"

"Let me check," I said, squinting as I scrutinized her sweet face. "You have a good nose, an excellent jaw line, but let me see your teeth." Kylie smiled wide revealing a little gap on her lower set.

"Let's take a look at your eyes . . ." I said, measuring the distance between them with the end of my paintbrush. "They're nicely spaced, and a very pretty brown." I frowned as if mulling things over. "Yes, everything looks in order, but—important question—are you kind to bunnies?"

Kylie put on her glasses. "So kind," she said, her lenses amplifying the earnest look in her sweet, brown eyes.

"And what about Harvey at daycare, the boy who took your crayon? Are you kind to him?"

Kylie wrinkled her little brow. "That's harder," she admitted.

"It makes you beautiful, inside and out."

"What if I'm just extra nice to bunnies?"

"It's a start, but . . ."

"It's not enough?"

"No."

"Darn."

"Okay, I'll try, but how will I know when I'm beautiful?" she asked.

"That's a good question," I said, stalling. I didn't know how to answer that question, especially when sometimes I doubted my own beauty.

"That's why I asked it," she said, her voice taking on a raspier quality.

"Um, well," I said, starting to speak before I knew what to say, "there will come a point in your life, down the road, when you won't have to look to others for validation. You'll be confident in who you are, and . . ." Her expression fell, and I knew why. Not only was I confusing her, it sounded like becoming beautiful was going to take forever! This little girl needed to feel pretty now. "Never mind that," I said, one of the easiest ways to know you're beautiful is if an artist asks to paint your picture, which is what I'm doing now. Kylie can I paint your picture?"

"But I'm not beautiful yet like Mommy," she said, pointing at my sketches of Britney.

"That's grown-lady beauty, which is followed sooner than we'd like by old-lady beauty. But what you have is little-girl beauty."

"I do?"

"Why else would Harvey steal your crayon?"

"Because he's a dumb."

"He's a dumb because you're beautiful."

"That doesn't make sense."

I shoved Britney's sketches aside. "To be honest, I'm sort of new to relationships, but I promise, boys do unusual things when they like you," I said, smiling a little as I thought of my dance floor out in the middle of Ed Hinckley's potato field. "But right now, Little Miss Beautiful, I need to know, can I paint your picture?"

"But you're supposed to paint Mommy's," she said, gesturing at my sketches.

I gathered them together into a stack. "Let's paint yours first and surprise her."

Kylie smiled, making the little gap reappear. "Okay!" she said, and the two of us got to work—Kylie painting unicorns, and me making sketches of her.

You would have thought that now that I was Walt's girlfriend, Sunday lunches at Flintlock would have stopped. They didn't. This was partly because Kylie insisted we come, and partly because, quite honestly, it's hard to beat Patsy's cooking. And so Sunday lunch continued, as usual, except now I was the one sitting next to Walt. I had expected brooding from Shailene, but the only difference in her behavior that I could tell was that she poked Walt less.

"How are things coming along?" asked Britney, glancing at me then back to her phone.

Kylie stopped eating mid bite, her eyes wide with worry, which wasn't surprising. Five-year-olds seldom have good poker faces. I winked, letting her know there was no need to worry. "I'm getting there," I said.

"Can we head up and see what you've done?" asked Shailene.

"I'm sorry, but no," I said. Patsy bit her lip.

"We're not trying to be secretive."

Shailene cut into her steak. "So you're succeeding without trying."

Kylie began to chew again, but her eyes only grew wider.

"Oh, please," said Walt, with a slight roll of his eyes.

"You have to admit that right now, Dogwood feels more cloak and dagger than art studio," said Shailene.

"That's a little dramatic."

"We're working hard," I said, "I mean, *I* am working hard, and trying to focus."

"Gramps used to have people visit him all the time while he worked. People came and went from Dogwood," said Shailene.

"Daddy used to say that Dogwood should be moved to the middle of the town park to save everyone the trouble of heading up the canyon," said Patsy, making LeVan mutter something grumpy under his breath. I was too far from him to hear what it was, but I shot him a disapproving look all the same.

"The difference is me," I said. "I don't do well with distractions."

"East Tibukin Orthodox monks make pottery during their month of isolation," said Clint, again sharing random information. "They have a shop just outside Missoula called The Lonely Cup,"

"If you don't do well with distractions then we better run this one out of town," said Hank, gesturing at Walt.

"Ha ha," said Walt.

"Would anyone like some more rolls?" asked Patsy, smiling brightly.

Britney put down her phone. "I can understand you not wanting visitors. I'm sure you have a lot of work to do in the next few weeks. But, tell me, what's going to happen between you two," she pointed at Walt and then me, "when you leave?"

My just-eaten dinner seemed to turn to lead. I'd been so focused on happier thoughts that I hadn't stopped to think about that. What was going to happen to us when my time in Bluegill was over?

Walt put his arm around the back of my chair and rested his hand on my shoulder. "Well, there's this invention," he said. "It's really quite fascinating, called an airplane."

"I don't want Lana to go!" cried Kylie.

"Quiet sweetheart," said Britney to her daughter. She then turned to Walt and me. "So, it will be a long distance romance,"

"We'll figure it out," said Walt, his confidence making my worries lift temporally, but after lunch, as Walt and I walked around Flintlock's grounds, they resurfaced. "Walt," I said, as the two of us followed alongside a creek, "what are we doing?"

"You're looking pretty and I'm," He pressed my hand to his lips, "kissing you," he said.

Tears leaked into my eyes. "You know what I mean," I said, my voice catching.

Walt folded me into a hug. "Whoa, whoa, whoa," he said, "Babe, don't cry."

This made me cry harder.

Walt ran his finger beneath my eyes, wiping away my tears. "Don't be sad. We'll figure it out."

We continued our walk, moving away from the creek into a thicket. "Walt, you're a farmer. You need land for that."

"It helps," he said.

"And I'm an artist."

"We're different, but that's okay," he said.

"But we're *so* different. Maybe artists and farmers aren't meant to be together."

"It's true you don't see a lot of dating sites for farmers and artists trying to meet, but what does that matter? I believe in us."

"Why do you believe in us?"

"Because," He looked at the mountains and then at me, "we are the makers of manners." I gave him a puzzled look. "I'm quoting Shakespeare."

"How classy."

"I've got a classy girlfriend so every now and then I've got to step things up. We are the makers of manners, it's a line from Henry the Fifth. Bluegill High put it on when I was a sophomore."

"Were you Henry?"

"No, but I had to listen to his lines a lot. I was soldier number four. My line was, *Here, here!* By the way, I killed it performance night."

"Good to know."

"But my point is just as Hank told Kate after conquering France, *We are the makers of manners*—It doesn't matter what anyone else thinks. We'll decide how this farmer and this artist can make it work."

A tear slid down my cheek. "You think so?"

Ya Znayu Chto tak "I know so," he said, and brushed my tear away.

Chapter
Twenty-Eight

Good days and bad days. People often speak of having one or the other, but seldom is mentioned the kind of day that is perfectly halved between the two, that is equal parts wonderful and horrible, but days like that exist. Trust me, they exist. The following Thursday started off well enough. The week had hummed along nicely, LeVan making progress on his panels and me working on Kylie's portrait. It was easy to forget that every minute of conversation with LeVan, every stroke of his brush was a miracle. He'd had so many good days it felt like they might go on forever—days spent painting at Dogwood studio with Carl stopping by to say hello, and Kylie's afternoon visits. Life felt, if you can believe it, normal. So normal that, at times, circling the base of LeVan's scaffolding with pillows slipped my mind.

Standing on the scaffolding, LeVan gestured at his panels. "I'm satisfied with where I'm at," he said, then began to slowly descend the ladder. Halfway down, his foot slipped off a rung, making my heart almost jump out of my chest, but he steadied himself and continued his snail-paced progress.

"Are you okay?" I asked.

"Oh, I'm fine," said LeVan. Both feet firmly on the ground, he squeezed a bit of black paint on a nearby palette and pulled a

clean, thin paintbrush from his overalls. "Not in any condition
to hoof it up on Broadway," he said, signing L. Hitchpost in the
lower left corner of the first panel, "but they're not offering and
I'm not asking." LeVan then wiped his brush clean, set it down,
and fell more than sat into a chair. "Besides," he said, his gold-
rimmed tooth glinting in the mid-morning light, "some doors
eventually have to close."

I gestured toward his mural. "You've signed it before it's
finished."

LeVan shrugged. "We artists have our eccentricities."

"And by eccentricities, do you mean a secret theatrical
career? Did you really try to make it on Broadway?" I asked,
sitting next to him.

"Oh, I wanted fame, but never the Broadway variety. My
hunger for it—fame, I mean, felt, at times, like it was eating
me alive. Had to look to be sure I still had my arms and legs. It
consumed me, that awful monster." LeVan ran his weathered
hand across his head then shook it. "But enough about me."

"Not enough about you!" I said, touching his knee. "I want
to know more. How did you deal with that hunger?" I leaned
toward him. "I'm your student, you're practically required by
law to reveal this to me."

LeVan crossed his legs, his hand gripping the table to steady
himself. "It's no secret," said LeVan, pointing at his work.
"I told you it's right there—the secret to a happy life, which
includes how to deal with all-consuming ambition, among
other things."

I looked at the three panels that comprised LeVan's mural,
their depiction of a citified man standing in a field, discov-
ering something seen only to him, and then weeping for joy.
"Hmm," I said, rubbing my chin.

"Has my swan song begun to speak to you yet?" he asked.

I tilted my head. "I mean, I like it," I said, then studied it
a while. "Didn't you say that in this piece you were referencing
one of the old masters?" I asked.

"Not one, *the*. Christ, himself."

Oh," I said, my eyes narrowing in study as I continued to look at his work, "so you're depicting one of his teachings."

LeVan raised a crooked finger. "All his teachings are important, but certain truths speak to you, become your touchstone, or *your* secret to a happy life, and for me that has been the parable of the hidden treasure."

I began to see LeVan's painting with new eyes. "Seek after pearls," I said. "That's what your mural is saying, and what you had me say at the barn dance." LeVan nodded. I leaned toward him. "But how do you know what or who is a pearl?" I looked at the third panel. In it, the man who had been nicely dressed now looks disheveled as if from a long day's work, and the watch he'd been wearing is now gone. "How do you know what to give all you have for?"

"You'll know."

"People get it wrong all the time, LeVan," I said, sounding every bit as nervous about the uncertainties of life as I felt. "They chase the wrong person, thing, or goal." Like a distant song, I heard my mother, her words to me inside the stern woman's office, *I'll come for you, my love,* she had said, *when things are better.* Better. She didn't explain what she was chasing, what "better" meant, and I had been too young and terrified to say something like, *What could be better than me! I'm worth giving your all for!*

I knew I shouldn't fault her. Young as I was, I saw the worry in her eyes. And I was happy with my life, its twists and turns—things that couldn't have happened if she hadn't let me go. Still, a part of me wished—and I was pretty sure would always wish—that she had chosen to keep me. Abandonment cuts to the quick, creating a river inside you with dangerous currents. There is no swimming across or stemming its tempestuous flow, but over that brutal water, with time, the good things of life can build bridges.

LeVan smiled, but that did little to lift the worry that pressed in on my chest like a cinder block. LeVan was spent, his color was off, and his breath labored. I would have to find a way to keep him from working the rest of the day. He needed a break. "You're wanting to be smart about life," he said.

"Yes."

"Wanting to make the right choices."

"Exactly."

"I've known plenty of geniuses who've led miserable lives, and it was because they didn't understand," He pointed at his mural, "this concept, that what matters most, the brilliant choice in life, is love. And I'm not talking about the cheap imitation that's the stuff of dime-store novels. I'm talking pure, good, kind, self-sacrificing, stretching, completing love. Finding that someone you want to walk alongside, and then push in a wheelchair when the day comes they grow too frail for walking. That's what—" Suddenly, LeVan's eyes narrowed.

I turned around. "What's the matter?" I asked, just as I saw Patsy Stock. She was hiding behind a bush that sat between the house and the studio, munching on a banana watching us through little binoculars, and wearing camo. "Oh. My. Gosh. LeVan, we have a stalker."

"Just like when she was a little girl," grumbled LeVan. "Spying on me for her daddy. Of course, that can't be the reason now, since he's dead, along with my dear Rosemary." LeVan pointed toward the ceiling. "Wouldn't surprise me if he's up there right now trying to win over my wife."

My mouth fell open. I had seen pictures of the old patriarch at Flintlock, sitting beside his wife, Annette, surrounded by their children. He had a thick neck, and the shoulders of a bar bouncer, but overall looked like a nice guy. Who knew he was a creeper? "Phil Love made a play for your wife?" I asked.

LeVan glanced at Patsy and pursed his lips. "Not exactly," he said.

"Wait, then why do you think he might now that they're both in heaven?"

LeVan began tapping his knees as if in time to a peppy tune. "Because . . ."

I rolled my wrists. "Because . . ." I said, coaxing him.

"I may have stolen her first."

"You stole her? But she was Ernie Snapp's girlfriend,"

"Fiancé," interjected LeVan. "They were engaged."

"Woah," I said, feeling how that shifted things into a weightier matter.

"Ernie Snapp was his boxing name. His agent said he wouldn't get anywhere in the sport with a name like Phil Love. They were high school sweethearts here in Bluegill. Love came to New York for a fight. Rosemary came with her parents to support him and buy her wedding dress. She didn't make it to the fight. We met that afternoon in an elevator in Rockefeller Center, and I asked her to dinner."

"And he never forgave you for it."

"I don't think her parents ever forgave me for it, but Love wasn't the kind to hold a grudge."

I threw my hands in the air. "Then what was the problem between you two?"

LeVan looked away. "We all have our faults, so allow me a few of my own."

"LeVan what are you saying?" I asked.

LeVan returned his gaze to me. "That I was the jealous one."

"You?"

"He'd grown up with my girl, been her beau, and I didn't want to be his friend. It should have been as simple as that, except he loved my work."

"But that's nice."

LeVan hung his head. "I couldn't have made it as an artist in Bluegill without his business, especially at the start. Months would pass with no sales, and then Love would walk into my studio, always buying whatever painting was most expensive. I suppose it was his way of saying, *She would have been better off with me.*

I glanced at Patsy still eating her banana. "You can't know that."

Maybe not, but he proved a smart investor. His collection at Flintlock is worth a pretty penny. Of course, he's dead, so a lot of good that's doing him." He waved a hand. "He was Rosemary's fiancé, and one of the biggest political dunderheads to ever head to Washington. A friendship between us wasn't meant to be."

"This coming from the man who just told me love is brilliant."

"And it is, in theory."

"I think we should invite her in the studio," I said, folding my arms.

"Who?"

"Patsy Love Stock, your arch enemy's daughter."

"She probably prefers hunching behind—"

"She has fed us lunch every Sunday since I arrived at Bluegill, and goes out of her way to make sure we're comfortable in her home. The least we could do is invite her inside." LeVan said nothing. I stood up, my fists balled in determination. "I'm really going to do it!" And when he, again, said nothing, I took it as a green light. Had he insisted otherwise, I don't think I would have pressed the point, but his silence gave me just enough courage to walk over to the glass door, roll it up, and, waving, say to Patsy, "Hi, would you like to come inside?"

The banana slipped from Patsy's fingers. She looked first to her left and then right, then pointed to herself. I nodded. As she stood up, I realized that she had been sitting on a three-legged camp chair. "I didn't mean to, I just wanted, I'm so sorry, I couldn't see much, but I just wanted to watch—"

"And you can do so far more comfortably inside," I assured.

Patsy looked again to her left and her right. "I wouldn't want to interrupt."

"Actually," I said, leaning in conspiratorially, "we could use an interruption."

"Well, if you're sure," said Patsy, touching her heavily teased and sprayed hair to check that all was in place, which it was. "That would be super."

Together, we walked into the studio. "LeVan, say hello to our visitor," I said brightly, perhaps too brightly, because I wasn't sure how much she'd seen, and so, playing it safe, I spoke to him like his mind was infirm. It didn't appear that Patsy heard this. Eyes wide with wonder, Patsy slowly walked toward LeVan's mural, taking in its vibrant color and masterful brushwork.

"Oh, my heavens," said Patsy, cupping her hand over her mouth. "It's magnificent." She spun around to look at LeVan. "But how is this possible, considering . . ."

"Considering I've been as nutty as a sundae the past few years?" said LeVan.

Patsy gulped. "Something like that," she said, her voice cracking.

Gripping the table, LeVan attempted to stand, but couldn't quite muster the strength. "Confound it, I'd stand to shake your hand, but I suppose I'm spent."

Patsy rushed toward him. "No need to stand," she said, then turned once again to gaze at the panels before shaking hands with LeVan.

LeVan looked at his mural, this last work of his that he'd been so determined to create. It wasn't finished, but he was close, and the work that he'd done was enough to see that despite his frailties he had had it in him—one last masterpiece. I had a feeling he didn't need anyone telling him to know it was good, but he seemed to enjoy seeing Patsy's admiration. "So you approve of my swan song?" he asked.

"It's magnificent," she said. "Every bit as good as True Horseman." Patsy bit her lip. "I don't suppose it's for sale?" she asked.

LeVan glowered. "This mural is for Walt. I certainly haven't given my all so that it can wind up at Flintlock, a whatnot of the wealthy. Your father never understood this, but you can't have everything!"

"LeVan," I muttered, wanting to say, *calm down, you're being rude,* but I didn't. I didn't say another word, not even to shrug off the awkward silence that had settled over us.

Some people meet anger with anger, striking back when they feel attacked. Patsy wasn't that kind of person. I don't know what I'd expected from her. She was rich. She wore to the church the kind of jewelry worn to the Oscars, and had a staff that took care of things like buying groceries and polishing door knobs. Yes, she was an excellent hostess, but sometimes such graciousness is just for show. That wasn't the case with Patsy Love Stock. She sat next to LeVan who was clenching his jaw. "But you're wrong, Bishop," said Patsy, her voice kind. "Daddy didn't think money will get you anything, but he did believe in spending big when you found something worth buying. It's no secret he loved your art, and at the dinner table he was fond of telling the story of the first Hitchpost art he purchased." It was a subtle change, but LeVan's jaw softened. "His money was tied up in land, and he'd just married Mama. As he put it, they didn't have a pot to pee in, and yet when he saw your painting, Westward Ho, he said he had to have it, even though it meant working nights at a meat processor and braving your sour looks."

LeVan huffed. "I don't know that my looks were sour."

Patsy laughed. "They weren't sweet!"

LeVan cracked a smile. "That's true enough."

"For months, he and Mama would live on meat scraps, and just when things would even out, he'd fall in love with another. It was a lot, this young couple, trying to put together the money to buy your paintings, especially since Mama wasn't entirely on board. She was more into porcelain dolls. But she loved Daddy, so she went along with it."

LeVan chuckled. "That poor woman, her house full of western art."

"She was plenty happy about their Hitchposts when she realized they were a good investment. And when Daddy's land deal panned out, she got her doll collection, but their Hitchposts were what she liked to show people when they came to visit, but Daddy and I were the true fans." Patsy touched LeVan's knee. "He wasn't perfect."

"He had a perfect left hook," said LeVan, cupping his hand to his jaw.

"Let's face it, he wasn't a gifted politician," said Patsy. LeVan nodded. "But he was a good man, and he thought a lot of you. *LeVan Hitchpost is the only one who has the nerve to tell me no,* he used to say. He appreciated that about you."

LeVan looked at me. "I don't suppose you'd mind climbing up on that scaffolding over there and finishing what I started? Patsy Love Stock is here and I'd like to visit. But you'll need to add you name when you're finished. It wouldn't be right for me to take all the credit."

"You're sure you don't mind if I work on it?" I asked, my eyes wide with surprise. "You were so determined to do it yourself?"

"I know what I said," said LeVan, "but blessed are the flexible for they shall not get bent out of shape."

I rubbed my hands together. "Okay then, I'll work, and you two visit." And for the rest of the morning, I painted and LeVan and Patsy talked like old friends.

Chapter
Twenty-Nine

There should have been an hourglass in the studio that morning, an hourglass with sand slowly, noiselessly slipping through its narrow neck, and piling up below to signal the coming end. Or at the very least, I should have seen, like dried leaves in the wind, the pieces of LeVan Hitchpost beginning to scatter.

"What a fine day this is," said LeVan, motioning at the glass door, "a truly fine day."

I stopped my work on the second panel to look at my watch. "Wow, I didn't realize it's time for lunch."

Patsy stood. "I'm afraid I've overstayed my welcome."

LeVan psshawed. "In the twenty-seven years I've lived here, I don't think I've enjoyed a conversation more."

I climbed down the ladder, guilt distracting me from paying attention to what LeVan had said. He shouldn't be going up and down this thing. It was too dangerous. I'd have to find a way to keep him off. "I'm starving!" I cried.

"Of course, you know you've lived here longer than that," said Patsy.

LeVan nodded. "Of course," and if I would have been paying closer attention, I would have seen in his eyes a look that said, *What is she talking about?*

"I'll let you two enjoy your lunch in peace," said Patsy.

"Please stay," I said, wiping my hands on a clean cloth, "we'd love to have you."

"No one can ever say I'm not hospitable to the Loves," said LeVan.

"In fact, I could use your help in the kitchen," I said. "My lunches aren't the best."

Patsy brightened at this request. "I'll see what I can whip up for us."

LeVan, though knitting his brow, looked comfortable in his chair. "I'll be right back, LeVan. I'm just going to show Patsy the kitchen."

LeVan stared straight ahead, a look of concern on his face, and thinking it had something to do with what I'd added to his mural, I lifted the glass door, and walked across the stone path with Patsy to show her the kitchen.

"LeVan, I know what you're thinking, I shouldn't have gone so golden with the color of the wheat," I said, before realizing that his chair was empty. "LeVan?" I said as my heart beat wildly. "LeVan!" I'm not the calmest when panicked and so I did the ridiculous, like look behind canvasses propped against the wall, and under the table, before I raced outside and found him by the mailbox in front of the house, the one marked Seventy-Two Dogwood Lane, opening and closing it.

"LeVan!" I cried, breathless.

He didn't stop his opening and closing to look at me. "It's going to arrive, I just know it. It has to," he said, tears welling in his eyes.

"What's going to arrive, LeVan!"

"You!" he snarled as he pointed at me, "and those do-nothing bureaucrats in Boise. Don't tell me she couldn't have survived! You don't know my girl! She's a fighter! Always sending me letters of apology, can't spend more government funds on another search! When is one of you going to send a letter to tell me that you won't give up! I've sent so many! Too many to count!" LeVan pushed me. "Get away from me," he said. "I know it's your job, standing between me and the men with the power, but I despise you all the same."

LeVan hadn't pushed me hard, but sorrow has its own blow, and it knocked me to the ground. "Patsy!" I cried. "Patsy!"

I heard the screen door slam, heard Patsy's hurried footsteps across the gravel, but couldn't see a thing. I was crying too hard. "What's happened?" she asked.

The subtle squeaking of the mailbox opening and closing stopped. "Annette," said LeVan, "I know I haven't always been the friendliest, but Rosemary is out there! They say there's no chance she's survived, that because her body wasn't found along with the others only means an animal got to it, but they don't know my girl."

I looked up to see Patsy put her arm around LeVan. "They don't know your girl," she said.

"They need to keep looking, hang the cost!" he cried, shaking his finger at the sky.

In a hushed and calm tone, Patsy spoke to me. "I need you to pull yourself together. Shut and lock the house and studio, and bring the truck here. Hurry."

I nodded, got off the ground, wiping my eyes on my sleeve.

As I raced away I heard her saying to LeVan, "You're right, we need to go into town and put together a search party. We can't waste a moment. We're going to find her."

"She's probably hurt!"

"Now, now," said Patsy, "we've got to think positive."

Rushing into the studio, I knocked over a small table, making tubes of paint scatter. Frantically, I looked around, my palm pressed to my forehead, as I tried to think where my keys might be, before realizing they were in my pocket. My fingers shook as I locked the studio and house, and started the truck, making the whole process seem to me to take an eternity.

I punched the gas, sprinting across the short distance to the mailbox, and stopping with a lurch. I had hoped that Patsy might have calmed LeVan down, but he was just as distraught as before. "Those do-nothings in Boise! I'm going to ring each one by the neck!" When he saw me, he snarled again. "What are you still doing here!" he cried.

Patsy patted his shoulder. "She's going to take us down the canyon and help us put together a search party."

LeVan stamped his foot. "I'll not work with her kind. All they do is drag their feet!"

Patsy put her hands on his shoulders, and looked him in the eye. "Sometimes you've got to dance with the devil to get things done."

LeVan knitted his brow. "You've said that before," he said.

"No, you've said it when you've had to work with Phil Love."

It seemed like LeVan was about to berate Patsy's father, when his face contorted in pain. "She's hurt! I know she's out there and hurt!"

"Then we'd better go," said Patsy, opening the truck door. "Rosemary needs us."

LeVan nodded at this. "She needs us," he said, and got in the truck, but not before Patsy and giving me another angry look. "So help me if you give me the runaround!" he growled.

"I won't give you the runaround, I promise!" I said.

"Just drive," whispered Patsy. "Get us to the hospital."

There are laws against driving while drunk, but driving while crying is perfectly legal, though it, too, is dangerous, especially on a winding canyon road. I took a deep breath, trying to calm myself, but I was certain the end had come. I would never again spend a day at Dogwood painting with LeVan, and I couldn't help mourning that loss.

Compounding my sadness was LeVan mourning anew the death of his wife. It was as if someone had pressed rewind, allowing me to see the full measure of his loss. Hunched and wringing his hands, LeVan's body heaved with the force of his sobs.

"Rosemary," he wailed. "My sweet, Rosemary!"

"Don't despair," soothed Patsy, her arm around LeVan, "she needs our hope."

"I can't do this," I said, wiping my nose on my sleeve. "You're going to have to drive. I just can't."

"You have to keep going," said Patsy, her voice sweet yet stern.

"I can't," I sobbed.

"Shh. Shh. Let me tell you something," she whispered to me as she patted LeVan's back, continuing to comfort him. "Do you know which of all my Hitchposts is my favorite?" She asked, just loud enough for me to hear over LeVan's wailing.

We left the mouth of the canyon and turned onto the road leading into town. I shook my head.

"It's True Horseman," she said as LeVan who had calmed slightly was hit by another wave of sorrow, filling the truck cabin with grief-stricken howls.

Again, I was overwhelmed by tears, barely able to see. "Just let me pull over," I cried.

"Keep going," said Patsy as she hugged a sobbing LeVan. "Deep breaths, deep breaths," she said, and though it occurred to me she might have been speaking to LeVan, I did my best to comply. "Shh. Take the next right. Do you want to know why True Horseman is my favorite?" she asked, leaning closer to my ear.

Tears falling faster than I could wipe away, I nodded.

"Because True Horseman was the first painting he started after losing Rosemary. This isn't how LeVan's story ends, not really. He pulled himself together. He painted, raised his grandson, did a lot of fishing, and a lot of arguing with my father down at City Hall. Rosemary's death sent him sprawling, but he got back on that horse and he lived. Do you understand what I'm telling you?" I nodded, sucking in a deep, shuddering breath. "Be happy for the life he lived, while he had his wits to live it."

As LeVan continued to sob uncontrollably, a picture of him, paintbrushes in his back pocket, climbing his ladder to paint as I scurried around placing pillows beneath him came to mind. "He is so stubborn," I said, smiling a little as I cried.

"You don't have to tell me that. He never did make peace with my father." Patsy pointed at a large white building in the distance. "Take your next right."

At the corner was a sign that said Intermountain Hospital, which, distraught as he was, I hadn't expected LeVan to read, but he did, and fractured as his mind was, he put two and two together.

The wild look of betrayal, the fury, his struggle to get out the truck, his screaming—both at us, and for Rosemary, followed by an injection, and him slumping, still sobbing, but slumping onto a gurney, and my emptiness as they wheeled him away.

"His heart," I heard one nurse say as she rushed passed me. "We need to settle him down quick."

Situations like LeVan's involve details. Papers must be signed, phone calls made. Maybe if Patsy hadn't been there, capably attending to dotting the *is* and crossing the *ts*, I might have found the strength to step in and help. But as it was, I was free to sit in a chair, bury my face in my hands and cry.

I heard Walt before I saw him. "Where is he?" he cried, "Where is he?"

I looked up and saw Walt across the ER lobby, his hands pressed to his head, as Patsy gently explained what had happened, and the fear in his eyes shifted to confusion, and then to anger.

"Why?" He cried, rushing toward me. "Why didn't you tell me?"

I flinched, as if—like the stern woman so long ago—he'd raised his hand to hit me. "I wanted to!" I cried.

Looking at the ceiling, Walt balled his fists. "He had a good day today and you didn't tell me!"

Barely able to look at him, I nodded.

He swiped a finger across his upper lip. "Has he had other good days?" he asked, his voice rising with hysteria.

I nodded again.

He held my arm, his grip firm. "How many, Lana," he demanded.

Sniffling, I slowly met his gaze. "A lot."

Walt stormed away, just a few paces, then came rushing back. "And you didn't tell me!" he cried, a wild look in his eyes. How could I tell him the truth, that his grandfather hadn't wanted him to know? I couldn't, and so I stood there, tears spilling down my cheeks, saying nothing. "He shouldn't have been at Dogwood!" cried Walt. "Why didn't you listen! And now he's in there, and his heart—"

"Mr. Hitchpost, we need you," said a nurse, her tone serious.

Worry flashed through Walt's eyes, and he rushed off with the nurse, but not before glancing angrily back at me.

Not far from where I stood, a hospital worker was typing, her long nails clicking with accuracy across the keyboard despite the many glances she sent my way. I shifted my weight from foot to foot. Patsy was on her phone, telling someone about LeVan. Soon, others would arrive, huddling together to share what they knew, and, like the hospital worker, steal glances at me. I felt the teeth of the truck key digging into my palm, cutting through my sorrow, reminding me that I didn't have to endure those glances. I rushed out of the emergency room to Walt's truck, hastily wiped away my tears, and started driving. Away. That was my destination, but when I realized I was headed for Idaho Falls, a plan started forming in my mind—park Walt's truck at the airport, leave the key under the mat, and buy a one-way ticket—leave everything and go home.

I had never indulged in the luxury of crying on my mother's lap. Leftover Siberian ice, as well as an anxiousness to be a good daughter, had kept my emotions in check, until now. Now, I wanted to rush into my mother's arms and sob until, eyes swollen and throat sore, I fell to sleep, forgetting, at least momentarily, everything. It didn't matter what it cost. I'd text Walt where he could find his truck, and let the Wilmington Trust figure out how to get me my things. Stepping onto a plane with just my wallet appealed to me. It simplified things, and right now I needed that. Life lately had been too complicated.

My phone buzzed, making me jump. I had been out of range for so long, I'd almost forgotten it could receive calls. Approaching an off ramp for Peak Pass, a quiet road without stores or gas stations, I pulled off the highway, grabbed my phone off the bench seat and saw Ingrid's name in bold letters on my touch screen.

It's strange how quickly the mind works. In an instant, I went from sad that it wasn't Walt to relieved that it wasn't Walt to happy it was Ingrid to annoyed she hadn't replied to my texts to ready to sob my way through an explanation of the past few weeks to deciding that it would be best not to overwhelm her, and to, finally, clearing my throat, taking a deep breath, and saying, "Hello?"

"Hey, Lana! Finally, you pick up!"

"I was going to say the same to you," I said.

"It's been crazy, Lan," she said, sounding giddy. "We just got back from Cabo!"

I shook my head. "Who's we?" I asked, feeling foggy, like I'd just been awakened from a sound sleep.

"Riley and me," she said, the subtle shift in her tone letting me know she'd just broken into a big smile.

"Cabo, as in Cabo San Lucas, Mexico," I said, sounding calmer than I felt.

"Yes, Cabo San Lucas! Riley found an incredible deal at an all-inclusive!"

I pulled over to the shoulder though there was little chance of another car coming my way. Peak Pass seemed to lead nowhere, at least nowhere that was paved. "Wait," I said, killing the engine, "you went to Mexico with just Riley," I said, hoping I'd heard her wrong.

I hadn't.

"It was amazing! I am literally obsessed with the water there; it's so blue!" she cried, and I knew her well enough to know that her enthusiasm for the water was just small talk, her way of leading into a much bigger conversation.

I could feel a vein pulsing in my temple. "Tell me about the tacos, "I said, because I didn't want to have a bigger conversation. I didn't want to hear her say what I already knew.

"Lana, I have something to tell you," said Ingrid, sounding suddenly like her no-nonsense father.

"No, you don't," I said, tears pricking my eyes.

"Lana, I'm a senior in college," she said softly, and at that moment I heard her, my old friend—the girl who, on that soccer bench, coaxed me into our first conversation, who helped me be more outgoing, who believed in me, complained constantly about me wearing black, and who, so long ago hatched a plan—made a promise, one that we'd both pledged to keep. I stepped outside, the truck cab suddenly feeling suffocating. Didn't she know how precious she was? That she was a daughter of God, and that she was worth more than Riley and Cabo and the bluest blue water. *How could she,* said a voice inside my head, *when you never found the courage to tell her?*

Below me, on the highway, cars rushed passed, their whooshing sound reminding me of waves breaking on Anna Maria Island. I closed my eyes, wishing I could go back, back to that wedding between two people I didn't know, and stop that beer from spilling—stop Ingrid from ever meeting Riley.

"No!" I shouted, objecting to all of it—LeVan's illness, Walt's anger, Ingrid's choice. "No!"

"Lana, we've already said we love each other," she said, frustration ever so slightly trumping her patience. "This is a serious, committed relationship!"

"We had a plan!" I cried, my voice tossing in the wind, and going nowhere, like our conversation.

"It was a middle school plan."

"We were in high school!"

"But it was unrealistic. If you knew Riley, you'd understand. He's such a good guy."

"You were supposed to wait!" I cried. "That's what you wanted!"

Ingrid took a deep breath. "Lana, this is good for me. I know you want the best for me, and I love you for it, but I'm ready for this. But what about you? How have you been?" she asked.

"Fine," I said, while sobbing.

Ingrid wasn't convinced.

"Lana, what's happened? Are you okay?" asked Ingrid, her voice filled with concern.

Just then my phone beeped. I looked at my screen; Lefty was calling. "I've got to go. I'm getting a call," I said, my voice flat.

"I love you, Lana," said Ingrid.

I clicked over to Lefty's call without saying good bye.

"Hello?" I croaked.

"What! You can't sound like that! I'm about to tell you good news!"

"What's the good news?" I sniffed.

"Russia loves you!"

Stunned, my voice swapped sadness for confusion. "Russia loves me? Why?"

"A producer at Channel One, a television station in Russia, saw your work when I was in Helsinki, loved it, did a little digging, and found out you're from over there. He wants to come to the Wilmington Museum Gala in the fall to see your latest works, and he wants to do a reality show about you."

"A reality show," I said, sounding and feeling numb.

"I know that doesn't scream artistic success in the traditional sense, but hear me out—this could be huge for your career."

"They want to watch me work?" I asked.

"Ratings need something a little spicier."

"Spicier?"

"He wants to run DNA tests to see if you're related to a famous artist or two over there. He's also got this idea of taking you back to the orphanage you came from, let the camera roll, and see if he strikes media gold. I know it's a lot to think about. How soon can you—" The wind made it impossible to hear.

My mind swirled like my hair in the wind. I pushed it out of my eyes, but it flew back. LeVan would have chuckled had he seen it—chuckled and recited some silly proverb about how the bald are blessed. *I wish he were here right now to tell me what to do*, I thought, and then it occurred to me that he already had. *Finish my mural*, he'd said. The wind blew harder, making it impossible to hear what Lefty was saying. I climbed into the truck and shut the door. "Sorry about that. What did you say?"

"I said when you get to New York I'll take you to Carmine's. Julio could tag along and take some pre-production video. By the way, Julio says hello." Outside the wind roared. "Dang girl, it's windy! Where are you?"

"Peak Pass."

"Well, get out of there!"

I started the truck. "I will, but let me get back to you about New York. I've got some work here I need to finish."

"I like your style, Lana. Getting it done. Can't get paid, if you don't get it done."

"And tell Julio hello for me."

"I will."

"And that he should have come. Tell him he missed out."

"Missed out on what, milking the cows?" asked Lefty with a chuckle.

I thought of the weeks I had spent with LeVan. "On media gold," I said, then hung up, and headed back to Dogwood.

Chapter Thirty

I dreaded returning to Dogwood, to what I knew I would find there—a husk of a studio, no longer pulsing with activity. I gripped the steering wheel and pressed on the gas. As much as I didn't want to return, I wanted to throw myself into finishing LeVan's mural and let questions about color, texture, and technique crowd out any other thought. I wound the truck up Dogwood Lane, noticing, despite my heavy heart, the brilliant traces of pink in the sky left by the now hidden sun. I would miss this place, its sweet air and cool mornings, and, most of all, I would miss days and nights spent painting with LeVan. Pulling to the back of the house, I put the truck in park and grabbed my phone, glad, for the first time, that it didn't work up here. I didn't want anyone calling me. Hope can be a fraying rope, and until I'd finished Levan's mural, I needed to believe he was still alive—still there for someone to tell him his mural was finished. Whether he understood didn't matter. *I* needed that moment. I would finish the mural, leave instructions for Walt, and then, without saying good bye, I would go. It would be better that way. There are certain things relationships can't bounce back from, like not telling your boyfriend his grandfather is experiencing a miraculous recovery from Alzheimer's.

In our rush to help LeVan, I had left the studio lights on. Keys in hand, I killed the head lights and leaned back on the truck's bench seat, taking in LeVan's mural, visible through the glass door. His brushwork, the richness of his colors, and his use of shadow and light—it was all incredible. Like the man depicted in his mural, LeVan had given his all. He had worked day and night. He could have done other things. *Like talking to Walt*, I thought bitterly. But he hadn't, because creating this mural was that important to him. What was it he'd said? I bit my lip as I started to remember. He'd said this mural would continue to speak for him long after he was gone. Of course, art and its meaning is always up for interpretation, but as I looked at LeVan's mural, aglow in the surrounding darkness, I heard, once again, LeVan telling me his mural's intended message. "Seek after pearls," I said.

My back tensed. It wasn't that simple! People chucked precious things all the time, not realizing. And then, when it's too late, spot their old whatever on Antique Roadshow where an expert announces its vast worth. I thought of Walt. He hadn't "chucked" our relationship yet, but he would. I saw, once again, the fury in his eyes and mournfully shook my head. The thought weighed on me like a thick blanket. Summoning my strength, I shrugged it off. There would be time for sadness later, but right now, I needed to focus.

The truck door slamming shut was the only sound—other than the distant hooting of an owl—that I expected to hear, but, soon, heavy footfall and a throaty growl told me I wasn't alone. Silhouetted in the darkness, I saw the bear, reared up on his hind legs, assessing me. Standing half way between the truck and the studio, I froze, as my brain, now slowed to a crawl, tried to remember Shailene's advice. Use bear mace! I looked at the truck, knowing there wasn't time for me to retrieve it from behind the front seat. I closed my eyes and berated myself for not taking Shailene's advice seriously. She hadn't been trying to scare me!

The bear lumbered toward me. What else! What else had she taught me! My breathing was shallow and rapid now, and in the heavens new stars seemed to be appearing. I forced myself to think. She had said something about not letting a bear smell your breath, if you'd eaten. I hadn't eaten but I squeezed my lips shut all the same. The bear was close now, close enough that I could smell his musk. I tried not to make any noise, but with danger so close, I couldn't help whimpering.

The bear reared up on his hind legs, as more of Shailene's advice somehow pierced the terror in my mind. She'd said something about size, that the smaller ones can be scared off. The stars in the sky seemed to pulse in time with my racing heart. I looked at the bear who was now moving in a slow circle around me, and decided that when he was on all fours, he wasn't massive. He must have been one who fit into the "small" bear category. I needed to shout! To harness all my frustration and sadness and let it out in one tremendous scream!

I thought of my past, my mother abandoning me, the stern woman's slap, the orphanage's crushing loneliness. I thought of the ice inside me that for so long had kept me from risking at love, and I thought of Walt, how hurt and frustrated I'd made him, then I opened my mouth to let it out—a scream from the depths of my soul. But nothing came. Other than the sound of my shallow breathing, nothing came out, which was okay, because while it might be possible to scare away one bear, it's unlikely to scare away four. Stepping out from the darkness, they moved toward me, one and after the other. A random thought crossed my mind, that their movements seemed choreographed. And then nothing. The stars blazed brighter, like light bulbs before bursting, and then all went black, and I fell to the ground. I'm not really sure how long I laid there, out cold. Ten minutes? An hour? Time simply ceased to exist, until the moment my consciousness returned, and I thought, *Oh good, I'm not dead.* Afraid to move, to even open my eyes, I listened, trying to detect the slightest noise that might indicate that bears were still near me, a crack of a twig, a faint growl, a snort, but there was nothing. Slowly, I opened my eyes, and even slower, stood. Some have asked me why I didn't make a dash for the truck and get out of there. The answer is simply salvation was inside. At that moment, *I* needed to paint more than LeVan needed me to paint. Art had always been my escape, and now more than ever, I needed a place to hide, so I made my move. Once on my feet, I sprinted to the studio door, unlocked it, rolled it up just enough to slip inside, rolled it down, then collapsed on the floor and sobbed my way through a prayer of thanks. I was safe.

I don't know what, under normal circumstances, you do after a bear encounter, but this wasn't a normal circumstance. I needed to pull myself together and finish LeVan's mural. Still trembling, I stood up, and got to work. Paintbrush in hand, my breathing soon returned to normal. Painting didn't take away my sadness, but it seemed to make my low less low. Even hunger and fatigue's gnawing lost their bite, and for the moment, painting was all that mattered. I worked until the night lifted and birdsong, once again, filled the air. And then I stepped down from the scaffolding, stood back, took in each brush stroke, and added my name below LeVan's.

I laid on LeVan's cot, thinking I'd rest for a moment, and found myself at Bushkaya #3, standing in the stern woman's office. She sat behind a metal desk, her face pulled into a disapproving frown. She was speaking to me, but it was barely audible over the sound of her clock on the wall behind her ticking. Reminding myself I was no longer a child, and had no reason to fear her, I straightened my shoulders and walked toward her, each step making a lonely echoing. "Why are you here?" she asked, in Russian.

"I'm here for my mother," I said in English, speaking, despite my best efforts, softer than her.

She cupped her ear. "Did you say mother?" she asked, and when I nodded, she laughed, exposing what was left of her yellow, rotting teeth. "I told you she wouldn't come for you, and she hasn't. And yet, you came all this way. You always were a strange, little girl. Go home, there's nothing for you here."

The clock's ticking grew louder. I strained my voice shouting, trying to be heard. "She loved me!" I cried, thudding my chest as tears began to slide down my face.

"I wouldn't know," said the stern woman, "that's not included in your file."

A light bulb flashed, the kind used on old cameras. I turned and saw Julio. He was standing next to Lefty, taking picture after picture. "This is brilliant!" He shouted, just loud enough to be heard over the ticking. "People are going to love this!"

This, I thought. *This* that you're talking about is my life.

"I have things to do," said the stern woman, looking down at some paperwork and dismissing us with a wave of her hand.

"You have things to do!" I shouted over the incessant tick tock. "I don't have time for this! I have a life! And I love that life!"

"Keep it going!" said Lefty.

The stern woman looked up from her work and pointed a finger at me. She was about to say something, but at the sound of a glass door rolling upward, she turned into a wisp of smoke, and was gone.

I jumped up, and wiped my drool with my sleeve.

"We knocked but you didn't hear us," said Britney, her eyes darting around the studio that was now filled with sunlight. She was standing next to Shailene, both in full hair and makeup. "Patsy wanted us to check on you, and get her car."

Shailene jutted a finger behind her. "Those are bear tracks out there," she said, her tone serious.

"There were four," I said.

"Did you use the mace?" asked Shailene, sounding slightly like a strict teacher.

"I fainted."

"And you're not hurt?" she asked, disbelieving.

I held out my arms and turned around for proof.

Shailene shook her head. "Well, you can't expect that to work every time." she said, then surprising me, added, with a note of true concern, "But beside that, how are you?

"Keeping busy," I said, rubbing my paint-speckled hands, then, summoning all my courage, asked, "How is LeVan?" and then braced myself for the answer.

"Alive, but not well," said Shailene, her bluntness somehow a relief. "By the way, you look terrible. I know you've had a rough twenty-four hours, but, wow, you're a total mess."

Make that, sort of a relief.

I ran a hand over my messy hair. "I had some work I needed to get done."

"Speaking of work," said Britney, walking in a little circle and scanning the studio, "It looks like you haven't started a certain painting you were supposed to start."

Irritation pricked my skin. "No, I haven't," I said, causing Britney to frown. Resisting the impulse to throw a paintbrush at her, I cleared my throat and continued. "But there's a good reason for the delay. I wanted to do this first," I said, walking to Kylie's portrait and turning it around for them to see. In it, sweet Kylie sat on a swing, waiting to be pushed.

"Holy moly," said Shailene, her hand slowly moving to cover her open mouth.

Britney frowned. "You made her look sad."

Shailene shook her head, then pointed at Kylie's portrait. "It's absolutely beautiful."

"I get that," snapped Britney, "but why does she look sad?"

"Because she is sad," I said. Maybe Shailene's honesty had rubbed off on me. I don't know, but I wasn't holding back.

"Kylie's not sad," said Britney, insistent, as if saying something made it so.

"Not all the time," I said, "she plays and laughs as a little girl should, but she misses you."

Britney threw her hands in the air. "I don't know what you expect me to do, my clients count on me! And besides, I'm with Kylie a lot, probably more than most mothers."

If I let her, I was pretty sure Britney could've talked herself into believing that she was a perfect parent, but I wasn't going to let her. "I didn't know it was possible," I said.

Britney folded her arms. "Know what was possible?" she asked, her eyes narrowing.

"Abandoning your child without actually leaving them, but you do it all the time."

"Ouch," said Shailene, which could barely be heard over Britney.

"I haven't abandoned my daughter!" she said.

"You hardly ever give her your attention," I said, my voice trembling, because brutal honesty is its own adrenaline rush.

"I have a business to run!" cried Britney, tossing her head, sending a few curls askew.

"And you have a daughter to raise!" I countered. "A sweet, kind, funny little girl who needs you! And if you were half as focused on her as you are your phone—" I had struck a nerve.

Britney grabbed a pen knife off the long table and started for Kylie's portrait.

"Stop!" cried Shailene, grabbing her cousin by the arm, preventing her from getting close enough to the canvas to inflict damage. "What the heck are you doing!"

"I hate it!"

"Brit, calm down," she demanded, still restraining her cousin. She pried the knife from Britney's fingers. "You don't attack the Mona Lisa because you're mad at Da Vinci." Britney stopped struggling, and Shailene let her go, but not before placing herself between Britney and Kylie's portrait, just in case.

"I hate it! I hate it!" cried Britney.

"Quit being so dramatic," said Shailene. "You said just the other day that you need to spend more time with Kylie."

"So now you think I'm a bad mother too!" she cried.

"Oh my gosh, pull yourself together," groaned Shailene. "Yes, Kylie looks a teensy sad, but Lana has painted a beautiful picture of your daughter."

"I know it's beautiful, but I don't like what it's saying about me," pouted Britney.

"Then do something about it," said Shailene.

"I don't have time for this," said Britney as she stormed out of the studio.

Shailene waited until she heard the car door slam shut. "That could've gone better," she said.

"She needed to know."

"Yeah, but, you could have used a softer touch."

I didn't say anything, but I knew she was right. Shailene ran a hand over her hair. "Don't worry, I'll talk to her, and smooth things over. Britney's not one to stay mad forever. By the way, the painting really is beautiful."

My argument with Britney had drained me. I gave Shailene a weak smile. "Thanks," I said.

"Mom said to tell you that you're welcome at Flintlock."

"Thanks, but I think I'm going to clean up and get going."

"But you have another week of your mentorship."

I shook my head. "I don't think I should stay."

"Certain people will disapprove," she said, and I knew she meant Walt.

"I'm not so sure about that."

Shailene gazed at LeVan's mural. "He really did this?" she asked.

I nodded.

"It's incredible. And he didn't have a screw loose for weeks?"

I nodded again.

"Such a sneak, so like him," she said with a smile.

She unholstered the can of bear mace on her hip and left it on the long table. "Just in case," she said.

"Thanks," I said, and then smiled.

Bear mace in hand, I headed over to the house, downed a bowl of cereal, then washed and swept and set everything in place. I scribbled down some instructions for Walt, telling him what should be done with the paintings, and nothing more, because I didn't want to cry. I explained that my completed works were propped on the right side of the studio and should be sent to the Wilmington's art museum in Nantucket. I told him, unfortunately, I didn't know anything about transporting art, but gave him Lefty's phone number, and assured him he did. One of my completed works was the painting of Kylie, and, if Britney and Hank were willing, I wanted it included. As for LeVan's mural, it belonged to Walt, and could he please tell LeVan it's finished. That would make him happy to know. I then signed it, Thanks, Lana.

Rolling closed the glass door, I heard the crunch of gravel under tires. Walking out, I saw Carl getting out of his car carrying three hot chocolates and a stack of newspapers. The sight made me cry.

"What? What'd I do?" asked Carl, his New York accent sounding especially thick. As I cried my way through an explanation of all that had happened, Carl placed everything on the gravel, and took my hand in both of his. "I'm so sorry," he said. "So very sorry. What can I do?"

"Nothing," I sniffed.

"What do you mean nothing. You just told me—mind you, through heaving sobs—that you're headed to the airport. What am I, chopped liver? Do I not drive for Uber? You're too upset. The least I can do is get you safely to the airport."

I sniffed again. "Thanks, Carl."

Carl put my suitcase in his trunk. I handed him the keys to the studio and Walt's truck, along with the address where to take them, and then I climbed in, my swollen eyes fixed on Seventy-Two Dogwood Lane until it disappeared from sight. The sun shone brilliantly, streaming through the chinks in a dark cloud and into the passenger window, making me warm and introspective. Things had not gone to plan, but then I had come to Bluegill without a plan, other than to paint. And in the weeks I had been here, Bluegill, the pearl of Idaho and its people had changed me. Yes, I was sad, the heartache seemed almost unbearable, but my heart was no longer encased in Siberian ice, and for that I was grateful.

Chapter Thirty-One

I've never run a marathon, but the pictures I've seen of runners collapsing as they cross the finish line is something I can relate to. After Bluegill, I was spent. I felt weak, almost baby-bird fragile. I honestly didn't know if I could take hearing that LeVan had died or that Walt was still angry, and so I did what made sense to me—I turned off my phone, went home and hugged my parents, and then caught a bus to Tallahassee to wait tables at Applebee's, a first, I'm sure, for any Yale graduate.

I was killing five weeks. Then it would be time to head to Nantucket for my exhibit opening at the Wilmington Museum, and meetings with Lefty Zaugg. Despite his charismatic cajoling, I had decided not to meet up with him in New York. I told him we would talk about my future in Nantucket, and until then, not to try and reach me. I had tables to bus. Work at Applebee's wasn't prestigious, but the tips were great, especially when I sketched a quick pic on the receipt, and it kept my days open for spurts of conversation with Ingrid and sketching.

Sometimes I sketched what I saw in Tallahassee, but mostly I sketched from memory the things that happened to me in Bluegill, and the people there I'd grown to love, until from this jumble of memories sprung the idea of creating a graphic novel. Not one that would ever be for sale, but one that would help me work through all that had happened. And so, with pictures and limited words, I told the story of my time in Bluegill— arriving at Dogwood and finding no one there, getting angry with Walt, falling for Walt, LeVan going from dementia to sly fox, working in the studio, Carl's friendship, kissing Walt while being heli-rescued, my dancefloor beneath the stars, LeVan's determination to finish his mural, Patsy peeking, everything falling apart.

I bit my pencil as I considered my story. I didn't like the way it ended. It felt like the ending to a foreign film, the kind where lives crumble while someone plays the accordion. Such movies were depressing, but maybe that was because they were truer to life. Certainly they were truer than fairy tales, stories where the couple lives happily ever after. I took the pencil from between my teeth and blew a raspberry. I refused to accept that sadness was the truest ending. That's the thing about a heart no longer encased in ice—it's far lighter, far easier to lift with hope, and so under my last picture, the one of Carl's Jetta driving away from Bluegill, I wrote, The End, and then, without hesitation, added a question mark.

I twisted my blonde hair into a wispy knot and stuck it through with my pencil, securing it, as Ingrid, her backpack slung over one shoulder, walked through the front door. "I don't think I'll ever get used to it," she said, letting her backpack slide from her shoulder.

"Used to what?" I asked.

"How beautiful you look with blonde hair." I stood up, rolling my eyes. "I'm not joking. Dying your hair dark for all those years. It was like—"

"Turning off a light," I offered.

She snapped her fingers. "Exactly!"

"Well, get used to it. I'm tired of your gushing."

"How can you be tired of my gushing? You've only had it done for a week. And I'll gush all I want. My best friend looks beautiful, even if she's wearing my shirt and it's dry-clean only," said Ingrid, leveling a gaze on me.

"Hey, you're the one who doesn't want me to wear black," I said.

"I've created a monster."

"A beautiful monster," I said, batting my eyes.

Ingrid placed her keys on the kitchen counter. "I don't know, maybe I should have let the goths in high school have you."

"This coming from the girl who just last night said we should live on the same cul-de-sac when we have kids."

"Live next to me and you can raid my closet all you want," she said, grabbing my hand. "I'm going to miss you, Lan, and honestly, I don't understand why you have to go. You could just fly to Nantucket for the opening and then come back. Austin said he'll hold your job for you, and even throw in a benefits package."

"A tempting offer," I said with a wry smile.

"You have a home here."

"I have your couch here, and I share it with your room-mate's Chihuahua."

Ingrid folded me into a hug. "Don't go, Lana," she said, rocking back and forth, being silly.

"If I don't go, you will. You're graduating next semester," I said, still rocking like a metronome. "And by the way, this is uncomfortable."

Ingrid let me go. "Promise me you'll—"

"No more promises," I said, "unless, of course, you want to promise to meet again with the missionaries."

"Ugh," said Ingrid.

"Should I take that as a yes?" I asked, knowing she had zero interest in learning more about my church. "We could set it up for the weekend so Riley could be there. They could talk about not having—"

"No promises!" conceded Ingrid who, though in love with Riley, had grown more private about their relationship since I'd arrived in Tallahassee, which I understood, since I had yet to tell her about Walt.

"Except for one promise," I said, holding out my pinkie to Ingrid. "We will always be friends."

Ingrid smiled and wrapped her pinkie around mine. "Always," she said.

"So where will you go after the exhibit?" asked Ingrid.

"I don't know. I don't know how my story ends."

"End!" cried Ingrid. "You're not at the end, you're at the beginning!"

"I like the way you think," I said, and smiled at my best friend.

Chester Wilmington was a tightwad, to be sure, but he was also a billionaire, and the night of the exhibit opening his billionaire side won out. Twinkling lights were wrapped around every branch of every tree lining the street in front of the museum, and in the museum courtyard, a party tent had been set up providing a place for the guests to socialize while enjoying an array of fresh seafood and listening to The Johnny Hart Band play hits from the golden era of Hollywood. I had expected something nice, but I hadn't expected so nice—the thick, red carpet leading to the museum entrance, the bouquets of flowers on each table, a tuxedoed staff meandering through the gallery offering guests hors d'oevre and champagne—it all took me by surprise, but nothing more than seeing LeVan's mural at the center of my exhibit.

Tears sprung to my eyes seeing it there, so beautiful, so complete, and so perfectly displayed. As the strains of Somewhere Over the Rainbow floated into the museum from the courtyard, I searched the room for Chester and Ethel, and saw them talking to . . . Patsy Stock. My eyebrows knitted in confusion, I began threading my way toward them, ready to hug her and pepper her with questions, until I saw them, Walt and LeVan.

LeVan sat in a wheelchair, a small blanket across his legs. He was gaunt, and his eyes had lost their glint, as if something inside him had been snuffed out. But beyond my wildest hopes, LeVan was here. He was here, and with Walt. I have no idea what a typical response is when you're stunned, but mine was something like paralysis. My mouth fell open, but words bottlenecked in my throat, making it impossible to speak, and though I wanted to rush toward them, that message somehow didn't make it to my feet, and so frozen, I watched Walt step toward me as he pushed his grandfather.

Love for Walt swept over me as he rubbed his upper lip. "Hey," he said.

My heart beat wildly. "Hey," I said, then bending down took LeVan's cold hands in mine. "Hello, LeVan," I said, my voice trembling with emotion. "It's so good to see you. LeVan stared ahead, his gaze unfixed. Standing up, I looked at Walt. "Thank you for including your mural in my exhibit."

"It seemed the right thing to do," he said, color rushing to his cheeks. For a long moment neither of us spoke. A thin membrane, like the skin of a bubble, seemed to surround us, buffering us from the passing platters of finger food, the genteel laughter, and pleasant conversations, allowing us to be surrounded and yet alone. "You look beautiful," he finally said, gesturing first to my blonde hair, and then my pale-yellow dress.

Self-conscious, I touched my hair. "Thanks," I said.

"But you always look beautiful," he said, looking at the floor. Returning his gaze to me, Walt continued. "I hope it's okay with you that we came," he said. "The Wilmington Trust sent us tickets. I tried calling you, but you wouldn't pick—"

Stepping around LeVan's wheel chair, I hugged Walt, and wrapped in his embrace, considered again the rightness of the top of my head reaching just to his shoulders. "I'm sorry," I said, my tears wetting his pressed shirt.

Walt kissed the top of my head. "No, I'm sorry," said Walt, then I tilted my face toward his and he kissed me.

"Hubba, hubba," said an old man walking by, a pin to our perfect bubble.

"Lana, this probably isn't the right time, but—"

"Lana!" Lefty cried as he clapped a hand on my shoulder, looking handsome in a tuxedo, "I've been looking for you. Maksim, the producer with Channel One, is here!"

I turned to Lefty. "Lefty, I'd like you to meet Walt Hitchpost."

They shook hands. "Nice to meet you," said Walt.

"Same," said Lefty. "Look, I don't mean to be rude, but Maks has a helicopter waiting, so if I could have Lana—"

"You can have Lana in a minute," I said, for some reason speaking in the third person. "Walt was about to say something."

Walt looked around the crowded museum. "Maybe I should wait," he said.

"Fantastic," said Lefty, nudging me toward the producer.

"No," I said, resisting his nudge. "What were you about to say?" I asked.

"Whatever it is, say it fast. Opportunity is about to knock," said Lefty.

"I love you," said Walt, catching my hand in his.

My heart, my ice-free heart, burned with happiness. "I love you too," I said.

"Aw, that's sweet, now let's go," said Lefty, tugging on my arm.

"Patsy says they have a room ready for you, if you'll come back to Bluegill."

"Go back to Bluegill, that's funny!" cried Lefty.

"Yes," I said.

"That's not funny," said Lefty, his voice instantly somber. "Excuse me, Walt, do you mind if I have a private word with your girl?" Walt nodded, then after giving me another kiss, took LeVan over to his mural.

Lefty waited until they were on their way, and then turned to me. "What is going on?" he cried, throwing his hands in the air.

I scratched my head. "I believe I just said I'm moving to Bluegill, Idaho," I said with a laugh.

"Move to Bluegill!" cried Lefty. "As your mentor, it is my responsibility to tell you that is highly unadvisable."

"Why?" I asked, picking up a mini quiche off a passing tray.

"Because a billion-dollar company in Russia wants to invest in you!" he cried, his hands again flying toward the pitched ceiling.

I bit into the quiche. "Yeah, I've been thinking about that," I said, then took a moment to swallow, "and I don't think Russian reality TV is for me."

Lefty put his hands out, as if ready to catch me. "It's a springboard, Lana, a brilliant opportunity. Think of the places it will take you!"

"Love is brilliant, Lefty, and the only place I want to be is Bluegill, Idaho. You should come out and visit when they have the grand opening for the Bluegill Museum. You could bring Julio."

"Listen," he said, shaking his head, "you want to live in Bluegill because you've fallen in love with that guy, Walt?"

I nodded. "That's right."

Lefty flashed his winning smile. "You could have ended up anywhere, had any experience. Walt's not someone to sacrifice for, he's the flavor of the month! If you would have ended up in Paris, it would have been another guy. Tokyo, another guy. Come on, Lana," he said, closing his eyes and rubbing his temples, "be reasonable. Maksim's waiting."

I looked at Walt, adjusting the pillow behind his grand-father's back as his grandfather stared blankly at his last masterpiece. "Seek after pearls, Lefty," I said, gesturing toward LeVan's mural.

"Are you trying to sound like me?"

"And when you find them," I continued, "give all you have to keep them."

"I don't get it."

"See you in Bluegill, Lefty. Tell Maksim the answer is no."

Smiling I walked up to Walt who now stood alone in front of the mural, Patsy having taken LeVan to go look at the other paintings. There he was, standing before me, Walt Hitchpost, tall, strong, handsome, and kind. As guys went, he was a pearl of great price, and he was my boyfriend. I sighed with happiness, and then I kissed him. "Hey," I said, slipping my hand in his.

"Hey," he said, then, opening our hands just enough, kissed my palm.

"How's your grandfather doing?"

"His mural is hanging at the Wilmington Museum causing a lot of buzz, and he's here at the opening. I'd say he's having a good day."

"That's true," I said, nodding.

Walt shrugged. "Physically, of course, he's been better. Can't get him to eat much, and he hasn't spoken since the hospital." Walt cleared his throat. "You could say he's on the downhill slide." I squeezed his hand. "Lana, did he talk a lot when you two were together?"

"Yes," I said.

"I don't suppose." Walt paused to get control of his emotions. "you could tell me everything he said?" he asked.

"Everything," I said, and kissed him again.

"That ought to seal it!" said the same, obnoxious old man who had commented before on our kissing. Well, I think it was

256

him. The moment was too wonderful, and so I had closed my eyes.

Walt glanced around the room. "Good turnout," he said.

"It is, and somewhere in this mass of people are my parents," I said, looking into Walt's perfect brown eyes.

"I should probably meet them, since I'm in love with their daughter," he said, his hands on my waist.

"And they should probably meet LeVan since I'm in love with his grandson."

Walking hand-in-hand through the museum, we found my parents talking with Patsy as LeVan stared with dull eyes at my portrait of him with Walt as a young boy.

Patsy and my parents were so engrossed in conversation they didn't see us approaching, and LeVan, of course, seemed equally unaware.

So, it was probably my imagination, how could it be anything but? But just as Walt reached out to shake my father's hand, just when I alone could see, I swear LeVan gave me the faintest of smiles and winked.

Acknowledgments

I wasn't sure Brush With Love would ever see the light of day. It was a tough story to write, because I knew nothing about being an artist and had only been to Idaho a handful of times. But, inspired by the life of Minerva Teichert—an artist who married a rancher—I dove in. My thanks to the very talented Heidi Darley for taking the time to teach me about painting. Hali Bird, thank you for pushing me to cut the fat. You are a tough task master, but *Brush With Love* is a better story because of you. Priscilla Chavez, thank you for your artwork. I couldn't imagine a more beautiful cover. Jessica Romrell, and the rest of the Cedar Fort crew, thank you for all you've done to bring this book to life. And, finally, my thanks to my family for your love and support. You are my pearl of great price.

About the Author

Lisa McKendrick lives in Florida and is the mother of seven children. When she's not writing she enjoys picking up original works of art at yard sales. Some of her favorite finds include, an etching from Salvador Dali, and two drawings from Al Hirschfeld. Lisa enjoys hearing from her readers and can be reached at lkmckendrick@gmail.com.